W

"It's no mystery why

it's got a sweet friends-to-lovers romance, a heroine whose personal growth you'll be cheering on, and a murder mystery full of twists. I enjoyed every nautical mile."

—Bellamy Rose, author of *Pomona Afton Can So Solve a Murder*

THE PERFECT ROM-COM

"Ferguson's (*How to Plot a Payback*) charming slow-burn rom-com is full of fun banter, lovable characters, community and family connections, and heart."

—*Library Journal*

"Melissa Ferguson delivers yet another sparkling, laugh-out-loud romance! *The Perfect Rom-Com* is a heartwarming story about chasing your dreams, discovering your voice, and finding love where you least expect it. With unforgettable characters and delightful humor, this novel is perfect for anyone who believes in second chances—both in love and in life."

—RaeAnne Thayne, *New York Times* bestselling author

"I loved this book! If you're looking for a heroine you can root for, a mean girl to boo, and a unique hero to fall for, this is your book. Bryony Page will keep you reading as she writes her way to the perfect HEA."

—Sheila Roberts, *USA TODAY* bestselling author of *The Best Life Book Club*

"In *The Perfect Rom-Com*, a successful ghostwriter longs to see her beloved book published under her own name. But her agent, who holds the keys to publication, also holds the keys to her heart. Don't miss this fun romantic romp into the intriguing world of publishing!"

—Denise Hunter, bestselling author
of *The Summer of You and Me*

"I can always count on Melissa Ferguson for sweet romances bursting with both wit and wisdom. Hilarious and heart-warming, *The Perfect Rom-Com* is comfy and cozy from the first page to the last."

—Bethany Turner, author of
Cole and Laila Are Just Friends

"This clever and adorable romantic comedy is brimming with warm humor and a lot of heart. It kept me giggling and turning the pages to see what came next. What a delight!"

—Rachel Linden, bestselling author
of *The Magic of Lemon Drop Pie*

"*The Perfect Rom-Com* contains two of my favorite tropes: friends-to-lovers and a road-trip romance. Melissa Ferguson handles both *perfectly*! I couldn't put this book down! And when main character Bryony finally clues in to the fact that Jack is not *just* her best friend, it's the sweetest, swooniest of moments."

—Suzanne Allain, author of *Mr. Malcom's List*

HOW TO PLOT A PAYBACK

"The perfect escape for lovers of dogs, second chances and swoon-worthy romance. Don't miss this one."

—Annabel Monaghan, bestselling author
of *Same Time Next Summer*

"Super cute! Melissa Ferguson's rom-coms lean more on the com than the rom, and this book is no different, delivering chuckles and giggles with an effortless writing voice, witty dialogue, and a cast of lovable characters. I was totally on board as soon as I read the premise, especially since it's a storyline I haven't already read more than a dozen times (give me all the fresh plots please!). You could say this is a grump/sunshine (although he's really not all that grumpy), enemies-to-lovers (although the hard feelings are only one-sided and misguided at that), slow burn, but I just call it a cute little romp of a book."

—Sarah Monzon, author of *All's Fair in Love and Christmas*

"It was so fun to sit in on the writer's room of a successful sitcom in Melissa Ferguson's delightfully charming and wonderfully quirky romance. There are so many sweet moments and wonderful characters sprinkled throughout, and I'm certain rom-com fans are going to fall in love!"

—Courtney Walsh, *New York Times* bestselling author

FAMOUS FOR A LIVING

"*Famous for a Living* is a heartwarming and funny read with quirky characters and the occasional moose. It takes the reader on a virtual escape to the mountains and hot springs of Montana and the lofts and busy streets of New York City. Melissa Ferguson has given us a sparkling, sweet rom-com with a lot of heart."

—Suzanne Allain, author of *Mr. Malcolm's List*

"Calling all fans of slow-burn, opposites-attract romance! Melissa Ferguson brings another fresh, delightful rom-com in *Famous for a Living*. Cat and Zaiah are an imperfectly perfect match with swoony chemistry and plenty of back-and-forth banter. The gorgeous national park setting provides a lush backdrop for this fish-out-of-water story as influencer Cat hopes to escape a media fallout and finds much, much more. Readers who loved *The Cul-de-Sac War* and *Meet Me in the Margins* won't be disappointed in Ferguson's latest read!"

—Emma St. Clair, *USA TODAY* bestselling author

MEET ME IN THE MARGINS

"*Meet Me in the Margins* is a delightfully charming jewel of a book that fans of romantic comedy won't be able to put down—and will want to share with all their friends. Readers will lose themselves in Melissa Ferguson's witty, warm tale of Savannah Cade and the perfectly drawn cast of characters that inhabits her world. This literary treat full of missed opportunities, second chances, and maybe even true love, should be at the top of your reading list!"

—Kristy Woodson Harvey, *New York Times* bestselling author of *Under the Southern Sky*

"Ferguson has penned a lively romance for every bookworm who once longed to step through the wardrobe or sleep under the stairs. *Meet Me in the Margins* brims with crisp prose and crinkling pages as Savannah Cade, lowly editor at a highbrow publisher, secretly reworks her commercial fiction manuscript with the help of a mystery reader—and revises her entire life. You'll want to find your own hideaway to get lost in this delightful, whip-smart love story."

—Asher Fogle Paul, author
of *Without a Hitch*

"Ferguson (*The Cul-de-Sac War*) enchants with this whimsical tale set against the evergreen culture war between literary and commercial fiction . . . An idealistic, competent heroine, a swoon-worthy hero, and delightfully quirky supporting characters bolster this often hilarious send up of the publishing industry, which doubles as a love letter to the power of stories. This is sure to win Ferguson some new fans."

—*Publishers Weekly*

THE CUL-DE-SAC WAR

"Ferguson offers an entertaining enemies-to-lovers story for readers who prefer a chaste romance. Imagine one of Sophie Kinsella's rom-coms made into a Hallmark movie."

—Booklist

"*The Cul-de-Sac War* by Melissa Ferguson is a humorous and lighthearted story about neighbors who are at war with each other . . . If you are looking for a fun, clean, lighthearted romance, then I do recommend this one."

—LifeIsStory.com

"Two neighboring houses, a big, slobbering dog without boundaries and one unwelcome attraction add up to a madcap romance in *The Cul-de-Sac War* . . . This kisses-only inspirational romance is a sweet treat with a soft center."

—*BookPage*

"Melissa delivered a book that is filled with both humor and heart!"

—Debbie Macomber, #1 *New York Times* bestselling author

"Melissa Ferguson delights with a grand sense of humor and a captivating story to boot! With vivid detail that brings the story roaring to life, *The Cul-de-Sac War* brings us closer to the truth of love, family, and home. Bree's and Chip's pranks and adventures turn into something they never expected, as Melissa Ferguson delivers another heartwarming, hilarious, and deeply felt story."

—Patti Callahan, *New York Times* bestselling author of *Becoming Mrs. Lewis*

"Melissa Ferguson's *The Cul-de-Sac War* is sweet, zany, and surprisingly tender. Bree and Chip will have you laughing and rooting for them until the very end."

—Denise Hunter, bestselling author of *Carolina Breeze*

"With her sophomore novel, Melissa Ferguson delivers hilarity and heart in equal measure. *The Cul-de-Sac War*'s Bree Leake and Chip McBride prove that sometimes it isn't the first impression you have to worry about—it's the second one that gets you. What follows is a delightful deluge of pranks, sabotage, and witty repartee tied together by heartstrings that connect to turn a house into a home worth fighting for. I was thoroughly charmed from beginning to end."

—Bethany Turner, award-winning author of *The Secret Life of Sarah Hollenbeck*

"Witty, wise, and with just the right amount of wacky, Melissa's second novel is as charming as her debut. Competition and chemistry battle to win the day in this hilarious rom-com about two people who can't stand to be near each other—or too far apart."

—Betsy St. Amant, author of *The Key to Love*

THE DATING CHARADE

"Part zany rom-com. Part family drama . . . a heartening read."

—*Library Journal*

"Ferguson's delightful debut follows a first date that turns quickly into a childcare quagmire . . . Ferguson's humorous and chaotic tale will please rom-com fans."

—*Publishers Weekly*

"*The Dating Charade* will keep you smiling the entire read. Ferguson not only delights us with new love, with all its attendant mishaps and misunderstandings, but she takes us deeper in the hearts and minds of vulnerable children as Cassie and Jett work out their families—then their dating lives. An absolute treat!"

—Katherine Reay, bestselling author
of *The Printed Letter Bookshop*

"*The Dating Charade* is hilarious and heartwarming with characters you truly care about, super-fun plot twists and turns, snappy prose, and a sweet romance you're rooting for. Anyone who has children in their lives will particularly relate to Ferguson's laugh-out-loud take on the wild ride that is parenting. I thoroughly enjoyed this story!"

—Rachel Linden, bestselling author
of *The Enlightenment of Bees*

"A heartwarming charmer."
—Sheila Roberts, *USA TODAY* bestselling
author of the Moonlight Harbor series

"Melissa Ferguson is a sparkling new voice in contemporary rom-com. Though her novel tackles meaningful struggles—social work, child abandonment, adoption—it's also fresh, flirty, and laugh-out-loud funny. Ferguson is going to win fans with this one!"
—Lauren Denton, bestselling author of
The Hideaway and *Glory Road*

"A jolt of energy featuring one of the most unique romantic hooks I have ever read. Personality and zest shine through Ferguson's evident enjoyment at crafting high jinks and misadventures as two people slowly make way for love in the midst of major life upheaval. A marvelous treatise on unexpected grace and its life-changing chaos, Cassie and Jett find beautiful vulnerability in redefining what it means to live happily-ever-after."
—Rachel McMillan, author of the
Three Quarter Time series

"Ferguson delivers a stellar debut. *The Dating Charade* is a fun, romantic albeit challenging look at just what it takes to fall in love and be a family. You'll think of these characters long after the final page."
—Rachel Hauck, *New York Times* bestselling
author of *The Wedding Dress*

Without a Clue

ALSO BY MELISSA FERGUSON

How to Plot a Payback

Snowy Serendipity: Two Christmas Stories

Famous for a Living

Meet Me in the Margins

The Cul-de-Sac War

The Dating Charade

Without a Clue

A NOVEL

MELISSA FERGUSON

THOMAS NELSON
Since 1798

Published in Nashville, Tennessee, by Thomas Nelson. Thomas Nelson is a registered trademark of HarperCollins Christian Publishing, Inc.

Thomas Nelson titles may be purchased in bulk for educational, business, fundraising, or sales promotional use. For information, please email SpecialMarkets@ThomasNelson.com.

Publisher's Note: This novel is a work of fiction. Names, characters, places, and incidents are either products of the author's imagination or used fictitiously. All characters are fictional, and any similarity to people living or dead is purely coincidental.

Any internet addresses (websites, blogs, etc.) in this book are offered as a resource. They are not intended in any way to be or imply an endorsement by Thomas Nelson, nor does Thomas Nelson vouch for the content of these sites for the life of this book.

HarperCollins Publishers, Macken House, 39/40 Mayor Street Upper, Dublin 1, D01 C9W8, Ireland (https://www.harpercollins.com)

ISBN 978-0-8407-1692-7 (epub)
ISBN 978-0-8407-1691-0 (TP)
ISBN 978-0-8407-1693-4 (IE)

Library of Congress Cataloging-in-Publication Data

Printed in the United States of America

25 26 27 28 29 LBC 5 4 3 2 1

RICKY

JACKIE

GORDON

NASH

Suspect List

CRYSTAL

HUGH

PIP

NEENA

To my mother, for a lifetime of support and love

CHAPTER 1

DID YOU KNOW THAT JAILBREAKING YOUR PENT-UP city toes from their Chelsea boots and surrendering your feet to the white-hot sand of Miami in February is good for you? That standing right where the crest of bubbly waves gently hugs your ankles before receding back into the blue-green ocean does wonders for your mental health?

But of course you do.

Just as *you* know, like everyone else on God's green earth, that the torturous act of waking up in an obscure conference center in San Diego at 3 a.m., missing your flight, rerouting your flying experience an extra ten hours through two more *extremely stressful* layovers (I don't have time for details, but I'm now missing one shoelace and definitely have a welt blooming on my hip as we speak), and becoming the ball in the great pinball machine of the United States is all worth it just to get to *this* moment?

But of course you do.

The beach is a miracle worker.

Any sane human knows that.

There are no words in the English language to properly describe the moment when you gulp in your first lungful of sea-salt air after months of particular grief and do precisely . . . nothing.

Nothing but stare out at the endless sea, listen as seagulls greet you gaily overhead, and feel the waves crash heedlessly all around.

No phones.

No agendas.

No mind-spinning movement.

Nothing but letting the senses take over.

It's worth it because of the ocean's intangible *something*, that mysteriously magical *something* that beckons you and heals you and envelops your heart in a warm blanket embroidered with the word *peace* and makes everything you've suffered to get here—everything you've suffered the past six weeks—absolutely worth it because of *this moment*.

Where the sea coos, *I know you were a splinter away from breaking down into total madness, but shhh, child, you are here now. Rest and find peace in my salty arms.*

That is what I came for. (Well, that and the small fact I'm paid to for work.)

This is what I'm supposed to be feeling right now.

Peace.

And in fact, until twenty minutes ago, that was precisely what I *was* feeling.

And then *he* showed up.

With that *THING*.

And I'm not entirely sure of how it's come to this point, how precisely point A led to point Z, but now here I stand, sensible twenty-seven-year-old Penelope Mae Dupont, with no criminal record or even so much as a speeding ticket, holding this stranger's portable boom box high over my head in knee-deep water and waves tossing all around—all while threatening to hurl his precious music box into the sea.

I've gone, as it turns out, completely mad.

Which both is and isn't surprising, given, as I said, I was only a splinter away before he came and ruined everything.

"Are you *insane*?" the man cries out, gesturing widely with his overtanned hands.

Then he utters some choice words.

And some more.

All of which I ignore.

A crowd is gathering.

But I, again in complete dissonance to my normal nature, don't care.

"I definitely think you've got me there," I cry back as the waves crash over my backside and send my green linen skirt twisting and choking around my legs like I'm a seaweed-laden mermaid. "Or who knows?" I toss out. "Maybe I've *been* insane all along. Maybe I've been insane all these years giving myself over to absolute delusions of who I was and who *he* was and what in life I was really bargaining for and maybe now, *right now*, I'm finally waking up. Who *really*, I wonder, has the authority to determine what makes us sane?"

My philosophical question clearly sails above the man's head.

After another cacophony of insults and a dozen commands, all of which I ignore, the man with the robust belly overtaking his pineapple swim trunks finally has had enough.

He drops his beer can in the sand.

The beach chair quakes as he pulls himself to standing.

I am fairly certain I've never seen a person more directly angry with me in my life.

I waver for a moment, then hold the boom box higher.

To be clear, I did not wake up today with intentions to

take on this one drunk man at two o'clock in the afternoon as representative of all that's wrong with society. I truly didn't. I'm not one of those people who ambles around New York with a water bottle sticker declaring *She Woke Up and Chose Violence*.

My stickers revolve solely around literary puns, the saving of trees, and cats wearing funny hats.

But he was here.

Dropping his slew of items *directly* behind me with a whole stretch of Miami beach around us, just to make painfully loud and alluding comments about "the view."

How beautifully green "the view" (a.k.a. my backside) was. How perfectly round "the view" (a.k.a. my backside) was.

And I was fine at that point. I was still a reputable woman in society, capable of ignoring his idiocy.

I was still Penelope Mae Dupont, summa cum laude graduate of NYU in English literature, lover of old books that crack when you open the spine and dogs that free-leash in Central Park at 8 a.m.

But then he cracked open what I guarantee was not the first beer of the day.

Made yet another leering remark.

And did the abominable. He turned on music.

Top-volume, angry, screeching, *repulsive* music that drowned out the beautiful keow of the seagulls, the laughter of children, the whistle of waves. A cacophony of sounds obliterating all the things I traveled thousands of miles through emotional anguish and physical distress *just* to experience.

He ruined . . . my moment.

"It's *my* music!" he demands.

"It's *our collective* experience you are debasing!" I counter, pulling away one of the long locks of my wildly disobedient hair that was trying to blind me and make me eat it for lunch. I gesture at the growing crowd.

To be utterly honest, they weren't exactly here before I made a scene.

Out of the corner of my eye, I see The Seven (minus Nash at the moment) in their little huddle, watching me. Suitcases are at their feet. Massive sun hats and sunglasses cover their faces. Sunblock is smeared on Gordon's nose like a vanilla Popsicle, the cruise ship we are meant to be boarding in a matter of minutes flapping its flags far in the distance.

Jackie nods approvingly at my word choice.

Ricky appears to be making a note of the word in his phone.

Crystal, well . . . her gaze alternates between me, my opponent, and her phone as she taps madly (attempting to write my current situation into a novel, no doubt).

"*Put it away*," I say fiercely, pointing at her.

She gives me a caught-red-handed look and pockets her phone.

Pineapple Trunks takes a thunderous step my way.

"You give it back now," he growls.

"Promise to turn it off," I counter.

I'm five feet even and half of my height is covered in damp, dark brown hair. Thick and twisty hair that has tried to mummify me in the salty wind. My long blunt bangs that reach to the top of my round glasses are plastered to my forehead, sticky and no doubt incredibly unsightly in the humidity. Most days I look screamingly academic, running around in maroon sweaters and juggling black folders full of Hugh's pages, but right now I look more like a horrifying creature who has emerged from the seaweed and is stealing people's beach cargo.

Which is . . . some could say . . . fair.

Nonetheless.

I can still see nothing but that same old loyal expression of fondness in The Magnificent Seven's—currently Six's—eyes.

But then something distinctive changes in Pineapple Trunks's look as he lets out another flash of outrage, and I cast a glance at the tide and wonder just how seriously I can outswim him.

Neena jumps in.

No, that's not correct.

Shimmies in.

"Okey dokey!" she cries out in a singsong voice, moving in between me and the man. "This has been a . . . well, a nice little surprise in the day . . . but I think we'd best all settle down. Pip, honey, give the man his nice boom box."

I open my mouth to protest, but she jumps in, adding, "And let me say, I'm *so* proud of you. This is great progress, and frankly, my dear, I'd love to sit this one out for as long as it takes. But the boat has made that honking noise three times now, and I'm afraid if we let them go on any longer, they'll leave us entirely."

"They won't *leave us*," Hugh says. "We're the ones putting on this cruise."

"Never leave people believing they play second fiddle to you, Hugh," she says, frowning at him. "It's impolite."

Hugh tucks in his lower lip, and Neena continues, "Anyway, I think it's probably time we give this man back his property—no matter how annoying he is or how many oxymorons he uses—"

"I'm not a *moron*!" Pineapple Trunks yells.

"Of course, dear," she says, with a *now let the grown-ups*

talk wave. "Or how generally wrong he seems to be in every way. It's still his boom box, and we must give it back."

"You heard her!" Pineapple Trunks pumps his fist in triumph and reiterates what she says very loudly, and much more forcefully, in my direction.

Neena gives him a simpering smile and, to everyone's surprise, pats his hand a few times. "I'll take it from here."

The man looks from his hand to her, this sixty-eight-year-old curvaceous woman in head-to-toe glittering purple.

And to everyone's surprise, he sits down.

She turns to me.

"Come on," she says then, beckoning me toward her like I'm some puppy being wooed from its cage. "Let's go, sweetheart."

"He's just so insensitive," I say.

"Very much so."

"And the music was so *abrasive*."

I take a tiny step forward.

The sparkling starfish clip in her hair glistens as she nods, and she reaches her hand out farther over the waves. "I heard it all the way from the pier. A true blight to the human ear," she agrees.

"And he was so . . . offensive." I take another step forward, the boom box lowering slightly to my shoulder.

"I have no doubt. But we all make our own choices, don't we? Some opt for a lifetime of meaninglessness. We can't force someone else to have a positive effect on the world."

"Can't we, though?" Hugh says casually. "With a little nudging?"

"Focus," Neena says under her breath, smiling through gritted teeth.

I take a step forward.

Neena takes a small step forward to meet me. "The important thing is to focus on what kind of positive effect *we* can have."

I nod, aware suddenly that the boom box feels heavy on my shoulder. The weight of this situation I put myself in is beginning to settle on me, and the fire in me that started this whole mess is fizzling out.

"I want to have a positive effect," I murmur and trudge through the waves.

My skirt is soaked.

My white blouse is dangerously close to getting soaked as well.

And my hair has twisted so far around me, I feel like a furry teddy bear.

I step onto shore.

"I know you do." Neena clasps my shoulder with one hand in *welcome home, soldier* fashion and grabs hold of the boom box with the other. Swiftly she hands off the boom box to Hugh, who hands it to Ricky, who hands it down the line to Gordon, Crystal, and finally Jackie, who hands it, with the kind of severe look only Jackie and very, *very* angry librarians can give, to Pineapple Trunks.

He takes it.

People begin to clap.

"What a *breakthrough*. I'm very proud of you, Pip." Neena engulfs my soaking wet, frizzy-hair-ensconced body in a hug (effectively soaking herself entirely) that lasts several moments too long.

Eventually, the clapping dies down.

And Hugh clears his throat.

I look and see Pineapple Trunks with a screwy look on his face, the look of a drunk man trying desperately to use his remaining working neurons to deduce whether this was a situation in which to call the police.

The cruise ship gives another honk.

And I realize I'm already gearing up to make a statement, quietly hoping for a female officer who's more likely to follow the thread of how discussion of a perfectly beautiful view has led to this.

Neena swings her wide smile to the man. "You know what?" she announces. "You look like somebody who appreciates a good fruit basket."

Crystal rolls her eyes.

"Fruit baskets are not the answer to everything, Neena," Jackie snaps.

They are, of course, to Neena, who firmly believes that a fruit basket is perfect in every situation from infant baptism to petty crime.

"Forget the basket. Consider this your lucky day, sir," Crystal, the youngest of 90 percent of the group by several decades, says. "You get a heck of a story and a group picture! Free of charge. That's worth a dozen fruit baskets and two dozen of your archaic boom boxes."

The man watches The Six begin nodding and mumbling in approval as though this is a most generous apology gift for an insane woman who stood in the ocean holding his boom box hostage.

"Ship's dropping ropes now," Ricky says, squinting at the cruise ship in the distance. "I think they're really going to leave."

"They're playing with us," Hugh retorts. He kicks his suitcase, which topples into the sand. "And two can play that game."

"Time for the photo op! Everybody in," Crystal says,

gathering the group together. Her eyes graze over the man dubiously. "Do your . . . swim trunks have a phone swimming there, or should we use one of ours?"

"All the sunblock's covering my makeup," Jackie protests, souring as she reaches into her handbag.

"Has anybody seen my hat?" Gordon says, twisting as he scans around him.

Pineapple Trunks notices, for the first time it seems, the crowd of bystanders with their phones all raised our direction.

"Who *are* you people?" he asks, as if we must be aliens freshly landed.

"Ah. The first intelligent question of the day." Hugh steps out from the group, a head taller than the rest. He takes off his hat. The sun glints on his silver and gray hair. His blue eyes twinkle. He looks distinguished and mysterious, even here on this sandy port shore, just like his author photo on the back of every one of his mystery books lining the shelves at every bookstore around the globe. "We're The Seven."

"The *Magnificent Seven*," someone murmurs, phone raised.

"And that girl there," Hugh says, pointing at me, "belongs with us."

CHAPTER 2

I COINED THAT TERM FOR THE GROUP, ACTUALLY. RE-marketed, more like.

For some awful reason, Hugh and the other six authors had called themselves "the group" for decades (painfully uninformative, I know), and I wasn't six months in before I changed the group's official title to something the book world had been calling them all along anyway: *The Magnificent Seven.*

The Magnificent Seven is exactly what they are: seven celebrated authors each in a different genre who banded together forty years ago to prop one another up as they carry the candle in their distinctive fields.

It's worked tremendously well, actually.

All things considered, it proved to be an ingenious plan to unite this unlikely group of authors together to cheer one another on. After all, fiction readers tend to read widely. What better marketing technique is there than for one famously good author to constantly recommend the books of the same six famously good others?

Lore is that Hugh and these six other stranger authors were all en route to a writing event and became stranded in an elevator with one random reader. Stuck together for hours, Hugh eventually asked the gentleman, "So. Which of our genres do you read?"

He replied with a hearty laugh, "What do you mean 'which'? I read you all!"

That day, a plan was hatched.

What if all of these completely distinct authors worked together to promote one another at events? Book signings? Presentations? Endorsements? What if they made an oath to promote one another—and one another *only*—whenever they were inevitably asked in interviews about their favorite book recommendations? What if, separate in so many ways and yet the same, they grabbed hands and pulled one another up as they all climbed the proverbial ladder? Together?

The Magnificent Seven.

And forty years later, the partnership is something of a fellowship of rings, all but two members (who recently retired and passed the proverbial baton) still the same. Rumors about the group abound, ideas involving secret handshakes, secret codes. The wildest one so far is that there is a secret passageway accessible via Hugh's library that opens to another room, where an underground ring of publishing elites gather with the sole purpose of skyrocketing The Magnificent Seven's books to the top of every chart.

For the record, there's no passageway.

At least, I haven't found one yet.

And if any outsider would know, it would be me, considering I've been working for Hugh and the group for five years.

There are seven genres under the banner of the group. Sure, we almost added the horror writer Aleksandar, but frankly, he was too scary in real life. Even if he did live in a legitimate castle and threw the best parties (part of the thrill was that you never really knew if you would actually make it home).

And here's the list:

Vibrant Neena, always handing out fruit baskets and throwing propriety in the air for the sake of the bold life. Writes romance. You know. The stuff with people drowning in satin dresses on the covers.

Prim Jackie, the definition of "antithesis to Neena," who considers being five minutes early as being late and collects—with particular *obsession*—pushpins from the 1700s. Like, ten-out-of-ten-level hype. Goes on and on about sharing a distant lineage with the king of England and uses that single fact to promote every single one of her historical fiction books. I once saw her holding up a Garfield souvenir T-shirt in quiet fascination. She caught my eye and dropped it like it was gasoline at a fireworks show.

Gordon, who is almost always in some costume or other. To say he lives for the medieval renaissance fair or a good Comic-Con is an understatement. Fantasy.

Crystal, twenty-two-year-old fellow NYC native who made one twelve-second TikTok about her book idea and it blew up to the point of becoming a Paramount movie. She's always missing important meetings because she's off water-sliding somewhere.

Ricky, who, I'll be honest, is totally creepy. Has a mysterious history working at Oak Ridge National Laboratory before finding his niche in thriller. Talks extraordinarily slowly and cautiously as though he's *seen* things. You never know what they are, and you never really want to find out, but you're absolutely certain they happened. *Things.* Rumor is he and Stephen King play chess on their phones together.

Nash, who . . . well . . . he's Nash. Everybody calls him dashing. Everybody thinks he's wonderful. Me too, of course. I'd be blind, deaf, and a liar not to admit it. He's been one of my closest friends in the past three years he's been on the team, if I really had to pin a title to us. Not that we have a title, of course. Not that we *are* anything.

Good friends feels like a stretch, honestly. I don't dare tell others that. He's far too, well, everything I'm not. I'm perfectly comfortable being the group's assistant and, by design, his assistant. I'm like his cheerful butler and he the delightful-to-everyone socialite. We laugh behind the scenes; we don't laugh in them.

And as if his career alone isn't leagues more extraordinary than my own, Nash grew up on a ranch. He goes off-grid at a snap of his fingers and tells nobody. Spends half his time somewhere out west, preferably under the canopy of a full sky and with absolutely no protection from beasts or rabid people except for his God-given muscles and a larger-than-life knife. Fun fact: He has worn Wrangler jeans, boots, and a cowboy hat in every single photo I have ever seen of him. Every single one—even the blurry paparazzi photos where people catch him at 7 a.m. heading into a coffee shop. I'm not sure, honestly, if he lifts weights, but if he does, I can guarantee it's while wearing a hat. Writes . . . unsurprisingly, Westerns.

And Hugh. My boss. Incredibly intelligent. Charming. Risk taker. Founding father of the group, whose brain is constantly whirring, taking in every speck of detail from the moment. Casually chatting with you about the tarragon in the sauce while mentally solving real live murders. Still works part-time for the police department. *Voluntarily.* As a "mental exercise," he says. Just to "keep his mind fresh" at seventy-five while being a benefit to society. Writes mystery. Not the kind with an apple pie on the cover beside an illustrated cat, but Agatha Christie. Dorothy Sayers. Convoluted stories. Surprising, sometimes bitter, sometimes bittersweet ends.

Nobody in the group fights.

There are no arguments. Not really. Not *actual*, shout-to-the-rooftops arguments over anything more substantial than where to eat dinner.

Just pure support year in and year out.

In my five years as Hugh's assistant and, by extension, assistant to The Magnificent Seven, I've never seen anything like it.

Honestly, if I didn't know them better, I'd say they were hiding secrets.

If I didn't know better, I'd say they had to be.

After all, they're human.

"Come along, Pip," Neena chirps. "Even through our mental breakthroughs, we cannot dawdle."

It takes approximately twelve more honks and thirty more minutes, but at last here we are, halfway up the gangplank with our luggage, sweat carving streaky paths down our sunscreened faces. My skirt is mostly dried. My hair is knotted in the ugliest let's-just-keep-everything-together bun alive. My blouse is missing a button.

I feel terrible they all followed me down to the beach, but as Neena says, "Once we saw the whole thing through Ricky's binoculars"—another question for another time: Why was Ricky watching me through binoculars?—"what choice did we have but to save our baby?"

(I'd ignore the reference to my babyhood and assert myself as a capable adult, except for the fact that at the time, I was indeed acting like a child and did indeed need a capable adult.)

Neena has put on her gigantic floppy beach hat, which

looks like it weighs approximately forty pounds. She turns toward me, and despite being a full three feet ahead, it whacks me in the face.

"He was gross. *And*," I add pointedly, "he was *inconsiderate*."

A far worse crime.

Somewhere along the way, driven by guilt mostly, I've added Neena's suitcase to my load.

It's not easy dragging our bags, considering her suitcase is not only one hundred pounds of glow-in-the-dark purple with a thousand stickers of her book covers smashed all about, but also twice the height of mine with a dodgy wheel. I'm lopsided, pulling along her protesting suitcase beside my modest (and personality-less) beige one.

And while I'm kicking myself while I'm down, I must note it reflects well who I am though, doesn't it?

"Of course he was inconsiderate. As men so often are," she says in a *we of the female population have resigned ourselves to this fact* singsong voice.

Hugh ahead raises his brow.

"Quite the statement for the romance author," I say.

It's funny because, for one thing, she's surrounded by the most trustworthy, upstanding men in the universe (minus Ricky?), and for another, her specialty is writing utterly unrealistic, nearly nauseatingly self-sacrificing and noble firemen-type males.

"Gordon and I are the same, honey," Neena says. "We both write fantasy."

Now it's Gordon who jerks his head back.

She's just trying to make me feel better. I've suffered from a male, ergo, she, too, will strike her fist in the air. I appreciate the move of solidarity. Even if it's a bald-faced lie.

She stops and turns, and I dodge another whack of her

hat to the face. "Would you like me to write him into my next book, sweetheart? I'll kill him off, if you like. Just for you."

Golly gee. What a treat.

"I appreciate the gesture, Neena. But that's more Hugh's genre."

"*The Pineapple Murder*," Hugh announces cheerfully. "Has a ring to it."

"How would you . . . have them . . . do it?" Ricky says with morbidly piqued curiosity. "I just read . . . a cyanide toxicity report in . . . fruit juices. Watch out, everyone," he says, casting a foreboding look at each of us. "It's too easy."

Too easy to what, Ricky? Kill someone?

Are these really things you should announce out loud?

This from Ricky, for the record, is normal. We are informed on a daily basis via email or otherwise how something can and will kill us. And it often ends with a statement about just how easy it'd be for he himself to do it. Reassuring stuff.

We all ignore him.

"The whole incident with the stereo is too funny *not* to use in a book," Crystal says. She hoists her camo backpack that's twice the size of her body higher over her shoulders as she strides alongside us, her little legs working like a seagull on a brisk walk. "It'd be a *travesty* not to show the world the hilarious moment of the Pip Breakdown. I'm working on a book set here in Miami—"

"Is that what we'll refer to this incident as?" Gordon says, ever the one for naming things. He has an entire language he's created for curse words, which he uses, in our real world, on the daily. "Binks" is one of them.

"Finks" if you're going for a low blow.

You should see Gordon and all his buddies at Comic-Con

in their wizard hats holding thirty-two-ounce sodas, each tossing their own made-up languages into the pile of conversation, each secretly, desperately hoping their made-up words will catch on.

And while Neena and Hugh and the rest carry on, arguing over exactly *who* is going to get the honor of using Pineapple Trunks in their next novel, I glance to the shore, back to the specific spot in the distance where I completely lost it.

Man, I really lost it.

In all the lifetime events of Penelope Mae Dupont, none will be as extreme as this. Mom likes to talk about how I once walked outside of my room as a three-year-old and peed on the carpet in defiance while in time-out. But that's the point. People who know me laugh, precisely because it's the exact opposite of something I'd do. I'm compliant and obedient.

I obey laws.

I give away cats when the landlord says they are no longer allowed (*difficult*, I assure you).

Hugh gives me a deadline for two days from now? I do it in one.

Hugh wants me to fly with him on a whim to an abandoned hospital in the middle of Nowhere, America, for some terrifying research? I say, "Shall I pack one bag or two?"

But that spot on the shore . . .

It seems that everybody's relieved I actually have a breaking point.

For weeks they'd been trying to get me to open up, to display any emotion, and I'd clamped my mouth shut.

I had composed myself.

I'd brushed my unruly hair until it went into a nice, neat ballerina bun. Every single one of my cardigan buttons was looped in place. I put on a polite smile and said to every single person who dared ask, *So how are you, Pip . . . really?*, "Me?" (as though it was funny they should ask such a surprising thing). "Oh, I'm doing well. Really well. Thank you so much for asking. And how are you, [insert anyone from distant aunt to secretly unsympathetic, gossipy downstairs neighbor]? How is your [dog, geranium, wart issue, whatever possible topic comes to mind to get the subject off me]?"

And I had just gotten to the point where everyone was possibly believing the ruse—including myself—when today happened.

The moment the man broke my perfect peace bubble and was so wholly *inconsiderate*, not thinking for a moment about how his actions affected the rest of the world around him, that I lost it.

Because the reality is, what you do with your life affects other people.

Thinking only of yourself comes with a cost, always.

You just may not be the one paying it.

People should know that.

Michael should know that.

Pineapple Trunks—and every other person on earth for that matter—should know that.

And be held accountable.

"Well, I think it's safe to say on behalf of everyone, we are all very proud of you, darling," Neena says quietly, bringing me back to the world around me. The beating Miami sun overhead. The blue and white bunting flags of the cruise ship snapping in the wind. Nothing depressing or unhappy in sight.

She's now got her arm wrapped around me as we walk several paces behind the others.

"I'm never dating again," I mutter as I grunt along, dragging our suitcases.

"We'll never date again, together!" Neena agrees in a tone that suggests, *Whatever you say here, I'm going to echo, darling. Because that's what you need right now. A good corroborating spirit over facts.* The captain of the ship glides past our periphery, and she follows his gait. "Except for men in hats," she says. "I've always had a weakness for a man in a good hat."

"You know, this could be an interesting start to kick up *your* novel," Hugh says cheerily. The fact that all my dirty laundry has been and continues to be so obviously aired in group conversation speaks volumes to my mental state right now. And to our group closeness.

Regardless.

"I don't have a novel," I say automatically. "There is no novel."

"Sometimes when you don't have the inspiration, you just have to make it," Hugh says in his *I'm guiding* voice. "Sometimes the best way to get your foot in the door if all the doors are locked is to simply build a new door."

My brows cinch together. These "words of wisdom" are frequent, by the way.

He's always trying to push me into writing and I'm always trying to push him out.

His brilliance just assumes everybody else's mind can work the same as his.

"What?" I say. "What do you mean by just build a door—"

"Butt out, Hugh. This is my pep talk, not yours," Neena says, shooing him off with her hand.

"You had to let it out sometime," she says, squeezing my shoulders despite the fact that I'm now (a) being pushed along on a gangplank, (b) dragging two heavy suitcases, (c) with gusts of wind trying to blow me over the railing and into the water below.

"Nobody can live very long with that kind of passion inside without it eventually blowing up and out. It's human nature. None of us are immune, no matter how much we sometimes wish it were so." She gives me a kiss on the top side of my head (blinding me in one eye with her hat while doing so) like the doting-but-eccentric grandmotherly figure she is.

"You know what, love?" she says in an entirely new tone. "This really might be the perfect time to let me see that novel of yours—"

"That's what I said," Hugh interjects.

"Get your mind off things," she continues, ignoring him.

"It's not a novel," I say.

"I heard you've got three chapters in!"

"I've been writing those same three chapters for three years."

"I heard you entered it into a writing contest and earned *fourth place*," she continues triumphantly.

"There were three contestants total," I reply. And after a pause, "Somebody's name was duplicated."

Neena purses her lips.

Yes, Neena. Try to find something positive to say about that one. The sad little "novel" I've been writing on and off (mostly off) for the past three years is nothing. *Really.*

Those evangelical pamphlets people leave beneath windshield wipers are longer than my "novel."

My new vacuum cleaner has a manual longer than my "novel."

It was stupid of me to even try to write a while ago. But it was like cigarettes, really. When *everyone* around you just so happens to be a literary giant and eat writing, drink writing, breathe writing, you can't help but pick up the proverbial cigarette eventually and say, "Hmm. What if I tried just *one?*"

The answer, in my case, was you cough and spasm and turn out to be totally, absolutely wrong.

"Hugh says one day you're going to take the mystery genre by storm. And he knows," she says, tapping her nose. "He has a sense for these things."

"That I do," Hugh chimes in.

"Shh," Neena says tersely, pushing him forward.

She stops us and waits 'til everyone moves on.

When he's shuffled ahead so far that he and the others are on board, she continues. "Hugh really does know, love. When he's right, he's *right.* He called out Bick Denton before he ever even picked up a pen. I thought it was crazy at the time, but sure enough, now he's *Bick Denton* and giving us all a run for our money." She smiles motheringly as she looks at me. "And he says the very same of you. Says your research skills are bar none. And I'll tell you what right now. It'd be a true pleasure to see you giving us all a run for our money too."

"Just because I can find him a unique set of weapons, means, and methods for his books doesn't mean I can piece all those facts together into anything cohesive. Believe me, Neena. I've tried. Researching pieces and parts for Hugh's books is one thing. Writing a masterpiece, as I have discovered to my great disappointment, is another. I can talk about dimethylaminopropionitrile all day long, but creating anything with actual creative genius is another."

"Hugh disagrees. He says you're talented."

"Yeah, well, currently my 'manuscript' is something between a journalistic piece and a medical dissertation, a bunch of technical terms gurgled up and emotionlessly splattered on the page."

She shrugs. "Hugh says though, love."

"Yeah, well, he can be wrong sometimes."

"That he can." She pauses. "But not when it counts like this."

Agree to disagree.

"Oh, you just need someone to push you off the ledge is all," Neena says, shimmying herself through the narrow entrance on board the ship, holding on to her hat like Marilyn Monroe. The silvery heads of several staff members turn.

An attendant opens his mouth to welcome us on board, but Neena raises a finger with a smile. He waits, gloved hand over gloved hand.

"I'm going to tell you a little secret, darling."

"I don't believe you are capable of secrets, Neena."

"We're all terrified when we first start. None of us think we have what it takes. You know what Hugh says: 'It's all about the first chapter. It's all as simple as getting down that first chapter. Once you've got that, you're nearly there.'"

How many times has Hugh said that to me? A hundred. A thousand.

When are you going to give me what I want, Pip? I want to see that first chapter. It's all as simple as getting down that first chapter.

"And that's where we differ, you and I, Neena," I say calmly. But it hurts, really. It hurts to have to defend the painful reality that I so wish were not true. "You actually had talent under that imposter syndrome of yours. I don't."

"You know," Neena says, looking at me with huge, eternally sympathetic eyes, standing beside the welcoming staff member with his now equally large, sympathetic eyes. "One of these days, I'm just going to break into that laptop of yours and read it myself."

I frown. "You wouldn't dare."

"I absolutely would."

"Breaking into laptops isn't really on brand for you, Neena."

"There's almost always more to people than meets the eye."

At a sudden gust of wind, she grabs her floppy hat and pushes it down firmly over her sparkling starfish clip. "Ah," she says with a sigh. "The sea. There is nothing quite like the sea."

The cruise ship is smaller than one of the giant cruise liners, bigger than a ferry boat and capable of taking on the open seas, but more manageably sized. Quainter. Classy. The hull and main deck are a gorgeous baby blue, the color of hydrangeas sweeping over Cape Cod porches in summer, the color of stately swinging French doors of old châteaus teeming with life in the countryside. Everything else is a pearly white, from the ornately designed railings with their graceful swerves and swoops, to the bow where a figurehead of a woman with an intricate golden crown smiles as she looks with confidence to the glistening sea. Crisp blue and white bunting banners flap everywhere overhead, stretching across the bow side with the glistening pool to the stern and the generously sized lounge chairs in striped blue and white on the other. Pagoda-style umbrellas in various shades of blue and white surround the pool, all with golden tassels shimmying in the breeze.

Waiters in deep blue waistcoats and blue feather bow ties glide around us, arms laden with crystal glasses full of fizzing amber and pink.

The cruise ship is straight from the twenties. It's classic glamour in a boat.

And, uncoincidentally, an absolutely perfect choice for the location of The Magnificent Seven's Inaugural Book Cruise.

I exhale as I watch the first impressions stretch across Jackie and the others' faces. Everybody's thrilled. Everybody is smiling in wonder at something—the waiter in his gorgeous purple-blue feather bow tie who just slipped seamlessly backward between two clusters in his polished black roller skates, the cocktail glasses in his hand not even so much as quaking at the shift. The slew of people—older women mostly—already stretched out on pool chairs on the sundeck, books (of The Seven, naturally) in hand.

Gleaming white marble side tables stacked with our team's books can be seen everywhere. (I thought it'd be a nice touch, but make no mistake, discussing mailing 2,500 books to the liner with express wishes to "thoughtfully set them around" was a more difficult conversation than one would think. Eventually we landed on a smattering around the ship and a neatly tied bundle on each person's pillow.)

The amount of organization and planning that went into this book cruise was heavy, to say it lightly. Over a year went into planning what I imagined would become our first of many book cruises: seven-to-ten-day excursions to stunning places around the world where readers could meet and share magical memories alongside their favorite authors. There were reasons behind this mad plan. Photography and film rights were included in the contracts. I'm hoping to capture so many perfect moments of the authors with their readers during this trip. There should be enough footage for news-letters, posts, advertising, and website management to last a year. And readers—of whom there are approximately three hundred on this ship—have been given so many books as part of this trip package, they'll be going home with a new library.

A win-win for all.

I round up the troops and announce that we will meet

back on deck in thirty minutes to go over the schedule, and then everyone departs for their rooms. Some attendants sail by while I'm not looking and take my bags—so sleekly, in fact, I thought for a moment I had just been robbed. Honestly, where did they hire these people? I can absolutely picture the CEO of this cruise liner tasking his underlings to loiter around the Eiffel Tower and find the smoothest pickpockets lifting wallets from tourists for the job.

My room is, in a word, *incredible*.

For one thing, it smells of lemon drops.

Plush pearly carpet looks like it was installed yesterday. Tendrils of gold are woven into the grasscloth wallpaper. The king-size bed overtakes the room, stuffed with a dozen plump white pillows of various sizes beneath a large, gilded oil painting of a water scene. What I expected from online searches was a head-shaped porthole. What I've received, however, and what makes up for the small space, are four floor-to-ceiling glass panels that take up the length of the room.

I pull open the door and immediately am washed in a breeze of warm, sea-salt air.

I step out to the little terrace, look down, immediately regret just how *far* down the tiny waves lap against the ship below, and step back inside.

Making a mental note here: Good to know. Avoid the patio.

When I step back inside, I notice for the first time my suitcase was somehow magically placed in my room.

How did they . . . ?

How did the staff know who I was when they took my bags? Or that I was in this room?

This is next-level hospitality stuff.

I gasp in shock when I lift the suitcase and feel it's empty.

I audibly say, "Wow," to the gilded wallpaper when I pull out a dresser drawer and see all of my belongings inside. Crisply folded. Down to the shaggy sweatshirt I wear at night with the gaping hole in the armpit.

Okay, I love this place.

I, even with terrifying balconies leaving nothing but a three-inch steel bar between me and certain death, am meant for a life at sea.

I jump in the shower to scrub off the sea salt and the airplane-travel memories of the day and put on a pair of black leggings and a sensible I'm-working-not-relaxing-here cream blouse. I don't have time to do anything but wind my hair into a wet bun, but at least I braid it first, then wind it round and round until it's one gigantic Celtic pancake at the back of my neck.

Sensible.

Little bit prudish.

Could easily come off as a cross schoolmaster at an all-girls school, but I probably need to look it after the day I've had.

I'm the first to get back on deck, and as I wait, I scroll through work emails and text messages that have piled up over the day. All of the family messages that have been coming in waves in the past six weeks since everything with Michael went down. An electric bill to be paid. Thirty-seven spam emails swiftly trashed.

There is one text thread that my finger keeps swiping over to as I sit perched on a creamy stool by a marble top, one plain black flat hooked on the lower rung, swiveling me slowly back and forth as a live band plays an old Sinatra tune. Why hasn't he responded yet? Where *is* he?

Hurry up.

He was supposed to be here an hour ago.

It feels like the day has dragged to a lifetime.

A new, most terrible thought occurs and my heart plunges into my stomach. What if he missed it?

What. If. He. Missed. The. Boat?

Sweat prickles over my body like an army of soldiers called to action by my hypothalamus commander.

Surely not.

Surely they wouldn't *leave* one of The Magnificent Seven.

And specifically *him* of all of them.

I'm about to break into a full sweat and commence running about, grabbing ropes and throwing anchors over ledges and full-on dragging us back to shore, when the bartender steps forward.

"For the lady."

I raise my head at the sight of a drink slid beneath my nose.

"Oh, no thank you, I—" I begin.

"Rhubarb and Rosewater Fizz Mocktail," he announces. "Very nice choice. It was new to me; I'll have to add it to the list. Recipe compliments of the man over there."

He points somewhere over my shoulder, but he doesn't need to.

I knew as soon as he said *rhubarb* that he was here.

How can you put into words exactly what it feels like knowing your coworker / favorite friend / person you've been fully allowed to enjoy interacting with during work hours / person who is *your* person for the proverbial nine-to-five but then erases into memory once the day is done and the weekend has come, or (as in this case) goes off-grid for a series of months, has just returned?

Elated doesn't do it.

More like . . . like a mother who loses sight of her kid at

a playground and anxiously scans the area knowing everything is *probably* fine, it *has* to be fine, surely it *is* fine, and
then—*pop*—there he is hopping out of the bottom of the
slide and you find you can breathe again.

Seeing Nash, well, it's like I can breathe again.

And I didn't even know I had been holding my breath.

The hours of exhausting emotional strain and physical
travel slip away as I push off the barstool.

Nash heads toward me, cowboy hat and jeans and all,
making his way through a cluster of women. His eyes are
linked on mine, but even so, he tips his hat toward the ladies in
one of those endearing little ways that makes women swoon,
because *oh, isn't he so charming and dashing and brave—and
he smells just like sunlit dew resting on a fresh hay bale.*

And to be honest, he does smell like that.

It's the jeans.

It's sort of baked into him in all his travels.

Least, that's my theory.

"You're late," I announce, far less enthusiastic than I really
am, as I rise off my stool to give him a hug.

"That painful without me, huh?"

"You have no idea."

"Who's to blame this time?" he says as he gives me a
squeeze.

"Me, actually. I'd tell you all about it, but I don't think I
could live through reliving it."

He's a foot taller than I am, and suddenly I'm swallowed
up in denim and his signature hay bale scent, and when my
feet are lifted off the floor, a few sighs of envious ladies escape in the distance.

Here's the thing about us.

I've never texted Nash outside of a work-related context.

I've never been to his apartment.

I've never suggested we casually get together "as friends" ever.

He, likewise.

But during the work hours I'm free.

I'm allowed to laugh at his jokes.

I'm allowed to stand by his side on the street and discuss in low and humorous tones exactly what I think about Jackie and Crystal elbowing their way to get into the taxi first. I'm allowed to confide in him and appreciate him and all the ways we have each other's backs while on duty.

He's just . . . my person.

My work person.

And up until six weeks ago, that was all he was allowed to be.

There. That's how I'd describe us.

Nash is my nine-to-five person who lights up my nine-to-five life in a way that makes me feel that all the joy of work would be sucked out of my life without him.

Simple, and exceedingly platonic.

When he has finally let go and takes a seat beside me, I'm out of breath again, but for entirely different reasons.

Wordlessly, the bartender holds up a chilled mug in one hand and plain beer in the other. Nash taps the beer and he slides it over.

"Today was . . . not the best travel day," I say, feeling more grounded in Nash's presence than I have in weeks.

This is what I needed, I realize, taking a steady sip of my rhubarb and rose.

Not the salt air.

Not the bubbly waves.

I needed this right here.

That poor (I mean, but we can only pity him so much, can't we?) man with the boom box went through it for nothing.

"Neena didn't make you listen to 'Desperado' again, did she? I told you, Pip. You don't have to listen to it—"

"I know," I say. "But she plays it through her phone—"

"You gotta stand up to her—"

"She thinks it's bonding."

"What part of 'Desperado' is bonding? No part of that song speaks to group travel. I don't know why she clings to it. How many times was it this time?"

"I lost count after thirty-seven."

He whistles.

"And that marked hour one. I told you," I say, then pull the drink to my lips, "it was a long day."

My phone dings with an incoming text followed three seconds later by ringing. Nash and I both lean in to see who it's from.

That, I think, might sum up Nash and me.

We are both unapologetically nosy about other people's calls—and don't mind.

We press speakerphone when we answer.

It's more like a secret third party on every call.

Neena's text is simple.

SOS.

Her name is also the one on the banner as it rings.

"How long have you been on board?" Nash whispers.

"Thirty minutes."

"Is that a new record?"

"Hardly," I say, then pick up the call. "Hi, Neena. Where are you?"

And as I commence working her through the twists and turns that would get her to the top deck, Nash makes small talk with the women who have been perched on the pool chairs, listening in.

Then he does something that stops me mid-sentence.

He takes off his hat.

Hooks it on his knee as one drops a hat on a hook by the door, one boot resting on the bottom rung of my stool.

And for a blink of an eye, he is rolling his shoulders and shaking out the glinting blond-brown locks of his shaggy (in a very nice way) hair, and I see as he rubs the back of his suntanned neck a look in his composure of one who is bone-weary. Of one who has just returned from a distant war to the squishy armchair of his living room, the one he'd dreamed of through all those cold and scary nights far abroad.

He's listening to one of the women drone on, nodding. Contented.

That's what he looks like.

Bone-weary but contented.

Like this is just where he wants to be.

Too.

A warmth blossoms in my chest and I quell it.

I listen as Neena somehow gets herself onto the wrong elevator and ends up in some underwater dining room. All the while, I'm remarkably aware of Nash's knee so casually touching mine.

How long have we been friends now?

Coming up on four years? And yet it feels like a lifetime.

Nash catches me looking at his knee and we lock eyes momentarily.

He clears his throat and pulls his knee back to his chair side.

I swallow my pride, forcing myself not to take it personally. Silly, really. We are *professionals*.

"Oh, I see some coattails," Neena says. "I'm going to grab on and not let go until he takes me up. Yoo-hoo!"

The line goes dead.

Moments after I break off, Nash picks up his beer and, after some polite niceties, the crowd of women drifts away, leaving us alone again.

He swivels my way.

"So," I say, "where was it to this time?"

"Buhl, Idaho. Down a tiny valley near Snake Ridge Canyon."

"Snake Ridge Canyon," I repeat with a suggestive lift of my brow. "Sounds charming."

I know the place.

I looked it up when he told me he might be going offline again a few months back, heading out beneath the wild sky to clear his head for book research and just general living. He juggles the states up quite a bit, but they all have some similarities: out west. Places either hot enough to melt butter or so cold you get frostbite (he's had it—twice). Humidity that you could slice through with a knife.

He brings his boots and his hat and jumps on a random horse with two saddlebags of canned beans and jerky and a tin coffee can and water and a notebook and his trusty computer and—let's hope—a toothbrush.

Sleeps on the ground with his hat over his head—just like in his books.

Drinks coffee that looks a lot like mudwater—just like in his books.

Pops into town to charge up his laptop every few days and grab a few more cans of beans.

Does nothing but muse in silence for days on end—and write his books.

He usually comes back with a half-written novel or, if not half, at least a quarter and a plan.

Every author has his method for inspiration, I guess.

"I thought you were going for four weeks this time."

"I went eight."

"You never go eight."

"This was a trip I needed eight. I had to . . ."—he pauses and his eyes jog away for a moment—"get away from it all for a bit. Get some perspective."

"About what?"

Nash hesitates.

Shakes his head.

"Just people. Work. Life. To remember my place."

He's shutting down over it. I can see it plainly in the shift of his body as he turns and takes a swig of his beer.

Well. I understand. If there's one thing, one tiny little take-away I've had drilled into my brain over the past six weeks, it's that I will never pry again. People can be well-meaning, but if I have to say, "I'm fine, and you?" while piecing my face into a perfectly effortless smile for their daily inquisition one more time, I just might throw a boom box into the ocean.

I shift the subject, keeping my tone light.

"Get bit by anything interesting?"

"Found a rattler in my boot one morning."

I make a face. It's revolting. His hobbies are *revolting*. "The number of times you've discovered living creatures in your shoes is really concerning, Nash. Have you ever, oh, I don't know, considered rolled-up towels in them or some-thing?"

"No room in the saddlebags."

"You have shirts."

"I have *shirt*," he corrects.

"You don't even carry an extra *shirt*?"

"If it gets dirty, you just take it off. Clean it. Put it back on again. Keeps things simple."

I laugh, picturing the twenty-*two* shirts sitting in my drawers in my room below at this very moment.

"Plus, a little threat of snake in your boots keeps you on your toes. You gotta have some adventure."

"Hey now," I say, putting up a hand. "I put three packets of sugar in my coffee at the airport this morning instead of two."

His brows rise amicably. "That so?"

"Darn tootin'. So. Any full moons? Any of those famous write-all-night-under-the-pale-moon-twenty-thousand-word spells of yours?"

"Couple. The stars were . . ."—he pauses, that little smile on his face he gets when he's conversing about something he likes—"you would've loved it, Pip. The whole sky was covered in them."

"You know, from what I read, the night skies out here are going to be pretty worthwhile too. *And*," I say, raising a finger over this very noteworthy bonus, "rattler free."

"I did hear something about that. It was your tactic to get me on this floating prison, after all," he says, and we pass a mutual grin.

In a moment of weakness, I did send him twenty separate text pictures of star-swept skies on cruise liners to sway him to go on this trip. And at least three articles on tonight's meteor shower.

I had to do some heavy-duty pleading for him to come.

For some reason, Nash in particular was resistant, unlike everybody else, who jumped when I said the words "book sales" and "free buffet."

And for Jackie, when I mentioned the sheet thread count.

And Gordon, with the magic show entertainment.

"How close are you to finishing up this book?" I ask, ever secretly amazed by how quickly Nash can throw out books.

"I'm close to the end of this one," Nash says, rubbing a hand up and down his stubbled chin. "A little bit stuck, though. I keep hammering on the page, but it never seems to make anything of itself."

"Case of the yips? No such thing with Nash Eyre."

"There's a first for everything, and I'm certainly living it."

"Even with a hiatus of snakes in the boots and rocks for pillows and everything?"

"Even with the snake," he says with a shake of his head. "I might just find one of those chairs and try to make an end to it tonight beneath that meteor shower of yours."

"I'll join you," I say cheerily.

It just pops out of my mouth.

A self-invitation.

There's an obvious pause.

"Yes. Can't miss this," Nash says, but there's something in his tone that carries a slight stilt. A wordless distancing. His boot ever so slightly shifts an inch away on the stool. "I can . . . knock on your door—"

What is that?

Is that too far over the line?

Daytime work friends, not alone-beneath-stars-at-night memory makers. I mean, what did I expect? I haven't seen him or heard from him in two months.

Immediately a warmth spreads across my neck, and I rub it subconsciously.

Stupid of me.

"No, *no*," I say in a casual rush, over-grinning. "I'll just meet you here. We'll have to duke it out with our elbows against the elderly to get a couple of chairs most likely. Don't worry about me."

"We're baaaaack," Neena says in a singsong voice, shimmying up to the two of us with the rest of the group trickling in behind. The time for Rhubarb and Rosewater is over.

"Did people break into your room and steal your clothes?" Hugh asks the group. "I went to the bathroom, came out, and it was all gone."

"Check your drawers," Gordon says cheerily. "They put everything away. Down to a very tidy arrangement of my hats by color and size."

Jackie sniffs. "They *wrinkled* my tweed blazer."

"It's been ten minutes. Can tweed really—" I begin.

"Sixty seconds," Jackie hisses. "You can ruin a whole wardrobe in *sixty seconds*—"

"Oh! Somebody grab me some pearls to clutch! The tea is *boiling*!" Crystal announces cheerily. "What'll be next at this diabolical luxury cruise? Unwashed slices of lemon in the water glasses? Lint on the bathrobes?"

"A dangerous thing . . . to do," Ricky murmurs in his painfully cryptic voice. "Breaking in . . . to the room of . . . a man so closely acquainted . . . with murder."

Nash gives me a look.

I give him one back.

"Okay, okay, everyone," I jump in before the conversation snowballs down this looooong hill. "In good news, Hugh didn't attack anyone trying to fold his laundry. I'll personally head over to your closet with an iron later, Jackie. And I have a tour to go over with you all. Move along."

I shepherd the group through a tour of the cruise ship in terms of workshops, meals, planning sessions, and free time. I lose Crystal to the slip and slide at some point and end up backtracking a fair bit to drag her back, but ultimately the day is smooth sailing (pun intended).

The big group introduction session goes as planned (except for Gordon, who loses his pet rabbit and spends the rest of the session checking under tables for a missing Holland Lop), and by dinnertime, we're all enjoying a feast of every meat under the sun in one of the big ballrooms.

The room is loud and jubilant with first-night energy. Nothing but sea and sunshine to the ends of the earth.

As dessert plates are being cleaned up, Hugh steps over.

"I need a word, Penelope. Just you and me," Hugh murmurs quietly with a touch to the elbow.

"We're just about to head to Coffee and Conversation in the parlor," I say with a *can it wait?* tone, but he just shakes his head.

"Okay," I say, swinging my head to the others.

Jackie is already halfway out of the room.

Neena, not even in view, is probably already there.

"They'll wait," he says, pressing me toward the back door.

There's no humor as we walk briskly down the hall, away from the others.

Which is odd, because Hugh *always* looks like he's on the brink of hearing a big joke.

I follow along the intricately patterned dark blue carpet, our feet making no sound. We twist this way and that until even I am turned around, and just when I think I *may* recognize an elevator in the distance, he pulls me into an empty room.

He switches on the light, illuminating gilded spines of books all around. Six stuffed red lounge chairs and couches circle the interior of the room, the blackness of night of three portholes soaking the view. A room of red, gold, and black. Fitting for the sense of dread coming over me.

I move next to one of the standing lamps, like a moth hunting for light.

He looks both ways down the hall, then shuts the door with particular care.

When he turns, I'm frowning.

"Is this about Jackie telling you not to eat the ice cream? I know she can be overbearing, but she's just worrying over you. It's the freakish way she shows she cares."

"No," he says, exhaling as he moves to a chair. He drops into it and beckons me to sit on the couch opposite. "No. But I wish it was."

He waits until I'm fully settled on the couch. Gives a look around as if expecting someone to be peeking out from behind the velvet curtains.

"Hugh," I say, because *honestly*, it's almost nine o'clock and everyone is waiting on us.

And he's starting to creep me out.

Working for Hugh, for the record, is not like other PA jobs. Other PAs print off copies. I print off copies while testing out how many seconds it takes me to snap the bullets of a .44 Magnum into place as research for his new mystery (he realized early on I was a handy amateur in all things crime, making me the perfect test subject for most of the characters who had normal jobs and lives before randomly murdering someone in his books).

Other PAs bring coffee. I bring Hugh three cups of coffee with sedative in one to see if he can guess which one knocks him out. And then test exactly how long it took him to actually be knocked out (oh, the pizza delivery guy who walked in on that one).

I keep him to his calendar. I remind him of deadlines and then drag him away from fun to lock him in his room to hit those deadlines. (Literally. His request.)

I pull the bayonet out of his sleeping hand and bring him his pills in the morning to keep his blood pressure down.

I am, essentially, the mother of an eccentric seventy-five-year-old author.

And now he needs reining in.

"We at least have to message them—" I begin, still thinking about how to salvage the event we're late for.

"I have reason to believe someone is trying to murder me. And it's one of The Seven."

I pause from reaching into my pocket for my phone. Squint at him.

"Hugh," I say again. "Come on. What's this really about?"

"I'm serious, Pip. I think my life is really and truly in danger."

The idea is so preposterous, so out of nowhere, that I laugh.

And yet he doesn't chime in, and after a few seconds, my laugh dies out.

"You can't be serious," I say.

He brushes a hand over his face, looking away to the left, somewhere in the distance. "I am," he says, more to the drapes than to me. "Incredible to believe, but I am."

I sit back, leaning against the upholstered pinches in the couch. Cock my head. Sit in silence for some moments.

"No," I say at last.

Can't be.

Not *them*.

"You have been working too hard, Hugh," I continue. "That's my fault a bit. I haven't been as attentive the past couple weeks, and you've gone . . ."

Mad is the word I want to say.

Manic.

Because that's another thing with Hugh. I learned early on that part of my job is to keep him from spending both too little *and* too much time writing. It's a thin line to balance and a long fall on either side if he missteps—and with Hugh, he tends to fall off the line every time without me.

Too little writing and pushing too far past the deadlines and the publishers come threatening.

Too much writing and escaping into his little office hole and he forgets to eat, sleep, bathe, and comes up with the most insane conclusions and ideas.

And the past six weeks, well, I've been chasing a rabbit down my own little rabbit hole.

I reach forward. Pat his knee and move to standing. "Come on. Let's do this recap and go straight to bed. You'll feel better in the morning—"

"I found a note."

That's when I notice Hugh's hands. Are they *shaking*?

"What did it say?" I ask.

"I went out yesterday from the office. Left my door un-locked as I always do."

Sure. And probably wide open.

"And when I came back, I saw the other door was open."

"What other door?" I say, brows rising.

"The secret door," he says, as though this was obvious. "The one we don't talk about."

"Wait. There actually *is* a secret door?"

"Have you not found it by now?" he returns, with a mild look of disappointment in me. "The point is, it was open. And on the round table—"

There's a round table? The gang meets up around a round ta-ble like medieval knights?! There is so much to unpack here!

"—was my book. With a knife stabbed right through it. And a note."

A chill runs up my spine. "What did it say?"

"'Off to sea but never stay, you will go home another way.'"

Okay. That is terrifying.

But.

But.

"But, and to go back to that note in a moment, that could be written by anyone—"

"It was signed. 'Of The Seven.'"

I stare at him.

"Where's the note?"

"In my top desk drawer."

"Did you take a picture?"

"No."

I rub my face.

Rub my face again.

He's expecting me to say something.

"Hugh . . ." I begin. "I don't know what to say. Maybe it wasn't one of them. Maybe it was someone else—"

"Who knew about the secret room? Come now," Hugh says, hands outstretched, "even you didn't know."

"But why would they do something like that? It makes no sense."

Warnings in mysteries, for that matter, *never* make sense. If you wanted to kill someone, go on and do it.

"Someone must've found out I know their secret."

"What secret?"

"I never should've allowed myself to get caught . . ."

"*What secret?*" I say with more urgency.

"I need you to do something for me," he says, grabbing me by the elbow. In his hype he's not listening. "Promise me, Pip, whatever happens, *should* anything happen, you'll get the note from my desk the second you get back to New York. Get to it. Hide it. It'll be little evidence, but there just might be something there for the investigators to go by."

"Stop it, Hugh. If this is some kind of twisted joke . . ." I say, winding my arm out from his.

"And no matter what, don't tell a soul. Pretend you know nothing. Keep yourself away from trouble. Not a soul, you hear me? That'll give you time to deliver it to the police without putting yourself in harm's way. *But no matter what, don't put yourself in harm's way.* I would never be able to forgive myself if I put you in a dangerous place because of my actions."

He rubs his lips.

His eyes dart back and forth, like he's reading through an invisible manuscript and watching this all play out. And he doesn't like the ending.

Hugh leans himself back suddenly. "You know what? Never mind. This is all too dangerous for you as it is."

He stands.

"Hugh. *C'mon.*" Now it's my turn to grab his elbow.

"You heard nothing," he says. "Stay out of whatever comes."

I purse my lips. "Well, now I obviously can't, Hugh. This is all insane." I stand too.

"Never mind, Pip. Just let it go." He pauses, his milky blue eyes roving round the room. "Just the ramblings of an old man."

I tilt my head as I look at him.

When did this transformation happen? How long has he been this pale and I haven't noticed?

Wasn't he laughing this afternoon?

There's a piercing look in his ice-blue eyes as I weigh the question.

The clock strikes nine on the wall, and he jolts his head up. "Ah," he says and pulls out his medicine from his chest pocket. The medicine he is *specifically* supposed to be taking at 9 *a.m.* every morning. He pops one into his hand and I grab it.

"These are for *a.m.*," I say. "Take one in the morning."

"Ah. Right." He grabs the pill back.

"Oookay then," I say with an exhale. My blood pressure is starting to drop. The black spots in my vision begin to clear. "Fine. Fine, Hugh. Should you mysteriously disappear by one of your lifelong best friends in a freak incident of the world flipping upside down, I promise I won't tell a soul. Happy?"

He swallows the pill dry.

There's a terrible dry gulp as it goes down and he opens the door.

Motions for me to go through.

"Tremendously."

CHAPTER 3

IT'S 2 A.M.

I stayed up, piddling around online mostly. Posting an edit here. Reviewing PowerPoints for various sessions there. Texting my sister about how things are going. Thinking about Hugh. Worrying over little nothings.

I checked my phone a few (hundred) times.

For a while I just flipped it over and took quick peeks as I focused on my work, but eventually I gave up and flipped the phone face up as I sat crisscrossed on my bed, typing— one eye ever on the time.

Maybe Nash wasn't even going to go. He was pretty raw at dinner; I wouldn't be surprised if he fell asleep and forgot about the whole thing.

Didn't matter, though, did it?

I was here to see the sky show, not him, great companion though he may be.

At two o'clock on the dot, I swing my legs over the four-poster bed, slip my feet into my furry loafers, and make my way up deck. It's quiet in the halls. The sconce lights are dim, and perhaps I'm imagining it, but I feel the tiniest sway of the cruise ship as the wallpaper goes up and down.

The sailor in the oil painting stares at me, and I stare back as I take the elevator up, my thoughts wandering.

When I reach the deck, Nash is standing beside a column, alone.

The moment he spots me his face does that little tilty smile of his and I smile back, like we're two kids at camp who agreed to sneak to the dock of a lake and watch the stars. It does feel oddly "not allowed" up here, all alone. But I mentally note his posture is an expectant one; he clearly didn't overthink any of this like I had.

To him? We agreed to meet. Watch a shower. Enjoy the moment. Nothing more.

"You ready?" he says, and before I can even answer, he pulls on a cord.

The rows of incandescent bulbs hanging overhead go off in an instant, leaving us surrounded by nothing but the tiny glow of floor lights at the pool stairs behind.

I blink a few times, my eyes trying to adjust.

Everything is shadows. The lounge chairs blobs. The pool glowing a peaceful Mediterranean blue. It's hard to distinguish just where the tasseled umbrellas end and the sky begins. I take a couple messy steps forward.

He meets me, his gait infinitely steadier than mine. "I've had them off for a while. I've adjusted," he explains to my wordless question.

I take a couple of shuffling steps, slow as molasses, watching the ground.

"Want a hand?" Nash asks.

There's a hesitancy in his question, as if to imply he's offering out of respect, not as a romantic gesture.

The way he always asks, with that border around his actions to say, "*We are friends, nothing more.*"

"Sure," I say with a breathy little chuckle, to show just how silly this is (but also yes-most-definitely-please).

I feel his rough, calloused hand slipping into mine. A hand that just very casually pulled a rattler from his boot, held the reins of a horse, made his own fire, and went on to write beautiful, emotional sonnets inside a big, beautiful head.

No big deal. Just ordinary things ordinary men do.

"We both know if you break your shins on one of these concrete things, they'll all be after me."

"Oh, they absolutely would."

Hugh and Neena and the lot of them would get after Nash relentlessly for turning the lights off and having me break my leg and fall into the pool and spend the rest of the week hobbling around. I can just see motherly Neena now, tsking with her arm wrapped around me, saying, "And to think she *just* went through that incredibly *awful* and embarrassing mental breakdown in front of the whole *universe* . . . *Oh*, you didn't hear about it, Nash? I believe Ricky caught the whole thing on camera, hang on . . ."

"They look like they bought out a dying ornamental garden store."

"I have wondered what this does to the weight capacity of the ship," I say.

By the time we've reached where he's landed himself, my eyes have adjusted and I can see he has indeed been here awhile, since leaving the parlor this evening is my guess.

His belongings are strewn across a pool chair beneath one of the umbrellas to our right. Closed laptop. Coffee cup. Discarded leather bag. Hat.

"It's just starting. I've already seen a few meteors," he says.

We skip the upright chairs and move out under the direct sky, popping our beach chairs down almost as low as they'll go, and gaze upward.

We watch for a few minutes.

Somebody slips around a corner, sees us, and slips back.

"We're going to get in trouble," I hiss, watching the server glide away.

"Turning off the lights. Terrible offense," Nash says, tucking his hands beneath his head. "I hear they have prisons on these ships."

"Or you walk the plank."

"Or they ration our pistachio pudding servings. Oh. There's one."

We both watch as a star streaks long across the sky.

He continues, "No, I think you and Jackie have successfully secured us one of those luxury cruise liners that'll let anything slide, so long as you've paid for your ticket. If you request they fill the pool with Jell-O tomorrow, their next question will be 'What flavor, miss?'"

"Benefit of being famous authors, I suppose."

"Benefit of paying a ridiculous sum for this excursion."

I smile to myself. That was the one fun thing about planning this work trip.

If I had to go, I might as well enjoy going somewhere insanely nice for free.

"After everything that's happened, I'm giving myself this one," I say. "I'm fully intending to eat all the pistachio pudding here and do all the paint classes. How do you feel about orange for the Jell-O pool?"

"I'm a cherry man myself."

"Alright. Cherry it is."

"So what happened?" Nash asks.

"When?" I say. And then remember. *Shoot.*

"You just said you're giving yourself a break this trip given what's happened. What's happened?"

But then I cry out and swing my finger toward the perfect diversion. Three stars burst simultaneously onto the sky stage and race with fiery competition to the other end of the world.

He turns.

Mission success.

The meteor shower goes on for another hour at least, and together we watch in quiet, taking it all in. Nash no doubt sees this stuff all the time, but for me it's breathtaking, a once-in-a-lifetime view, and for an hour at least I'm wholly satisfied. My breath slows, my eyes begin to droop, and somewhere in there a fluffy pool towel ends up covering me. I lie there for who knows how long, in peace.

I fall asleep, and I tell ya what. My sound machine by my bed has nothing on the real thing.

Nash doesn't break my moment, but somewhere along the way I hear the quiet clacking of his laptop, a calming rhythm to the stillness of the world around me.

The first thing I see when I wake up is the stars, brilliant but unmoving.

The show is over.

I look around.

Nash has moved himself quietly over to the table. His laptop is open. The glow of the screen lights up his face, and he looks up mid-typing, catching my eyes. I begin pulling up the back of my pool chair and sitting up again, and he shuts the computer.

"Sorry. Realized a new piece for my ending."

"Sure," I say, totally getting it.

I totally don't get it.

Personally, at least. But I do have two eyes and have watched plenty of times the extreme means by which Hugh works in words.

And Neena.

And all the others.

Inspiration strikes and suddenly they're gone, usually physically, but at the very least mentally.

No matter how inconvenient.

In the middle of lunches. In the middle of important Zoom calls. In the middle of award shows.

Just . . . in the middle of anything.

They all get this look and—*poof*—they're gone.

Which reminds me.

"Have you noticed anything off with Hugh lately?" I say, tucking the towel under my chin to keep out the chill.

"It's Hugh. How would you define *off?*"

"Oh, you know, different. He's been . . ." I hesitate, not sure of what to say. "Strange tonight."

Nash shakes his head. "Hugh's always strange in that luring sort of way. It's why we all follow him. The whole group would follow him off a bridge."

"Well, I don't know about a *bridge*, but I know what you mean. But this was . . . it was different. Tonight he . . ."

And then his absurd promise he had me make comes to mind, and against all better judgment, I shake my head.

But *obviously* Hugh doesn't mean Nash.

Then again, it was *obvious* he couldn't really be serious about anyone—Gordon, Neena, Jackie, Crystal, or Ricky.

Okay, maybe Ricky.

But not everyone else, surely. *Surely.* The whole idea was just beyond logical.

"I know Hugh's been dealing with a block on his next book. It's been driving him crazy," Nash says, filling in the gap of silence between us.

I nod, knowing all too well about the "book that will kill me" as Hugh has repeated at least ten times a day the past four months. "Yeah . . . there is that . . ."

Nash shifts in his chair. "The stress is getting to him."

"Maybe . . . the trip will do him good," I say, still unsure. "Give him something else to think about for a while." I drag my knees up on the lounge chair now, abort the stars, and face him fully. I consider my words. "I worry about him."

And to this, Nash laughs. "The man is seventy-five years old and sharp as a tack. I don't worry about him. I worry about every other poor soul he's ever made contact with."

A.k.a. me.

Him, too, and all the other authors who have endured some crazy things for the sake of "research."

"Sometimes I wish he wrote romance," I say.

"Yeah?"

"Absolutely. Be forced to go to plays and try out new coffee shops for research. Suffer through five-star dining at the top of the Eiffel Tower. Be forced to have breakfast in bed overlooking Fifth Avenue at the Peninsula. Be a grumbling plus-one through Christmas-themed train rides across the country."

"Go diving at exotic islands."

"I did that, remember? Hawaii. Last November," I say, lifting my finger. "It was horrifying. Not the cutesy foot-long snorkel kind. The *here, Pip, just hold your breath and swim through this cave underwater in under thirty seconds while the tide's in or you die* kind of thing."

Nash laughs. "You? No."

"Yep."

"No."

"What choice did I have? It's my job."

"Plenty of choice. You could've told him no."

"I can't tell Hugh no."

Once I stood outside at three in the morning beside the 65th Street train in Queens with a mysterious paper sack I was ordered not to look inside, and when he strode in at 3:20 a.m., he was both deliriously excited and irate that (a) a character he'd created just like me would actually be so dumb as to obey direct orders, and (b) I, Penelope Mae Dupont, was actually so dumb as to obey direct orders.

I never heard the end of it.

"And how does that work out for all of us?" I say. "Saying no? Does he ever really lose? Anyway, I had to go to therapy afterward. For the record."

"Not a fan of closed spaces anymore?"

"Not a fan of closed spaces *underwater*," I correct. "Let's just say I didn't ask Hugh permission to spend an obscene amount of trip money for bedrooms above sea level."

"I did wonder if the wallpaper was real gold."

"It's actually possible for what he—or really, you all— spent. Sorry."

"What do I write for, if not for you to enjoy wallpaper made of real gold?" he says with a little smile.

His laissez-faire words flip around in my stomach.

I purse my lips.

"Well," he says, rubbing his nose, "for what it's worth, I'm sorry he made you do that diving trip. Sometimes he gets himself so wrapped up in his ideas he drags us all under."

He looks away to the black distance of the sea beyond, and I see a little squint between his brows that makes my brows crease as well. "Heavy talk for one of the fabulous Seven, Nash."

When he looks back at me, though, he stands up, brushing away the moment. "Ignore me, Pip. I'm just dead tired. I don't think I've had a good night's sleep in a week. Walk you back?"

He gathers up his things while I fold the towel and put it on a stack with the others.

"You don't need to follow me all the way to my door. I think it's fair to say I've made it," I say, pausing at Nash's door.

"You sure? I don't mind."

I laugh. Swing my head left. Spy my door. Look back.

"I'm five doors down. I think I can manage."

He shuffles his feet uncertainly, as though seriously pausing to think whether he'd be neglectful if he let me walk thirty feet alone. It's so humorous I pat him on the shoulder. "Good to see chivalry's not dead, though. Good night, Nash. Or . . . enjoy those good three hours before we have to do this all again. See you for the eggs and bacon."

"And pistachio pudding."

"And pistachio pudding."

He chews on his lip thoughtfully as he watches me walk safely down the five doors, his hand on the knob of his own door. We've claimed the whole wing up here, eight doors for the seven authors plus myself. The library beyond it that will be used for our morning meetings and evening recaps, the dining hall around the corner. It's the only spot on the ship with double-locked security: keys for entry once you get off the elevators; keys to get inside your rooms. It makes sense, I guess. The most luxurious rooms reserved for the guests with the most money, possessions, and, consequently, paranoia.

As I'm turning the key to my room, he calls out, "Er, listen, Pip. I haven't said it before, but you know you can always count on me, right? If you ever need anything, anything at all, I just want you to know that . . . I'm here."

For a moment, I don't know how to reply.

"Thanks, Nash," I say at last. "And . . . I know."

CHAPTER 4

GLORIOUS NEWS.

Nobody died last night.

No dire phone calls came.

No suspicious text messages.

No screams for help.

I did order Hugh a nice homeopathic herbal tea to be delivered to his door in the a.m. that's supposed to do wonders for stress relief, and all in all, with regard to last night: 1 point for the rational PA, Pip, and 0 points for Hugh.

I slept like a log, actually—when I finally did fall sleep, that is.

The soft purr of the cruise ship as we cut through the ocean was quite the sleeping aid—though I doubt it helped poor Jackie, who's been downing Dramamine like it's water.

No, for me, the crisp white satin sheets and thick downy comforter were like slumbering in the comforting arms of a kind, rocking polar bear, and the dreams that fell in likewise were nothing short of extraordinary.

It was the first good night's sleep I've had in six weeks.

Perhaps my spell was broken, my curse over.

The star shower healed me. The beauty, the peace, the fact that I was so far away from all the troubles behind . . . the conversation with Nash . . . it was all restorative. Being back with Nash alone did something to me, quietly closing the door and setting me back in place. I hadn't even realized how off I'd felt with him all the way across the continent for so long, out of reach of our usual conversations.

But listen to me. I sound like I'm in love.

It's not love. It's just . . . well, it's hard to explain. I guess all I can say is, Nash fills a specific place in my life that nobody else can, and when he's not around, a part of my life is lacking.

Simple.

At any rate, coffee calls.

I push the sheets off me and rush through the prep work of the morning. Shower. Teeth. Run a comb through my unruly hair. Don an olive-green sweater to go over my black leggings. Take tiny scissors and give my bangs a millimeter trim so they just barely graze my glasses.

Everything to scream I don't really care about my appearance and am willing to do the bare minimum as a professional . . . until I swing back and give my blue eyes an extra deep line of liner to make them pop. Another layer or two of mascara until my lashes (annoyingly but prettily) hit my glasses every time I blink.

I look like a deer. A surprised deer that's spotlit by headlights and about to get run over. But still, a cute doe-like deer.

Done.

Somewhere between stepping out of bed and out of the shower, a cream envelope has been slipped under the door.

My name is on it, in the kind of handwritten calligraphy brides-to-be fight over.

I rip it open.

The weather across the transatlantic will be brisk today, I'm informed, reaching a blustery high of 56 with partly sunny skies. There's a list a mile long of extracurricular activities, all continuing on the outskirts of our book cruise program. Half of the happenings go on in the deepest part of the ship, which, thanks to my lovely new claustrophobic situation as a thank-you gift from cave diving with Hugh, I skip over.

I check my phone one more time for any missing messages needing attention, check my reflection one last time, and shut the door behind me.

The Seven walk into the meeting lounge in various states.

Jackie with one handkerchief over her mouth while gripping a wastebasket. The sea doesn't welcome her, it appears.

Gordon in what I can only refer to as a sheepskin dress, carrying a wooden Samurai sword.

Neena in full glam from the neck up, but wearing a satin nightgown with robe sashed around her waist.

Ricky, who, after I ask about his whereabouts, slithers out from behind a wingback chair (which means he also overheard the private conversation Neena and I had about her hemorrhoid cream situation).

Crystal, who slinks in after my fifth call. She was in her room playing video games (no surprise).

And Nash, who looks particularly sober this morning.

I try not to take it to heart when he seems to purposefully ignore my gaze.

He's just exhausted. Days of little sleep will do that, of course.

Oh, and Hugh.

Where is Hugh?

"I'm going to check on him," I announce, picking up a second cup of coffee for Hugh from the coffee cart after pocketing my phone.

It isn't like him to miss my calls, I mentally note, with a little chill.

Nobody really answers me.

I cast a look at everyone in their various positions around the room.

Some are looking at the library books.

Some are lounging on the couches.

Some stand beside the heavy velvet curtains, inspecting the deep maroon.

Geez. A bunch of weirdos before eight.

"Hugh?" I call as I rap twice on the door.

I wait several seconds.

Rap again.

"Hugh?"

A full minute goes by. I shift my weight, following the intricate patterns of the carpet with my eyes as I wait.

Sip my coffee.

The cups are getting hot in my hands.

At last, I set a cup in the crook of my elbow and go for the knob.

I wasn't exactly expecting it to open, but when I give it a turn, it goes easily, and I pop the door open just a respectful inch.

"Hugh," I call a bit louder now.

I step inside.

I take a couple of steps, slowly.

"Hugh?" I say again, but my voice cracks.

Stop it, Pip.

Stop it now.

Everything is just fine.
The door just happened to be unlocked.
And Hugh hasn't come to the meeting, but it's still early.
And you're on edge because of what he said last night, but—
Then I see the lump.
And scream.

CHAPTER 5

THE ROOM IS PERFUMED WITH THE SCENT OF BLACK coffee, which I realize is because I have dropped both cups from my hands.

A dark stain is blooming on the red carpet as I stand frozen.

My shoes are splattered in coffee.

My leggings, from the knees down, are covered in coffee.

The floor where I stand is covered in coffee, just beyond the little hallway of Hugh's room, where his bed had just come into view.

And there Hugh is.

Face down under the pristine white covers now covered in blood, one lifeless arm reaching out from beneath the sheet.

I stare at the motionless arm and the back of Hugh's silvery head for a full five seconds, then *sprint*, one hand clasped over my mouth.

They will know what to do.

They will . . . they will *fix* this.

They have to *fix* this right *NOW.*

The fifteen seconds from bedroom to library last a blink. I'm out of breath as I burst through the door.

Gordon is seated beside the chessboard, playing a game with himself.

Jackie is standing at the large bookshelves, one of the books in hand.

Neena is in the midst of adjusting the purple scarf around her neck as she drapes herself across a bookshelf, Crystal taking her picture.

Ricky is staring intently, morosely, at nothing as he sits by himself in the wingback chair.

And Nash is standing stiffly with his back to the door, looking out at the deep blue sea beyond.

All of their heads, except Nash's, turn sharply toward me.

"Penelope?" Neena says. "What is it?"

"Call somebody!" My words tumble out between raspy breaths. "Come quick! Something's wrong! *Something terrible . . . has happened to . . . to . . . Hugh!*"

And then when I've officially given over the words, I feel an immense pressure on my chest, and tears overcome me.

For a moment there is stunned silence, and through the blur of tears I see Jackie look to Gordon, Crystal to Ricky, Neena at Nash, and Nash, looking incredibly piqued, clenching his fists and breaking off to stare back out the window.

Neena shifts her gaze to Gordon.

And with now not one but *two* women pressing their gazes hard on him, he unsteadily stands.

"Oh! How awful!" he cries out in a pained voice, dropping the king chess piece in his hand. "I'll find someone . . . right now!"

He races out the door and shuts it behind him.

I turn to the others.

"We can't stand here. Let's go!"

I rub the tears from my vision.

"*C'mon!*" I yell again, and this time several people jump up.

Getting them to move is like one of those frustrating dreams, though.

One of those dreams where you are being chased and *need* to run but your legs are Gumby's and moving like they're stuck in quicksand. No matter how hard your heart is racing, you can't get them to work.

It takes an eternity to get them just to stand.

"*Let's go!*" I'm flailing my arms, trying desperately to get the group to move faster.

But they are molasses, slowly getting up, gathering things.

Nash doesn't even move.

"Are you all *serious*?" I scream. "FINE!"

I turn in my panic and violent frustration and rip open the door, making to rush back to Hugh myself, to face him and see what can possibly be done, when I feel a strong grip on my wrist.

I turn to see Ricky gripping me by the shoulder, and in my stunned surprise, I feel my feet being dragged with him back inside the room.

The door clicks shut behind him.

He gruffly turns me around.

Everybody has shifted their position to face Neena, who stands up from the couch now in her beacon of purple. She smiles nervously at me.

Her fingers are steepled together. "Okey dokey," she says in her singsong voice. "We tried but we can't do this. Somebody call Hugh and tell him it's off."

Crystal pops her phone from her pocket and strides to the corner of the room.

"What?" I say. My gaze is moving madly from face to face around the room.

Neena walks to me.

"I'm so sorry, honey," she says, putting a hand on my shoulder. "You must have had such a fright. In my defense, I *told* him this was a terrible idea."

"A . . . what?" I say.

"I told you all," Nash growls lowly. He looks so guilty and defeated he barely makes eye contact with me before breaking away.

I'm still sobbing, I realize belatedly.

I hadn't realized it was so loud until I see Neena putting a hand on my shoulder, but it bounces up and down against my choky breaths.

Jackie wordlessly hands me one of her handkerchiefs.

This is the equivalent of a hug from her, given she despises emotion (probably because at least half of her characters die of polio in any given book). And I'm pretty sure she cares about her vintage handkerchiefs more than the lot of us.

She winces slightly and moves away as I blow my nose.

"This is all . . . all some kind of . . . game?" I say, my heart refusing to slow down as it pounds in my chest.

"A *horrible* idea of a game," Neena says, pursing her lips. "He thought it might be good for . . ."—she hesitates—"the ship. Play a sort of live-action murder mystery game."

"People like to *know* if they are in a murder mystery game!" I say. "That's kind of a *key* factor."

"And there's his fault, I know." She tsks. "We all told him it was a bad plan. He was just so convinced."

"And you didn't *stop* him?!" I cry out. My tears are rapidly evaporating.

She shrugs. "Well . . . he bound us to it. It's not like we really had a choice." She pauses. "*Oath* wise."

Again with the mysterious rules of being The Magnificent Seven.

"You do realize that's the kind of thing people in *cults* say, Neena. This is real life. My real *life*."

"Yes," she hedges. "But . . ." Her words wander off in a *but we're part of The Seven, and we were bound—what really could we do?*

I can't argue with her.

You can't argue with crazy.

"If he had wanted to bind you to *murder*, would you all have blindly followed along with that too?" I cast a fiery gaze around the room, landing indignantly on Nash.

"There's more to it than you know. He was very insistent," Neena jumps in. "And really, at the end of the day, it wasn't hurting anyone . . ."

"It hurt *me*! It traumatized *me*! Gah!" I rub my eyes. "The image of him *dead* is going to be brandished into my nightmares forever. Thanks, guys. Successful authors are *freaks*."

They're all wincing before me now.

Like the guilty little ducks they are.

Neena looks especially sorrowful. "We're so *sorry*, Penelope. He only broke the plan to us last night. We didn't hardly have time to think."

I roll my neck.

He probably messaged them after dinner. Right when he played *me* with all that nonsense about someone being after him.

He was messing with us all.

"I hate to see you angry, honey. Especially after how well you were doing after yesterday's breakthrough."

"What breakthrough?" Nash says.

"From *The Incident*," Neena continues in a hiss.

"What incident?" Nash says.

"She was angry then too," Jackie points out.

"But that was a *different* angry," Neena trills in a tone that says *don't butt in, Jackie.* "That was *constructive* rage—"

"And this is . . . unconstructive rage," Jackie says slowly, scrutinizing me as if I'm a lab rat that she just can't quite understand.

"I don't know," Crystal says, "she was pretty ragey yesterday in an *insane woman stealing boom boxes* kind of way."

"Who stole a boom box?" Nash interrupts.

"Well, you can't blame her with everything that went on with Michael," Neena says, ignoring him.

"What happened with Michael?" he says louder.

"I don't know," Crystal says, her phone still pressed to her ear. "I've dated plenty of guys and haven't once tried to toss speaker equipment."

"I don't have any RAGE!" I cry out. "I'm a totally rational person." I fling my hands toward the door, *where my boss just pretended to be dead.* "This is a TOTALLY RATIONAL RESPONSE!"

Crystal, whose hand is now to her lips as though really trying to think it through, looks to Jackie. "Noooo," she muses. "If I were in her place, I don't know if I would really *fling* the door open like that. Feels a little unhinged to me. What about you, Jackie?"

"I walked in on my aunt dead once," Jackie replies cooly. "I didn't need to make a whole scene over it. It's a bit—"

"Pretentious?" Crystal says.

"I was thinking self-absorbed. But I approve the synonym." Jackie gives a curt nod.

"One hundred and seventy-one thousand people die . . ." Ricky says slowly, drawing a chill breeze to the back of everybody's neck, "every day."

Nash takes off his hat. "What happened with Michael?" Nash says louder, this time craning his neck in the air.

"No answer," Crystal announces, pocketing her phone. "I'll just go get him."

"No, if anyone sees him first, it's *me*," I say, wiping the last remaining tear vigorously from my eye with the palm of my hand.

I hand the handkerchief back over to Jackie and stalk out into the hall.

The rest of the group trails after.

Waiting at the subway with a mysterious package for Hugh for research was one thing.

Diving through terrifying sea tunnels was one thing.

Baking an apple pie with arsenic and then taking a bite and spitting it out before it killed me to see if I could really "taste the poison" was one thing.

Playing with my heart for *sport* is another.

Gordon jumpstarts from playing the little *Tetris* game on his phone as he sits on the ground.

Guiltily he pockets his phone as he stumbles to standing. "Called them! They'll be here any minute!" he trills.

Neena gives him a stern look. "For goodness' sake, you had one job!"

"I'm going to kill him for this!" I announce, stomping down the hall. "And I'm going to kill *all of you* for going along with this!"

"Hugh's very persuasive when he has a plan, Pip," Neena says.

"Don't care."

"I don't think it's really fair to pin any of this on us," Jackie says.

"You know what, Jackie?" I say, spinning around, "I *found*

that vintage Rosenthal Sanssouci replacement dinner plate you were hunting for—"

"Oh?" she says, her voice rising. "With the gold trim?"

"And was *planning* to give it to you for Christmas," I continue, "but no more! No vintage Christmas plates for *you*, Jackie!" I raise my finger, announcing as an afterthought as I swivel back around, "*No Christmas presents for any of you!*"

The shuffling behind me is loud as we march by door after door.

Heads are bowed.

They deserve it.

I'm an excellent gift giver, for the record.

They *should* be highly disappointed that my *incredibly* thoughtful gifts they receive year after year will be no more.

"To be fair, Penelope," Neena says, "we never thought you'd be, well, quite *so* upset."

I halt.

Turn.

"What is that supposed to mean?"

"But of course that's our fault," she continues hastily as she cinches her robe tighter around her. "It's just . . . with a missing note . . ."

I raise my hand. "I'm sorry, Neena, but Hugh being dead on the mattress with pools of blood on the sheets around him is anything but *unconcerning*. *Of course* I would react this way. Any *sane* human *should* react this way—"

"Blood?" Gordon interrupts. "No, he was just going to be missing. Leave a note."

"What do you mean there was blood?" Neena says, stepping closer to me, her eyes growing wide in alarm.

"I mean there were *pools* of blood!" I cry out. "*Pools.*"

We all stare at each other for one long moment.

Then Neena pushes me aside.

They all, for that matter, push me aside and race toward the door.

"Hugh?" Neena calls out loudly, heedless of the volume of her voice or the time of morning. "Hugh, come on now! It's time to give it up—"

And then she, and we, all skid to a stop as we reach the door and bump directly into the rough blue uniform of a man backing up.

"Out of the way," he says gruffly, and then in our collective horror we see on the stretcher the figure of a man outlined by the cover of a white sheet, running all the way up to, well, to . . . *Hugh.*

"That'll do it," another man in uniform says, snapping a pencil into a notebook and pocketing it in his back pocket.

The gurney moves another foot or two backward and then the officer calls out, "Wait," and takes a couple of steps forward. He covers Hugh's face with the sheet; the lifeless, bloodied face that every single one of us has known for what feels like forever.

The officer pats the metal of the gurney, and the man continues moving it out of the room.

And that's when Neena faints directly into Gordon's arms.

CHAPTER 6

TO FIND OUT YOUR EMPLOYER AND ONE OF YOUR closest companions is dead once is horrifying.

To have to go through the experience all over again fifteen minutes later is enough to cause your own heart to stop indefinitely.

Neena recovers, comes to, remembers what's going on, and faints again.

Jackie chases after the gurney angrily.

Gordon keeps asking the same questions on repeat to nobody in particular.

Ricky slips off silently, keeping his brooding thoughts to himself.

Crystal and Nash take to cornering the officer, demanding every single detail, all with a vague tone of accusation.

As this is my second round, I just sit on the hallway floor, staring into nothingness.

Nothing makes sense.

Nothing.

At last the officer who directed the gurney away gathers us all together like sheep—even Ricky from his morose position behind a curtain—and herds us back to the library. He's older, bald, built like a concrete block, and walks like a man accustomed to the dark side of existence. The deep etches across his forehead follow the trail of his permanent-looking scowl.

"Sit down. Now," he instructs, gathering Ricky from the back of his collar before he can slip off again. "I wanna be able to see each and every one of you."

Jackie, Gordon, Neena, and Crystal sit on the long leather sofa, Ricky to the side, and Nash and I find ourselves standing behind it. Nash looks from the officer to me, and after seeing my face, the burning look in his blue eyes cools.

He closes the gap between us.

Wordlessly rests his hand over mine.

"First off," the officer begins, glancing from one face to another, "allow me to give my condolences."

He says this begrudgingly, like a flight attendant spewing out a script that's required and hating every moment. He speeds up. "This is a shocking experience for everyone. May the deceased rest in peace.

"My name is Ralph Carragan. Feel free to call me by any name you like. Officer. Security. Ralph. Carragan. I'm the head chief of security on this vessel and will be your point of contact here on out. And as for you all, I know who you are. No need to fill me in."

He shifts his weight. "I'm given to understand each of you were supposed to be providing guest author sessions today in your appointed conference rooms. Can I presume each of you are under enough emotional duress that you will not be able to attend to your preregistered sessions in good mental health?"

He pauses.

The group nods.

"Fine," he says shortly, then beckons the other man in uniform and whispers something to him behind his notebook. The man nods subserviently and whisks himself out of the room.

"And who's in charge of organizing these events?" he says, scanning each of our eyes until he comes upon mine.

I raise my hand.

"You, Miss . . ."

"Penelope," I say. Then, when that doesn't seem to satisfy, I add, "Dupont."

"Well, Dupont, several hundred fans of this group have spent a sum of over four million dollars collectively for this vessel experience. This is a . . . unique situation the ship is in. No insurance measures cover something like this. The higher-ups have requested—no, insisted—I continue the vessel forward on its journey. The police on land, likewise, find it . . . convenient . . . to continue. And to that end, the less people know, the better. Can you distract them?"

"What? Like pull off a one-man show?"

The image of me tap-dancing across a stage for the next ten days while the rest of them cry in their rooms floods me.

"I can't do that," I say.

"Well, you need to figure out something."

I raise my brow. "*Me?* What would you have me do?"

"I don't care. Just do it in such a way that they are satisfied. Watch a movie. Read aloud these people's books. But whatever you do, the important thing we need to maintain here is a sense of normalcy."

"So just what?" Jackie says, sniffing indignantly. "You want us to pretend nothing happened?"

"Ma'am, we have a murder on the ship in the middle of the Atlantic. Everybody's stranded here with a murderer. Yes. We need *not* cause mass panic."

The image of three hundred women in their late fifties in seashell flip-flops and tropical skirts screaming and running away from each other while gripping steak knives comes to mind.

At the word *murderer*, Crystal vomits into an umbrella bin, then slips out of the room.

"As I was saying," he continues, but Neena, who has been loudly sobbing into one of Jackie's hankies, jumps in.

"The police say it's convenient to just . . . carry on?" Neena says. "How is that"—momentary pause for sobbing—"How can you be thinking of convenience when"—another pause for sobbing—"How is that in any way convenient for us?" (More sobbing.)

"Oh, not for you," Carragan cuts in. "No. The convenience is on our end entirely. See, on land, we have the disadvantage of picking through thousands of miles to find a criminal. Here?" he continues, and the tiniest, almost imaginary flicker of a smile crosses his face. "Here you're trapped."

He says it like he's not speaking to all of us but to the murderer directly.

Like he's thrilled.

Because some idiot made the idiotic plan to kill someone while being trapped like a rat on a ship with no way out.

A silent electric shock jolts through the room.

So far we've all just been focused on the fact that Hugh is dead. It hasn't registered to anyone—except perhaps Ricky sullenly regarding us in the corner—exactly *how* that death happened.

It feels like we just stumbled into a second death.

Because somebody here is our enemy.

Neena faints again, right on Gordon's lap, to Carragan's blistering groan of annoyance.

After two minutes of absolute silence, followed by fifteen minutes of sheer chaos—Gordon and me trying to revive Neena, everybody talking over one another about the insanity of that statement, defending themselves, defending each other, crying out about the impossibility of Carragan's statement that a murderer is on board the ship, Crystal coming through the door, seeing the room in chaos, looking ill, and slipping out again—Carragan pulls Crystal back inside, shuts the door, turns, and in a loud voice says, "*Quiet!*"

He frowns. "This is *seven* of you," he snaps impatiently. "Imagine what this level of chaos would be at *three hundred*. Now, here's how it's going to go. Today, your"—he waves a vague hand at me—"organizer will create a casual, *believable* message of a change of events on the calendar. Meanwhile, we will block off the front of the ship and the rest of this hall for your leisure. I will question each of you over the course of the day. You are to stay away from all other people. Except, and if you choose to risk it, one another."

My eyes flicker down at the tiniest shift Crystal makes away from Gordon on the couch. Neena wordlessly offers back Jackie's handkerchief.

Jackie jolts at the sudden movement.

I look to Nash and realize his hand is back on mine, and my arms, my whole body, in fact, is numb.

He's the only one who looks resolutely defiant in this group, resolutely angry. "Nobody in this group did it."

To which Carragan looks entirely unsurprised, as though there's *always* someone in his slew of suspects who says so.

"Of course none of you did it," he says dryly. "Then riddle

me why we have a locked entrance on both sides of the authors' hall and *only* the seven of you have the keys? There was no forced entry."

"Someone could have stolen a key," Gordon puts in.

Carragan steeples his fingers over his stomach. "Unlikely. The reality is, the killer is most often found in the path of least resistance. Follow the thread. Find your killer. And we don't have a broken point of entry. We don't have anyone who called the front desk complaining about stolen keys. But what we do have are seven people right here with a load of plausible motivations. Point is, you're all guilty until proven innocent—"

"Shouldn't it be the other way around?" Crystal interjects.

"What are you, a freshman criminal justice major?" he snaps. "In the courts, sure."

"And shouldn't *you* be following that mentality, if so?"

Carragan smiles at her. Momentarily drops his notebook to his side. "How old are you?"

Crystal raises her chin. "Twenty-two."

"And what's your full name?"

"Crystal." In defiance she keeps her lips sealed as for her last name.

He lets the silence stretch between them.

"Well," he says at last, "Crystal of a staggering twenty-two years with no last name, you can keep that mindset if you like, but I can tell you right now, I can't count on one hand how many suspects of mine with your same . . . *mentality*, if you will . . . ended up in a less than favorable position when *push came to shove*, if you get my meaning. Do what you like, it's your life, but just know, were it me, I'd be locking my doors at night. Now," he says, looking to the rest of us, "like I say, we have nine days left on this ship, and I made a promise to the higher-ups to get off it with someone in some brand-new metal bracelets. Today I'll question each of you."

"And tomorrow?" Nash says.

"Tomorrow you all will return to your jobs while I do mine. Smile. Entertain your fans. And me? I'll go find a killer."

CHAPTER 7

THINGS CAN'T GET ANY LOWER THAN THIS MOMENT, right?

Right?

I, without question, am living out the exact second I'll look back on and think, *Yup, that was definitely rock bottom.* Can't get lower than discovering your boss murdered, twice, being a suspect while stuck on a ship with the real murderer, and *still having to work.*

The next three hours are a manic-induced blur.

And while everybody else kept to their rooms, I spent the majority of the day racing around, trying to come up with different activities for each of the authors' workshops that sounded believable and totally not made up on the fly.

No time for grieving.

No time to hang out in the land of shock.

Creating a Fantasy World 101 Workshop from noon to 2 p.m. with Gordon?

Not anymore.

Now it's a "Magical Scavenger Hunt" that ultimately

results in women charging the decks and kitchens, scouring through pots and pans, pressing elevator emergency buttons, and, in one case, breaking into the captain's bedroom, hunting for clues that mirror Gordon's latest fantasy release. (For the record, all of my clues were in logical, legal places, and 85 percent of the ladies involved ended up looking in the exact opposite places. The crew was quite upset.)

It was hard going.

It was hard to convince three hundred avid readers who spent their hard-earned money to specifically see and interact with their favorite authors that no, they didn't *really* want to shake hands with Ricky Gables and hear intimate details of the time several Romanian *politia* came upon him when he was sleeping on the floor of an abandoned Transylvanian castle for research, that instead it was *very exciting* to do this puzzle shaped like a hot-air balloon while *talking* about our favorite books. Isn't that equally exciting? Isn't that worth every penny?

Let's just say I ended up pulling a lot of strings and making a lot of phone calls.

I don't want to pat myself on the back too much given the circumstances and all, but the substitute activities turned out to be pretty great.

In Ricky's case, Stephen King did in fact play chess virtually on a projector screen (with *me*, and as it turns out, I am *really bad*) while fielding questions about his writing life.

For Neena's class? Debbie Macomber crocheted on-screen from her plump sitting chair overlooking Puget Sound and shared stories about all her Christmas books that became Hallmark movies.

Teen heartthrob Harry Bailes took fifteen minutes out of his day to video chat about his fiction-to-screen role from Crystal's book *Castaway City*. Fifteen legendary minutes that made me realize I am indeed *very* good at my job.

I included a notice in the changes that Hugh was ill and would be kept to his room, although who knows how long I'll have before I start hearing complaints about *that*.

All in all, by the time six o'clock rolled around and everyone was leaving to go into the dining hall for dinner, I finally stopped to realize I hadn't eaten all day. In fact, I'd hardly taken a breath all day. Or had a moment to think. About much of anything. At all.

Which of course was partly intentional, a parting gift from what I experienced the last two months over Michael. I am now very good at stuffing emotions deep, *deep* down through the power of distraction.

A breakup, of course, is nowhere near as gut-wrenching as a murder. But at the same time, there is a certain kind of death to both. And in my case, in both cases, Hugh was critically involved.

"You primed the pump, so to speak, Pip. And for that I'll be forever grateful."

"I-I'm sorry, Michael?" I stammered into my phone exactly six weeks ago. "You're leaving me . . . after everything . . . on public *television*, for a girl with a high ponytail *you have never spoken to in your life*, and the entire planet is deciding to root for it, and all you can say is, 'Well, at least you can give yourself a pat on the back, Pip, knowing you *PRIMED. THE. PUMP?!*"

Michael was my boyfriend of eight years. *Eight.*

An elementary school education is eight years.

An Olympic cycle is eight years.

A full term in political office is eight years.

The time it takes to go through med school and residency

to become a *doctor* is eight years, *including* a bonus fellow-ship year.

The entirety of my adulthood. Spent with Michael.

Waiting on Michael.

Rooting for Michael—even when that meant positioning myself against everybody else to be on his side.

We were together practically since the day I walked into his sports medicine class sophomore year at uni. He was twenty-seven then. I was three weeks shy of nineteen. He was the adjunct professor of the class. And to say it was a challenge wading through the reality of his very forward romantic pursuit while being forced to be discreet under professor-student bylaws is an understatement. I eagerly missed out on years of college experiences, trading sorority life and dances and football parties for eating pizza in his dim apartment. Sacrificing a thousand college activities and precious future memories because (a) "It's not really that mature now, is it, Pip?" and (b) "I really can't be seen with you or I'll lose my job, but . . . if you really think it's *that* fun to go without me, then go."

I supported him as he spent his days teaching part-time at the small college that paid so little we couldn't afford to go hardly anywhere—even if we could.

I supported him *choosing* said part-time job so he could pursue his actual dream where he spent the majority of his time traveling: baseball.

I.

Supported.

Him.

And *when* he made the minor league after all his hard work and moved last year to Detroit, I.

Supported.

Him.

Why?

Because we were in love and soulmates and were going to get married and have babies and live happily ever after. Obviously.

As had been *his* stated plan. On repeat. Since I was three weeks shy of nineteen.

We were meant to be.

So obviously it was an unfortunate fact that here I was, eight years later, still without a ring on my finger. But as he had so "thoughtfully" articulated over the years, he wanted to make sure it was the right time.

It was never the right time.

At first it was because he wanted me to finish college.

My parents would want that (though he never met them and I never dared tell them).

Then it was because he wanted to be in a financially stable place before he asked for my hand. He wanted to make sure he was "worthy" of me.

I didn't care, for the record.

I would've said yes by month three of my sophomore year.

I was head over it all for Michael.

I was so lost in him I would've followed him anywhere.

So imagine my surprise when on the *one* day I'd schlepped Hugh's candy-apple-red 1964 Pontiac GTO uptown to one of the few remaining gas stations in NYC existence, I discovered, at said pump, a slinky woman with an overbright smile and massive lips announcing on the pump screen the "trending moment of the day" and then showing a clip of *my* Michael, clad in his baseball uniform standing over the wall from the fans, flirting intensely with this blonde girl who looks *half his age*. As she tosses him the baseball she caught, he—to manic cheering all around—grins as he catches a Sharpie someone has thrown at him, scribbles his number, and *tosses it back.* All while the slinky woman with big lips narrated the entire scene and summed it up with, "The video that's breaking the internet. I'm Elissa, and you saw it right here on Bright News TV, exclusively good news for a brighter day!"

And then, to shut the casket door entirely over my head, I saw a blurry video clip by an amateur do-gooder videoing the two of them in a dimly lit restaurant hours later, and Michael, *my* Michael, kissing her.

"It seems dreams really do come true!" the woman announced merrily as I set the pump back in place and the screen clicked off before my eyes.

The earth sucked all the air from my lungs in that moment.

I could feel it, all the air leaving my body, taking all the thoughts in my brain with it.

I couldn't think.

I couldn't breathe.

I was just . . . nothing.

And then, twelve eternal seconds later, my brain recharged with *vehemence* as I heard that woman's grating voice again. "I'm Elissa, and this is your Trending Moment of the Day!"

My head shot over to the pump beside me, and there she was on the screen, retelling the story as the man pumped his gas. The camera zoomed in again on the girl in the stands, and on Michael's bright, charming smile as he caught the Sharpie and began to scribble on the baseball.

". . . and this is your Trending Moment of the Day!" I heard at the pump behind me.

". . . and this is your Trending Moment of the Day!"

". . . and this is your Trending Moment of the Day!"

I yanked the car door open and slammed it shut as "Dreams do come true!" rang all around.

This was . . . The Incident.

Hugh and the others had found me in the hallway of his office when I was on the phone with Michael. They had just gotten off the elevator on the seventh floor, and there I was, fifteen minutes into the worst conversation of my life. My hands were shaking. I still had my key in the lock of the office, the key long forgotten as I listened to Michael on speaker.

Trying to swallow this conversation.

Trying to make sense of it all.

"You showed me what love was, Pip. You got me to love again. Even if . . . you weren't . . . you know . . . the final destination."

I'm not . . . *the final destination?*

"I'm a vehicle, Michael? That's what you're saying. You appreciate me because I transported you from point A to point B."

Everyone took a collective few steps toward me on instinct, surrounding me. They were mom and pop birds wanting to spread out their wings over me, to protect me from the torrential downpour. Even Ricky proffered a creepy, wispy hold on my elbow. It didn't take long for them to get the gist of what had happened.

Eventually Hugh got my cue and put a steadying hand on my shoulder, gave it a comforting squeeze, and turned the key in the door for me. They retreated inside to give me privacy—Neena the only resister, being dragged away by Hugh. The rest of the conversation was the same, a slow slit to the throat as I bled out little by little.

Just your normal, very average, very common confession of betrayal.

Just your normal, very average, very common death of an eight-year relationship, a once living thing.

And if I could survive that death, be it of far less weight than this, I know I can survive this too.

As for the others today, though . . . well . . . their mental health is another matter.

"How long has it been like this?" I lean over and whisper to Nash.

We're sitting at the long table in the dining room, quite literally roped off with a cream and golden rope that looks to have been plucked straight from a unicorn's tail. Carragan has apparently decided that we've all had enough "time to process the unfortunate news" and it is now time to act normal.

With several hundred heads looking our way. Expectantly.

It isn't going well.

Neena, for one, just screamed when Ricky picked up his steak knife.

"Everyone's lost the plot," Nash says grimly, picking up a roll from the untouched basket on the long table. "It's too much to ask of them. I think they could handle losing . . ."—there's a pause in his voice before he adds—"*him.* But then to pit everyone against each other? It's too much."

He scrapes his knife across the butter, and Jackie on the other side of him winces.

Her glassy blue eyes stare as he scrapes for a full five seconds, then suddenly she blinks three times in rapid succession, stands, and leaves the table.

Now that I sit here, I realize Nash and I are the only ones sitting within arm's reach of each other.

I lean in closer to him and say lowly, "What did everyone do today?"

"Stayed in their rooms, mostly, and waited for Carragan to call them in for questioning. He spent thirty minutes on all of us, down to the minute. Then they went back to their rooms."

"With nothing to do except become more paranoid," I muse.

Nash tilts his head at me as if to ask, *Have you met them? Paranoid doesn't begin to explain it.*

"Maybe it's good to go back to normal then. Maybe it'll be good for everybody."

"Another twenty-four hours like this and I'm convinced they'd all accidentally kill each other."

I purse my lips. "Surely it wouldn't get that bad."

"They're authors. Half of their brains are dedicated solely to the imagination. It's bad, Pip."

I raise a brow.

He looks at my reluctant expression and puts down his knife. "Watch this. Oops."

The roll falls from his hand and, like a soft miniature bowling ball, begins a path past me, the braised beef plate, two large vases overflowing with peonies, and the stemware glasses of champagne everybody assumes are poisoned and nobody has touched, finally landing on the floor beside Neena's purse.

Pandemonium ensues.

Chairs tip over, champagne glasses spill, somebody cries out about a bomb, and the group bumps into, and then even more desperately away from, each other like bumper cars at a carnival of death.

Nash lifts his plate and fork quietly from the table just as it's being turned over.

Crystal ultimately ducks behind it as some sort of hideout.

I watch in absolute shock as terror fills the entire room.

It's like one of those movies where a food fight erupts at a summer camp, only everybody's seventy and the plates are fine china.

It's not until thirty staff members jump in threatening to tranquilize everyone that things calm down. Everyone is dismissed to their rooms after a thousand assurances, and nobody is quite certain how the chaos itself began.

"See?" Nash says. He and I are the only two who remained seated—or even with upright seats for that matter.

"Carragan was right," I say. "The ship would sink."

Both of our phones go off simultaneously, and we reach into our pockets.

It's a group text.

From Carragan.

He's not happy.

Meet in the library. NOW.

As we move along the hall, Nash's hands are stuffed in his pockets. "Will you tell on me?"

A whisper of a smile lifts my lips. I can absolutely see him as a first grader, wooden slingshot behind his back, paper ball in the teacher's hair.

And it's funny, because a part of me couldn't imagine it possible to ever smile again.

When we get to the room, Nash turns the knob.

The door swings open.

It looks just like the cover of a Clue board game.

Carragan is standing with his hands on his hips to one side of the velvet couch.

Ricky is beside the curtain.

Neena stands beside the bookshelf, gripping a hardback book like a weapon.

Jackie is clenching her handkerchief between tight white knuckles by the lampshade.

Gordon sits at the chess set, looking up and over his

shoulder at Jackie as though ready to knock the pieces over and use the board as a shield at any moment.

And Crystal, facing everybody with her back to us, is drowning herself in her phone.

I look at the bold letters at the top of the article she's reading. "Ten Easy Ways to Use a Water Bottle to Kill in Self-Defense."

Super.

Great to see everyone is handling this like champs.

CHAPTER 8

CARRAGAN GIVES EVERYONE THE LECTURE OF A lifetime.

Shouting about how we have to "act natural or get ourselves all sunk."

Yelling, "You all—excluding that lady over there [me]—are authors who make up characters in your books all the time; just pretend you're one of those *sane* people over the course of this trip!"

Honestly, I've never seen an officer so insensitive, all things considered.

But I guess that isn't part of the job description.

Nash is right.

The group has wound themselves into such a fit of worry that by eight o'clock, they look like they are trying to tiptoe on the point of a knife.

Leaving them alone did them no favors. I may have had three momentary panic attacks over the day, but something about staying busy at least let me keep my wits about me.

"You're up," Carragan grunts at the end of his long lecture, motioning to me. "The rest of you"—he waves his hands in the air in an *I couldn't care less if you live or die* way—"go to your rooms, stay here, end up on deck, I don't care. Miss Dupont, I'll follow you."

He motions for me to walk ahead of him, to my room I presume.

Makes sense.

Nash had said Carragan spent half of his interview poking around the pillowcases looking for clues.

I cast one glance back at the group and (aside from Nash) see the hollow, frightened, and frankly suspicious glares.

I frown at Neena, who is looking at me like she's never noticed before how suspicious five-foot-even girls who overbuy stocking gifts for friends' cats are.

Really, Neena?

Et tu, Brute?

My room is in tatters from rushing around all day. Clothes are strewn across the floor. Drink cups empty and discarded.

Turns out, neat freak behavior has no manners.

How neurotic can you be, Pip? A man just died.

And yet I begin hastily picking up papers and tidying up my bed as Carragan steps inside.

"Here. Let me just—" I begin, snatching up a pillow from the floor, arms loaded.

"Tell me, Miss Dupont, when exactly did the hate for your boss begin?" Carragan cuts in, pen in hand.

I stop abruptly. A pillow falls. "Excuse me?"

"That was your motive, wasn't it?" he continues, scribbling something down. "Hatred? Or perhaps . . . jealousy? Jealousy tends to be a big hitter when dealing with someone this successful. Unless . . . did you have anything to gain, perhaps? Has he put you in his will?"

He says it like he's musing aloud, not even thinking for a moment about exactly with whom he's talking. Like I'm some . . . some random coworker instead of a *real, live, absolutely affected person.*

Ugh. I've read about this type of investigative questioning a thousand times, this aggressive rushing in like a bull on fire, but when it's directed at *you* about a person *you* care about, it hits entirely differently. A fire builds in the pit of my stomach. A shot of adrenaline zips around my body, desperate to defend myself against such unholy accusations.

It's stupid.

It's stupid and I *know* what he's doing. But I can't help myself.

"How dare you insinuate something so . . ." I fumble for the words. "So . . . *false* about me. I have been *nothing* but dedicated to Hugh for five years. He was a *friend*—"

"What does being friends have to do with anything here? Half the murders I come across are people who were 'friends.' And I imagine some half-witted gold digger running around getting him coffee like yourself—"

I round my shoulders back.

This man has absolutely *no right.*

NO. RIGHT.

I point a finger at his chest.

Actually, if I'm being totally honest, I irresponsibly and irrationally put my finger *on* this security officer's chest, and I push a little. "Now *look here*, sir. I have *read* all the books Hugh's written. All seventy-two of them, multiple times. I myself have edited twenty of them. I have spent a thousand nights working through detective dialogues *just. Like. This.* And I can tell you right now you will absolutely *not* play such a petty, aggressive trick on me to get me to crack, because there is *nothing to crack.* And if there *was* something to crack, you'd better be smarter about it, because believe me, after working under Hugh for this many years, I know every trick in the book. So please, at the very least, question me, but don't insult my intelligence."

Carragan and I share in a sort of stare-down for some time. I make sure he's the first to look away.

"Fine," he says, flipping a page in his notebook. The tiniest smile flicks on his lips. "If you're so smart, Miss Dupont, lead the way. Break it down for me."

I holster my finger back at my side. "Break what down?"

"What you think I should ask. How I get can the information out of you that I need. You think you *can* do that, right?"

"Absolutely," I say with less certainty. I cross my arms over my chest.

"Then do it. Do my job." There's sarcasm in his tone.

I hesitate for a blink, then forge ahead. What option do I have? My dignity is on the line.

My mind flips through various conversations I've pored over in Hugh's books, lands on the first question I can remember, and I wing it. "Alright. I'd say, 'Let's begin by walking me through your day. How did your trip begin, Miss Dupont?' And to that I'd say . . ."

Turns out, I'm not half bad.

I tell him the questions he was planning to ask, including the information he was trying to squeeze out of me, and answer them in turn. I can anticipate what facts from my words he wants to pull out and write down, and sure enough, I'm right 90 percent of the time.

Isn't it incredible how fiction can mirror reality?

Even Carragan begrudgingly gives me a little respect in the form of tiny nods as he writes things down. Or was this his plan all along?

Thirty minutes goes by in conversation. Forty-five. An hour. Why am I different than everyone else here? Does he actually think *I* am the one who did it?

"Tell me, Miss Dupont, what would you have to gain from Hugh's death in this instance?" Carragan says eventually, cutting in.

I frown. "Nothing. I'm out of a job."

"Not nothing entirely, though, is it? You are well known for being the assistant to Hugh Griffin. A lot of people are desperate to know about the inner workings of a successful man like that. You were close enough to touch the oven itself, if you catch my drift."

"I could go out and find another assistant job, if that's what you're saying. But that's not a perk. At best, that's a parallel move."

"Oh, I don't know about that. I'm sure lots of authors would love to have the assistant of Hugh Griffin for themselves. The keeper of secrets. The front-row viewer of his success. Perhaps you've learned things from him you could go forth and share with others. Perhaps you could use those secrets to propel your own writing success."

"*My* writing success?" I say with a laugh. "I'm not going out to have my own name on a shelf, and I definitely don't need to kill anyone to begin writing. The only thing I've learned from Hugh was that he was a mastermind with skills I'll never possess."

"Oh, I wouldn't say that's all you learned. Of all the people I've interviewed, you come out the one most capable of getting away with murder."

Me?

Me?

"He was bluntly stabbed in the back and now is stuck on a ship," I reply curtly. "This isn't mastermind work. If it was up to me, I'd have a timed alibi, use foxglove to mimic a heart attack, and be the last person to walk in on him dead this morning. A stab in the back is crude work."

Carragan's brows shoot up. He scribbles something down.

Right.

Mental note: Moving forward, avoid sounding like Ricky.

You are a dumb assistant. *You get confused about which paper to put in the printer and scroll for hours at your desk.* Be. Dumb.

"And you say you share an apartment with two other roommates on 102nd Street between Broadway and West End Avenue? Must be tiring, taking the subway all the way to Tribeca day in and day out. Doing all that heavy lifting for Hugh just so that he can live among the cobbled streets with the stars—"

"Hugh loves the subway and spends—spent—four out of seven days of the week sleeping on an old couch in his office." I frown deeper. "Look, Mr. Carragan, let me cut to the chase on this. I had nothing to gain from this. *Nothing.* Jealousy didn't get me. I had $8,615 in my savings account before this happened, and $8,615 now. I will continue to take the subway. I happen to *like* my roommates. I wasn't in love with Hugh. I didn't hate my job to the point of putting myself in danger either. I never killed ants with a magnifying glass as a child for fun. And I have never had so much as a speeding ticket. I am just the lowly assistant to an incredible person, and happened to be the unfortunate first-person witness to a terrible tragedy."

Carragan purses his lips.

Shuts his notebook.

Grabs his belt buckle and adjusts it as he stands.

"Seems you got it all figured out then, Miss Dupont."

"I have nothing figured out. I just know I didn't do it. And I'm tired of this conversation."

I follow him to the door. The clock on the bedside table now reads 8:30 p.m. The man has a particular ability to wear people down until they have no civility left. I suppose that's his aim, and in that sense, I have to give him credit where credit is due.

He may be irritating, but he's irritating with purpose.

He pulls the door open, and when one foot is out in the hallway, he turns.

Pauses.

"I do wonder, Miss Dupont . . . if you seem to have it all figured out, maybe you can help me with one thing."

"What?"

"If it wasn't you, who do you think did it?"

I swallow.

Pictures of The Seven (now Six) fly through my mind. I suppose I could come up with some crackpot ideas and incentives if I had to, but I won't do it.

I'd never do that to them.

I shake my head. "It's more likely that you are the murderer, Officer Carragan, than any one of them."

"Unwilling to rat anyone out, are we?" Carragan replies, without surprise. "Never mind. I've figured out who did it anyway, and I intend to bring justice to light in the morning."

"You knew it wasn't me all this time, did you? Then why'd you keep me so long?"

He smiles a little. "A detective always does his due diligence. Good night, Miss Dupont."

"Good night."

He turns to go. I bite my lower lip, hesitating to ask. *If you are so sure of who it is, who is it?*

"And Dupont?"

I look up. Realize he's turned around. "Hmm?"

"I got a daughter about your age, and I can't help saying it one more time. Keep your door locked tonight. And for your parents' sake, I wouldn't open it for a soul."

CHAPTER 9

IT'S JUST PAST 2 A.M. WHEN THERE'S A RAP ON MY door.

I jolt out of the anxious, needling sleep that's been mocking me the past few hours, slip out of bed, and slink silently toward the door.

Somewhere along the way I've unconsciously picked up a little table mirror and now hold it in front of me like a weapon, poised.

Oh, good grief.

I should've read Crystal's article.

I'm holding my breath, I realize.

A part of me has been holding my breath since Mr. Carragan left with that eerie message hours ago. I mean, what sort of person tells a young lady with roughly zero self-defense skills that a killer may be lurking outside the door, but "don't worry, rest well, and just do your best to keep the bolt locked"?

A bolt is a two-inch-long piece of metal.

Do I look like a person who has the ability to stay calm and trust a two-inch piece of metal?

Somebody raps a second time, this time louder.

My stomach starts punching me internally and urgently, urging me to get down.

I hesitate, then peek through the peephole.

Well, that cinches it.

I really and truly am the kind of girl who would walk toward the sound in the basement and get herself killed.

"Pip." Nash's voice comes through the door. "I can hear you breathing. Like one of my old asthmatic horses, I might add. Open up."

I pop my hand over my mouth, frown, then quickly unbolt the door.

A little smile lights up his face when he sees me standing in my pajamas, one hand over my mouth, the other with a hand mirror pressed tight to my chest.

"What are you planning to do with that?" he says, nodding to the mirror.

"Self-defense," I say. "And what are you doing here?"

"Giving actual defense to the girl with a plastic mirror. Mind if I come in?"

I feel a sudden surge of adrenaline rise from my stomach to my throat and quickly tamp it down.

Because.

Well.

Isn't that nice, though?

There's something . . . well . . . rather nice in the way he's come to think of me, lady in distress and all. And then, of course, adrenaline in the fact that the deepest part of me is saying, *Yes! PLEASE come help me. I'm absolutely a child at heart and don't want to deal with this situation with a brave face.*

I swing the door open wide.

He steps inside.

Walks down the length of the hotel room as if assessing something.

Tells me he'll be back. Goes the several doors down to his room. Returns with a pillow, some sheets and a blanket, and his computer.

"What are you doing?" I say, standing over him as he begins setting up a little bed on the floor.

"You only have one bed. And I wanted sheets."

"And a pillow?"

"My neck still has a crick in it from the rock I slept on three weeks ago. So I'm softer than the readers are led to believe. Sue me."

"And your computer?"

"For writing. Obviously."

I fling a hand out. "So . . . you're just planning to sleep here then?"

He drops the pillow at the head of his makeshift floor bed, leans back on the heels of his boots, and stands. "Yes. Well, you didn't answer your phone."

"You messaged?" I begin, reaching for my phone on the nightstand.

"And I figure if I'm going to get any sleep, I'm just going to have to be in here myself."

He puts his hands on his hips and looks from the floor bed to me.

Well, well, well.

The cowboy rescue genes are strong in him.

"What about Crystal?" I say. Or Neena, for that matter. Or Jackie.

"Crystal's terrifying. She can hold her own."

So I can't hold my own then.

Fair.

I cross my arms over my chest. "And what exactly makes

you believe that *I* am up for this?" I say, gesturing to the bed on the floor.

I am totally up for this.

I am exhausted and adrenaline hungover and already feel my limbs starting to sloop toward the bed up for this.

"You could be a murderer," I point out.

He laughs as if it's the wittiest joke he's ever heard. "So could you. So that makes us even. Excuse me, I'll just . . ." And then he goes off and drops his toothbrush in the little bathroom.

"You know, I was given strict orders not to open the door for anyone."

"More the reason it's clear I need to be here. You like to keep this on? It's like a Walmart in July in here," he says, standing by the lamp switch. I realize I've moved myself back to my bed. I'm sitting on the edge of it, my shoulders leaning backward, begging me to draw toward the pillows.

"No." I pause. "Not anymore."

Nash flicks the switch, then quietly moves around the room, turning off each of the others.

I let him. "Thanks, Nash," I murmur in the dark, my eyes already closed.

There's silence.

"Anytime."

An hour later, I hear it.

I'm just leaving the bathroom as silently as I can (thank you, nerves) when I hear in the utter silence something just, well, *less silent.*

It's *wings flapping on a bird high overhead in a forest* level silent.

Never would I have heard this sound in the middle of the day, under normal circumstances.

But now?

On high alert?

When I was already so quietly stepping around Nash and careful not to wake *him*?

I stop abruptly just beside the door.

In the darkness, I check through the peephole.

Pull back.

Close up again.

Who is that? *What* is that?

The mash of gray and sheer purple pulls away and I see Neena standing in the hallway, one massive purple-satin arm resting on what appears to be the jamb of the door, the other hand pulling her slipper on.

I can't hear what she's whispering, but there are definite whispers as she looks forward in the blurry, extreme close-up of her robe and talks to somebody else outside of range. Some short words, a whisper like, "*I'm coming*," or better yet, knowing Neena, "*Hold your horses.*"

And then she's gone, the peephole suddenly clear again and showing nothing but the wallpaper opposite and the textured hallway carpet.

I bite my lip.

Swivel round.

Look at Nash's sleeping body beneath the bundle of sheets on the floor. The good soul, who has gone through days of exhaustion and was still thinking of me.

Should I wake him?

What is Neena doing up right now?

It may be too late to wake him and *then* catch whatever clue I need to see.

My hand is on the handle, hesitating.

But who knows? Perhaps somebody is waiting just out-side right now.

Perhaps this was some kind of ploy.

I was told on no account to open the door.

And yet.

Quiet as possible, I slowly inch the handle down, down, down until there is the faintest of clicks.

Even that click, however, is enough to stir Nash, because he pulls up instantly on his elbows.

"What are you doing?" Nash says in the darkness.

I put a finger to my lips, and without need for further prompting, he quietly stands. Alert. Ready.

I feel his breath tickle the back of my neck as I turn the knob further. His head is directly above mine as I pull the door open millimeter by millimeter, and we look out.

Nothing.

I pull the door open farther.

Nothing still.

Once the door is open by a foot, we look out to the right. Then left.

Nobody, and still nothing.

The hallway is just one long stretch of muted light, a dozen dimmed sconces to the very end.

"What was it?" Nash whispers above me.

Carefully I shut the door.

I pull away from it before I begin speaking. I'm starting to get paranoid myself here.

"Nothing. Maybe. But Neena. She was in her robe and she was in the hall. And she wasn't alone."

Both of us wordlessly look at the clock on the nightstand: 3:35 a.m.

And I'm positive we're both thinking, *Why is Neena—the person who passed out when Ricky tried to hand her a biscuit*

*at dinner—doing the very thing Carragan told her not to do
and loitering out in the hall, in the middle of the night, with
somebody else? And more specifically, with whom?*

I'm living the classic chapter 8 of Hugh's *November in
Red*. Chapter 12 in his *Four Endless Days*. I'm Terry Frost
in the middle of Hugh's most celebrated work, *Peril's Last
Case.*

I'm the character who goes against all logic and blindly
follows the shadow in the hallway.

I'm the character who either gets killed or solves the case.

"What are you doing?" Nash whispers in a tone of *have
you gone mad?*

"What does it look like? I want to find out what's going
on," I say, pulling on my flats. "Are you coming or not?"

Please come.

And I guess that's two things I've discovered about myself overnight.

The first is that yes, I am the scared girl who would walk
herself into a basement when she hears danger. I'm the terrified girl. I'm no stranger to fear.

But the other is that in the case of fight or flight, I am not
the kind of person who can just let things go and slink off in
the distance. I'm brave and afraid.

I need to know what's going on, for better or worse.

And I entirely intend to find out.

CHAPTER 10

THE HALLWAY IS SILENT AND NASH IS TWO MINUTES behind.

Sconces glow softly, the fabricated flicker of the antique-looking flames giving an unnerving glow.

Even Nash for all his nonchalance has his hands at his sides, as if halfway expecting to have to knock something or someone down at any moment.

But nothing jumps out at us.

We even go back to Neena's door and listen a minute or two.

Nothing.

There's a list of activities inside a gold frame next to the elevator.

Nash scans the list.

"They have three things still alive this time of night," Nash says, then sees my face. "Sorry. Not the best choice of words. Caree's Casino. A piano bar. And the Blue Lagoon Lounge. Want to take the elevator down?"

I shake my head.

"I can't imagine Neena breaking out in the middle of the night to go to a piano bar. Either she's made her entire life a lie and she's a killer, or she did the same thing we did and broke into Gordon's room for safety. I'm banking on her going to Gordon's."

I scan Nash's face.

He nods wearily and I feel a pang of sympathy for him. And a bit of guilt for having dragged him out of bed for nothing.

"I'm sorry. I shouldn't have gotten you up for this. Let's just go back to bed."

Nash and I turn back.

Nothing, not a fingerprint on a doorjamb, not a hair out of place, is anywhere for us to find.

It's depressing, actually.

It's never this slow in the books.

There's always a most convenient clue just lying about.

A perfect imprint of a soggy boot left by the doorway.

A scream sounding right at the moment of the fireworks that you still can just vaguely hear.

But no. No fireworks this night.

The door is still cracked when we return.

Nash noticeably cuts me off to step ahead of me.

Enters first.

Checks it all out.

"And you're sure you saw her?" Nash says in the quiet, taking a tentative step toward the bathroom and pushing the cracked door open in the dark. The clock on the bedside table glows 4 a.m. now. Another night on this ship with no sleep.

Another night with Nash, I can't help noting, but for two vastly different reasons.

"I mean, I wouldn't gamble my life on it," I say, then correct myself. I rub the bridge of my nose. "I don't know. I would've sworn I saw her, but it was so close up, I guess it could've been anything." I throw my hands up. "Or nothing! I don't know. I really could just be hallucinating at this point. Everything I say should be taken with a grain of salt. Nash?"

I realize that Nash has turned his entire attention onto something at the edge of the bed. Shoes.

But wait. That can't be right.

Nash is wearing his boots.

And if Nash is wearing his boots . . . whose *shoes* are they?

And suddenly, the little table mirror now in Nash's hand, he steps forward and—

CHAPTER 11

TWO DEAD MEN.

It's *unbelievable.*

I'm pretty sure at this point I'm never going to sleep again, even if we did vacate my room that is now surrounded in caution tape and migrate over to Nash's. And while, yes, the sheets are clean, the room's an identical shade of interior design perfection, and the bed doesn't carry a dead man underneath, the effect is the same: I will never sleep again.

I even at some point around 8 a.m. google that question. *Exactly how long can someone live without sleep?* The answer, for the record, is eleven days.

I stir my freshly poured cup of coffee from the coffee cart in the corner of the library as I listen to Cedar Pogache, the second man in command (more like very, *very* new adult); the one who carried the stretcher with Hugh just yesterday. He's much younger than Carragan, and several strands of his long blond hair bounce unwelcome over his eyes every minute or two like a cat batting at a toy hanging in the window. He's got adolescent acne on his forehead. He reminds me of a childhood cat I once tried to dress up in a colonial dress. His clothes swim over his bony limbs. He fumbles over half of his sentences and takes pains to avoid using words with more than two syllables.

"Shouldn't you be writing this down?" I say at last, trying to tap into what little reserves of my patience are left. Pogache has been pestering Nash with questions for the past half hour and has yet to open a notebook. "Or recording it. Or *something*."

He halts in mid-pace. Puts both hands on his hips.

Is his goal to look intimidating?

He doesn't manage it.

"Record, yes," Pogache says swiftly, lifting his finger. "And I *am* doing that." He pats his chest, as if to say the recording device is inside.

I bet.

"So," Pogache continues, casting his eyes uncertainly around, "if that's . . . all . . . I think it's time we take a recess now. And you should go about your . . . activities," he says unsteadily.

"Activities!" I cry out, waving a hand at the group of us. "Your security officer and boss is *dead* hours after he told me he figured out who did it. We can't go on and have our normal *activities*. Clearly the time for *activities* is over."

The group members are perched back at their misery stations now.

Jackie with her nose in a handkerchief by the bookcase.

Gordon at his sturdy chess set.

Crystal trying to slink out of the room entirely.

Ricky standing by/behind the curtains. (Note: Is it possible for a man to cling to curtains as a sort of security blanket? Is this telling of some holes in his childhood? My one semester of general psychology is coming up short, but I think there's something there.)

Nash is, as is becoming a norm, by my side.

Everyone is the same except Neena, who's fidgeting with an unruly charm on her glittering bracelet.

"I think Pogache is right," she says. Neena glances at me briefly, then waves a hand. "There's nothing else to do, Penelope. We've got to fill the void of time *somehow* until we get to land and this wreck is all over."

Wreck. *Wreck?!*

"You can't be serious, Neena!" I exclaim. "Carragan was murdered!"

"And we're stuck here together another eight days, I know," she says. "Now, I don't know a whole lot about murder here, but the only thing that jumps out at me is that both times they were alone. So as far as I see it, I'm not going to get in a position where I'm alone ever again while I'm here. Possibly the rest of my life."

"Tasty Tom's does have incredible spring rolls," Gordon notes. "It'd be a pity to miss out."

"I'm sorry, have you *all gone mad*? There is a killer on the loose, and the very least you could do," I say, looking to Pogache, "is arrest all of us suspects so that none of us end up, oh, I don't know, *killing* somebody else."

Nash clears his throat.

Leans in.

"Would you like to volunteer to be in handcuffs together under the care of that kid?" Nash whispers behind my ear.

Agh.

Fair.

He does look like he'd lock us up deep in the basement in handcuffs *together* and forget where he put the key.

No sense in being handcuffed *with* a man on the loose.

"Rest assured we have cameras everywhere."

I frown. I'm fairly astute at this point about cameras, and I have yet to see one anywhere. "Where are you hiding them?" I say. "Somewhere in the pictures?"

He ignores me.

"Uniformed people—"

"You mean those in uniform," I interject.

"And . . . well . . . *not* . . . uniformed people—"

"Undercover staff," I say.

"Will be watching you the next few days. You won't have anything to fear. You will all be . . . be—"

"Safe," I interject, my frown so deep it's going to slip off my face.

Oh. My. Gosh.

Somebody take away his driver's license. I don't even trust him behind the wheel.

"While I finish up this investigation. As far as this goes, you all just go about your business. Let me take it from here."

Pogache fumbles to put his notebook in his back pocket and on the third try gets it in. He nods at us. Shuts the door.

"That kid is traumatized," Gordon says.

"Well, how could he not be? He's probably next," Jackie says. She sneezes into her handkerchief.

"And . . . he knows it," Ricky says, shaking his head slowly. "Knows that looking too deep into that . . . notebook of his supervisor's . . . may very well be the death of him."

"Well, I'm about ready for breakfast. Anyone else?"

All heads turn to Neena, who is focused at the moment on smoothing the wrinkles from her bright purple skirt. She moves to standing, her eyes bright. Clear.

"Anybody?" she says, turning in a circle.

We're all silent in return.

"Oh, come on," she says. "Cheer up. Man's on the job. This'll all get settled soon enough. Besides, I simply can't go another day without eating. Yesterday about killed me. I'm never going another four hours without *some* sort of protein."

I cast a glance over to Nash.

My eyes say it all. *You see this too, right? Catching her moving around the hall in the middle of the night and then this?*

"Have you lost your mind, Neena?" Jackie says incredulously. "Yesterday you *threw* a glass of champagne at the bellhop. For, according to you, 'looking seedy.'"

"I stand by that," Neena replies. "The man *was* looking rather seedy."

"He was looking at his phone while we got off the elevator."

"Plotting *murder* for all we knew," Neena retorts, then flutters her hand in the air. Her eyes cast around us. "So I didn't like Carragan. I'll admit it."

I put my forehead in my palm. "*Neena*," I hiss, "*you can't say things like that about the dead.*"

She shrugs, as though we're disagreeing over something as trite as how well to cook meat. "What? We all thought it. I'm just saying it."

"Yes, but he was *murdered*. And we're in the middle of an investigation!" I shake my head. "Neena. Honestly . . ."

This is all getting out of hand.

"Don't take anything she says seriously right now; she's gone temporarily mad," Gordon says. "It's the summer of '03 all over again. The Flash Mob in the Mall incident on repeat."

"Ah." Jackie nods, tapping her nose, as though it suddenly makes sense.

"How long did it take her to come down from that one, Jackie?" Gordon says. "Three weeks? Four?"

"I know it wasn't until she got that call from her editor with the latest numbers," Jackie says. She shakes her head critically. "*I* for one don't even look at my numbers. It's demeaning work, catering your self-esteem to sales."

"Oh, I wouldn't call it *demeaning*, Jackie," Gordon says, taking up Neena's defense. "A little pathetic, really, but not demeaning."

"You're all wrong . . ." Ricky slips out from the curtains and flashes a morose, totally miserable expression at all of us. "It's the pills."

We all turn.

"What pills?" I say.

"For her nerves . . . most likely," Ricky says. "I saw her this morning . . . popping them . . . like candy."

"I'll take whatever she's having," Crystal says, reaching for Neena's purse as Neena snatches it out of her hand. "C'mon, Neena. I want to check out of this trip too."

Neena pulls herself toward the door. "They're *prescriptions* for this trip." She raises her chin. "So I get a *little* nervous before traveling. That's allowed. And now, apparently, my fears are fully realized and turn out to be entirely possible and we are living in a nightmare. So I'm taking them. Yes.

"The fact is, we're stuck here now, so the way I see it, I might as well continue existing best I can. I'm going to eat breakfast—and drown my waffles in all the syrup I can get. Then I'm going to meet my readers—and gab with the charming butler at the pool."

Gordon frowns.

Everyone, for the record, is frowning.

"And yes," Neena continues, "most likely I'll go Hula-Hooping this afternoon during a reader workshop. I'm taking this trip by the horns, and my plan is to pretend none of this is happening until I'm back in the safety of my therapist's couch when this is all over. You can all join me in the dining hall, or you can sit here miserably in the company of a murderer. The answer is clear to me which of the two I'm going to choose."

And then to prove her point, she pulls a pill out of her purse and pops it in her mouth. "Seize the day!"

I look to Nash.

Then the others.

No.

We can't do it this way.

We *can't* just go with the flow.

As she makes to open the door, I call out, "Stop!"

Neena halts. Turns.

Everyone looks at me, and I shuffle toward the center of the room. Put my hands on my hips as I muster up a plan.

"Neena is right." I turn to face everyone. "The reality here is that like it or not, we have a murderer on the loose and a teenager with peach fuzz who just mispronounced the word *forte* fumbling around trying to solve things before something worse happens. Maybe you all can just sit here and let the chips fall where they may, but . . . well, I can't. This is a textbook issue. I know what happens when people do nothing—at least in books. Someone else dies."

Gordon spins the pawn around in his hand. "Well, what do you propose we do, Pip?"

He's asking genuinely. He really wants to know.

"Well," I say, taking a fortifying breath, "the way I see it, we need a proper investigation. We're stuck on this ship, going nowhere. And it's clear we're not going to get any help on the outside. So then . . . we'll have to do it ourselves." I look around the room. "One of us needs to play investigator."

I might as well have just asked a bunch of kids who wants to go first and they all put their fingers on their noses. Everybody except Nash becomes immediately fascinated with the objects around them. I try in the silence to get someone to connect eyes.

"Fine." I throw my hands out. "I'll do it. I've read enough of Hugh's books. I can piece together an interview. Do some sleuthing. So you all go off and do your classes, go about life as normal, and we can agree that I'm going to talk with each of you, one by one, and see if I can figure out what exactly made Carragan come to his realization."

"He *did* find a killer among us?" Jackie says, horrified.

"He said he *thought* he had," I say.

Nash's brow furrows. "Or we should all"—his glance to me is subtle but telepathically communicates *except us*—"separate. Get as far from each other as we can on this ship and stay that way."

"And remove ourselves by what? Three hundred feet?" I say. "We're on a small ship in the middle of a big ocean. And yet, someone has still broken in a locked door once and left dead bodies underfoot *twice*. The unfortunate fact of the matter is, if someone really wanted to find us, they would. So go about your business. Stay in pairs or groups of three *at the very least*." I cast a tiny glance at Nash to message telepathically *except us, naturally*. "Let's keep a running text of where we are and who we're with so . . ." I hesitate. "If by unfortunate circumstance, someone we're paired with did want to do something . . . nefarious . . . there would be a running log on our side of who we're with that would keep unfortunate actions at bay."

The group doesn't look too happy with that, so I continue.

"Look, the reality is, we're a smart bunch. Every single one of us may be many things, but the one thing we all have in common is intelligence. And if there's one thing I've learned in my years under Hugh, it's that people kill for four reasons: love, hate, greed, or just plain craziness. But there's a vast difference between *how* you do it. Stupid or smart. And yes, there may be one among us who has a secret motivation that is shocking and something we'd never suspect in a million years. Fine. But there's one thing I do know that gives me confidence: One of you may be evil and willing to commit unearthly crimes, but no matter what, you are also intelligent. And intelligent people don't kill other people without an alibi. Carragan was alone and was murdered for knowing something we don't. Hugh was alone and murdered for something I have yet to discover. So the way I see it, none of you are at risk if you keep to yourselves, communicate where you are and with whom at all times, and go about your business. The only person who has anything to worry about"—I look around the room—"is me, I guess. And that's a risk I'm willing to take."

Silence follows.

"Well, Pip's got a plan, as always!" Neena cries out cheerily. "Now, what do we say? Waffles!"

CHAPTER 12

IT'S UP TO ME NOW, I GUESS.

The assistant who doesn't have a clue.

There's a certain level of motivation that comes from having a purpose like this, at least, something that feels right if compared to just filling out workshops and scheduling social media posts. I mean, Neena's clearly not in her right mind, and what could Crystal do? Waterslide an answer to this?

No, if there's one thing I can help with, it's this.

I know poisons.

I know core motivations for murder.

I know how to erase fingerprints, just as I know how to find them with nothing but a little cocoa powder in your pantry.

Just as I know how to forge them for someone else (a skill best left unsaid at the moment).

This is just another one of Hugh's books. That's the way I'm going to have to chase this, or else I'll never be able to take it on.

Surgically.

With all emotion removed.

One page at a time.

And, I guess, with a knife behind my back and one eye over my shoulder.

"Easy there, Pip."

I pull out of my mental resolve moment and realize I'm gripping the sugar spoon over my coffee like a knife. Jackie, sitting opposite me at the breakfast table, looks entirely appalled.

Nash gently takes hold of my hand and lowers it.

We're back at the dining hall, all carried off by the breakfast march with Neena in the lead. To be fair, nobody really wanted to stay behind in the author/murder wing alone.

Nobody, I've realized, seems inclined to want to go back to the "safety zones" of our bedrooms—or that doomed hallway—ever again.

The sun is bright over the horizon, giving the room full of windows a heavenly sort of air. Light glints on everything. The chandeliers above. The gold-rimmed glasses. The heavy silver platters heaped up with egg casseroles and bacon. A harpist plays in the corner.

You'd never in a million years imagine a corpse, or two, below deck.

Jackie frowns at me and I realize I'm doing it again, this time choking the sugar packet. She moves over to the other side of the table. It's just Nash and me now.

"Okay," Nash says, "who are we going to interview first?"

"We?" I say, screwing up a brow. "Who's 'we,' cowboy?"

"Yes, we. You do all the talking. I'll just be in the background."

"You have a workshop this morning. There is no 'we.'"

Nash frowns. "You can't imagine after everything, I'd let

you do an interview alone with a potential killer. There's no
way—"

His voice goes distant. He simply shakes his head.

I imagine the mental image of Carragan on the floor, face
down, is fresh in his mind.

"No," he says simply. Firmly.

Is this what it feels like? To have someone so staunchly
by your side? A knight in shining armor, if you will?

I've seen it in the movies.

Read about it a few times in books.

But man, it feels good.

A small smile slips up my lips.

"What about your workshops?"

"I don't care about my workshops."

"*I* care about your workshops."

"Why do you care about my workshops?"

"Well, the people came to hear your workshops."

"So?"

"And the ship is expecting you to carry on your workshops."

"So?"

"And I'll deal with potentially a four-million-dollar demand for refunds and a thousand angry messages and be
harassed by both the ship and the guests here with no way
out if you don't do your silly little two-hour workshops."

"Fine. But for the record, aside from all that, I just care
about survival. That's all I've got in mind. Survival. How to
get us out of here. For that to happen in the *room* we were
in . . ." Nash shakes his head.

It's clearly gotten to him.

"That's fair. Survival it is." I load up another piece of
bread with butter.

Nash tilts his head, watching me. "Hey, who's this calm,

composed Penelope right now? You're steadier than I am in all this."

I shrug. "I guess . . . I feel like you can do all the worrying for me. It's oddly comforting."

"My fears are oddly comforting?"

"Grounding, I'd say."

"My fears are oddly grounding," he repeats, more to himself than me.

"Yup. You're shouldering the worry. I appreciate that."

Nash takes a minute, and then a smile cracks on one side of his face. He rubs his chin and lips with his hand. "Shouldering the worry. Smooth wording, Pip. I might have to put that in my book. Hey . . . so why didn't you tell me about Michael?"

My knife slips.

He's shifted his weight forward in the pearl-rimmed upholstered cream chair, all flannel and boots in a seat made for a tea party.

"You got the whole story?"

"Uh-huh."

I look back to my bread and knife. "Who told you?"

"Neena. Sometime after the delirious crying spells and before she went to Candyland."

Neena's making her way round the room now, squatting at a table of readers, chatting her heart out without a care in the world.

She's wearing a purple feather boa.

"For what it's worth, I'm not sorry." Nash is looking back at me now.

I tilt my head.

Cock a brow.

"Well, I gotta say, I've had a lot of responses. Not being sorry for me is a first."

"Let me finish," he says calmly. "I've held it in a long time."

And there it is. A jolt of electricity up the spine. "Yeah?" I say calmly. "What?"

"And I've held my tongue through the years, but now it's nice to finally say it."

I set the knife down.

Turn to give him my full attention.

Everything in me. My cardigan giving him full attention. My hair that's been wound up into a too-tight bun that I'm really regretting right now. Even my shoulders are leaning toward him a little, like daffodils reaching for the sun.

He takes a breath. Cricks his neck like he's prepping for some real conversation. "Yeah." He's leaning forward now, elbows on knees. I'm now the sun to his daffodils too. "It's a relief really. I hope you can allow me to say this even though it's not . . . well, it's not the best time."

"Go for it," I say automatically, more breathily than I mean to. Yes, it's *terrible* Hugh is dead. *Terrible.* Lifetime of therapy terrible. But this is Nash. "If there's anything to learn from all this," I begin, while thoughts of *All's fair in love and war, There is no time like the present*, and *Seize the day* poster bubbles spur me on, "it's to live fully and in the present. Say anything you want, Nash. I'm listening."

He nods.

I've given him full permission.

Three hundred people surround us.

The hum of excitement as waiters begin to stream out toward the tables, carrying curiously elaborate yogurts in cotton-candy pink and blue.

But I've never been more focused in my life.

A knife could whiz by my head and I wouldn't move a muscle.

Nash takes another breath. Rubs his hands together for a few seconds. And plunges in. "I'm not the kind of man to put another man down, but . . . Michael was worthless. I've come across a lot of filthy people in my life, but, and I mean this with all my heart, he's the absolute worst. I'm glad he did something so brazenly stupid you couldn't possibly ignore it before it was too late."

. . .

Wh—

. . .

What?

The little flutter of wings in my chest falls flat, dead on the ground in the pit of my stomach. Whatever thing I had *hoped* he would say was obviously not said, and instead was replaced with . . . well, with . . . *this.*

"I'm not an idiot," I say, pushing my coffee cup away from me on the table as if it's at fault and not *him.*

"I know," Nash says quickly, putting both hands up in a stop position. "That's not what I mean. I just . . . he's been a . . . well, when he didn't meet you on your birthday, for instance. What was that? Two years in a row—"

"He told me he missed the flight," I reply heatedly, cheeks flaring.

I *know* there were signs.

I *know* all the things people have said to me, thought about me over the years.

Doesn't he *know* how embarrassed I am?

I was glaringly the girl who gave excuses.

I once made excuses for him for ducking out halfway through a *funeral.*

That I was attending for someone from *his* family.

Don't I know what an idiot I am?

I know what he's doing. He saw an open door during the middle of a rocky relationship and he's desperately sliding in big brotherly words of wisdom before the door shuts again and I go back. He's desperate to help the idiot girl who can't stand on her own two feet before she gets whisked right back into the darkness.

Yes. It was rocky. But I'm *done*. Really done.

My face is beet red. I know it. I can feel it. It's precisely the shade of red that women get when they *thought* they were being told something infinitely flattering, and they *thought* they were fulfilling a dream they never thought possible and haven't consciously come to terms with, and instead are *blasted* with the sense that they are actually quite a child and are being publicly embarrassed, and by the way, everyone watched you be *incredibly stupid* all along. They were talking behind your back about it.

They had conversations that started with, "Oh, silly Penelope . . ."

He's the *very* mature, successful adult man with brilliance and personality, and I'm the girl who . . . well, who can *organize* things *almost* as well as ChatGPT.

The room feels suffocating and I stand.

I've got to get out of here.

"Listen, Nash, if you want to pull together a bandwagon to tell me how you knew he was a bad guy all along, don't bother. There's already one and I've heard it the past six weeks from everyone in the world but you. Congratulations on being the last person in humanity to accomplish the task. Who knew? Who knew that all this time there really was something in the world every human on the planet could agree about?"

He makes a grab for my wrist, but I pull away. "C'mon, Pip. Please. Let me start again—"

"I was desperate, if that's what you want to hear," I say, crossing my arms over my chest. "I was a stupid girl who wanted so desperately for someone to love her unconditionally—"

"That's not a crime. That's admirable—"

"That she put on blinders and made excuses for years until it was inexcusable. I'm sorry that I believed him when he first told me I was . . ." I swallow. I will *not* let my voice hitch. "Special. And I'm sorry that I believed his words and wasted all the adult years of my life on a guy who ultimately told me I should be grateful that I 'primed the pump' for him. I'm sorry that I have an incredible knack for deluding myself. So yes. Hooray. Let's celebrate a win."

I feel the warmth of my cheeks and turn, positively mortified by the swift change of emotions flooding over me. Positively humiliated because I've just, yet again, let emotions take the helm instead of holding tight to what little self-control I had left.

I am becoming full-fledged Boom Box Girl.

Normally I could keep my composure.

For years, I had composure.

In fact, what makes all of this *worse* is that composure was the one thing—pathetic as it may be in a long list of talents—that I *did* have.

In a world of people with outstanding skills like writing, and singing, and casually ordering your food in fluent French to the surprise of all the people around you (Gordon), I had *this*. I had composure.

It wasn't a flashy talent.

It wasn't something you'd probably announce to someone when saying you liked them. You wouldn't go off and say, "Oh, Cheryl, she's about five foot five, brown hair. Great composure."

But it's what I had. People couldn't quite put a finger on

why I was someone they liked to hang around, but I could tell them: It was because in any series of events, nothing ruffled me. I could watch a meteoroid flying straight for our high-rise and calmly organize a plan.

People like composed people. Especially celebrated authors who themselves usually had a dash of crazy to get them where they were today.

It was my one, single gift I could give away in exchange for friendship.

My trade.

But what happened with Michael broke me. And now Hugh. And now Carragan. And now with Nash saying, quite frankly, the *opposite* of what in my delusion I'd hoped, and now my filter is gone and I'm completely out of control.

I purse my lips, holding in a terror that has quickly come over me.

Nash is going to hate me now.

I once spoke back to Michael half as honest as this and was put through the silent treatment for a month. (And *yes*, I'm going to have to work through unwinding just how toxic my relationship with him was and how that *wasn't* normal, but still. The fact is, sometimes people react this way. And I have a dreadful, gut-wrenching fear Nash will too.)

I've screwed up, and snapped at him, and showed my true colors.

Is that really logical, Pip? If he really does hate you for this, doesn't that mean he's not that great either?

I don't know, I tell myself. *And right now, I don't care.*

The point is, all along he has thought I'm this nice, sweet little friend of his, the fun-loving partner among this group of seven.

And now he sees the truth of what I am.

I'm not that sweet.

I'm not that fun.

I'm a screwed-up mess just like everybody else who has a tornado of troubles swirling just underneath the surface, ready to let loose.

I'm not, after all, a reliable good time.

And that was all I had to give.

"Nash Eyre!" a woman exclaims from a distance, announcing her arrival twenty feet off. Her hair is pulled up in tight, perfect silvery-white curls around her face to match her tight, perfectly wrinkle-free suit dress. Her knees march in tight rhythm (unsurprising, given the suit looks like it's cellophaned to her body) as she ticks her way toward Nash in rhythm with the clock hanging on the wall behind. "I'm Melody Carlton," she says, stretching out her hand. She smiles brightly. "Your moderator for the group panel."

I pull away from him in the fraction of time he's turned his attention away from me and reach for my purse.

Now's the time to make a break for it.

I can already see how it's going to play out.

Of course, Nash will be a gentleman about it.

He's going to step back politely. Give me the distance I'm "asking" for. A distance I'm saying I want but don't really.

We'll move to polite niceties.

We'll be the kind of "friends" Ricky and Jackie are, polite but without substance.

The kind of friends who hold the elevator for each other but don't invite them inside.

The woman, Melody, tackles Nash with questions while I pull my purse over my shoulder and set down my coffee cup. One last hot sip of caffeine sizzles on my tongue (fitting, for how it's betrayed me) as I lock eyes on the exit doors.

I'm not sure where I'll go.

I can't go back to the room.

Not . . . not after everything.

For that matter, I can't bring myself to go down that hall again.

Everything about it feels cursed.

I'll go toward the light.

I'll find my way to the upper deck, the sunlight, and wander around aimlessly until it's time to get sound on everyone's microphones for their panels, make sure everyone is set up securely, and then in between sessions, find time to interview each in turn.

Anxiety rises in my stomach as I take a first step for the door.

Wasn't *I* the one to say to be smart, to move in pairs?

Wasn't *I* the one to volunteer myself to interview everyone?

This is how people die in the stories.

It's not so hard to write after all, really. You just give a person a stupid fault like mine and—*bam*—we kill ourselves from our pride. Or shame. Or humiliation.

Emotions make humans stupid.

Or, I guess, bowing to our emotions does.

I'll just . . . walk quickly is all. I'll be so quick people can't get me even if they try.

Right. And how many victims fall prey with that genius plan?

I take another two steps toward the door.

Then feel a firm grip on my sweater.

I turn and see Nash chatting away happily with this Melody woman, his hand all the while firmly gripping the cardinals stitched onto my cardigan.

Melody's beady eyes drift every now and again to his hand clamped onto me as she talks through the smile plastered on her face.

Nash, for his part, looks entirely unbothered.

I take another step and find myself yo-yoing back toward him.

"And . . . um . . ." Melody says, her eyes jumping to me, "with regard to . . . the origin story behind your writing . . . Do you need to . . . do something? Are you alright?"

"No, no, I'm fine. You were saying?"

I take another step. My face is prickling with a hundred tiny pins.

We are in a *workplace* here.

I know *everything* about this trip has been shattering, but we are *professionals*.

"Nash," I begin, my tone expressing, *I'm a very organized, very professional assistant to Hugh, creative genius, who has spent a year planning this trip,* and not *I'm Pip, dealing with a heat wave of overwhelming emotions and handling it like a child.*

I smile politely like I'm not currently at the end of his tether. "If you'll excuse me, I have to get Gordon set up for his session."

"What session?" Nash says.

"Gordon's *next* session."

"You're not excused," Nash says equally politely, eyes still on Melody. "Oh, well, I'm not sure I have the grandest of origin stories out there, but you're welcome to ask. Somebody always does."

Melody nods fervently.

Too fervently, as she scribbles quickly and says, "Keep the origin story question. Got it. Good. And, um . . . well, are you sure I'm not holding you up?"

"Nope."

"Absolutely sure?" she says, eyeing me like I'm a rabid raccoon in a cage he should probably deal with.

"Can't think of a thing."

"Nash," I whisper-hiss.

I feel Jackie's eyes fall on me from across the breakfast table, see the disapproval in the little crease forming between her brows.

Her words fly telepathically from her gaze and land on me. *Even in times of being distraught, one must keep one's composure.*

She flaps the napkin at her seat to prove her point and resets it in her lap.

"Not at all, this is a fine time," Nash says. "Although I do think"—he flips over his wrist, which also happens to be part of the arm holding on to me, and my whole body is jerked sideways. He checks his watch. "No, I've got another thirty minutes until my first session. Plenty of time."

Fine. I'll work around him.

"I'm going to go now," I say politely, my words aimed at Melody this time.

"No, you're not," Nash says to me chipperly, eyes on Melody.

"Yes, I *am.*"

"You'll rip your cardigan."

"*You'll* rip my cardigan."

"And we don't want us ripping your cardigan," he continues, as if we both absolutely agree.

Something is happening.

The shame of the moment is receding as my confidence starts to build.

I make one more move for the door, and this time his arm lassos me and pulls me in, all the way in, the scent of burnt coffee on rough Carhartt jacket scraping all up one side of my face. His arm is heavy as it wraps around the whole of my body, round the shoulders, and huddles me close. We look like we're posing for an awkward prom picture. Or perhaps like a cat who's caught a mouse.

At this new situation, Melody purses her lips with uncertainty. Her eyes jet over toward the other authors, catch Jackie, who parallels her expression, and flash back.

She looks entirely out of her realm.

"Is everything o . . . kay here? You know . . . I didn't know if I should say something . . . but it seems like everyone is just a little . . . off."

Her eyes flicker, and ours too, to Ricky, who is seated at the end of the breakfast table, suspiciously watching a waiter serve him more coffee while visibly gripping a champagne glass in his hand cocked and ready to blow.

"Of course," she says quickly with a laugh, "I know authors are known to be . . . well, *uniquely* them . . . but it just seems that everyone here is a little edgy. And we haven't even had an appearance from Hugh Griffin. At *all*."

"We are *fine*," Nash says breezily, putting on full charm. "Have you ever been to Writer-Con? *That's* the place to go to see all the authors in full character."

She pointedly looks at his arm python-wrapped around my body.

"So you've caught me. I'm a codependent author," Nash says. "Pip here is just my lucky star. And once you find your lucky star, you aim to always keep it in your sights. *If you know what I mean.*"

"Oh." Melody's eyes soften a little, the creases at her temples deepening as she looks at me with fresh interest. "*Oh*," she says with more meaning.

I give a forced smile.

Mostly because of Jackie's stares.

And a little, I realize, because . . . of what's happening in this moment.

"Well. I think I have enough to go off of for the session. Very nice meeting you . . . two. I'll see you soon!"

"Yes, ma'am." Nash smiles with that winsome smile of his as he tips his hat at her with his free hand (sending her hand fluttering to her cheek).

Amazing.

Women quake at Nash Eyre's charms even when he's *currently holding a woman captive in his arms.*

"Phff," I blow out.

"What was that?" he says, looking down at me.

I purse my lips. Shake my head.

It's a little annoying, if I'm being honest.

"What?" he says again.

"I said, *phff.*"

"I got that. And?"

I consider not answering, then gesture at the woman. "And. It's just . . . look at her. You've got me standing *right here* and she *still* is blushing with your little thing you do."

Nash looks amused. "What thing?"

"If you let me go, I'll show you what thing."

He shakes his head. "Clever try, but no can do; you're a flight risk now. I'm going to have to keep you close. Now, who do we interview first?"

I take a breath.

I know what he's done.

It's a little hard to get my head wrapped around the past ten minutes, but it feels like I've been through a storm and the sun has finally risen.

Emotions, I have learned in the past two days, rise to the surface before realizations.

Emotions race faster to the forefront of the brain than logical deduction, and before I have time to process everything and work through exactly what just happened and why, there is one thing I can and do find myself relying on in this moment: It's okay.

Everything is *okay*.

The worst that I thought was going to happen *isn't* happening.

And as that one piece of information falls like a leaflet to my brain, with big bold letters across the page, I process in words what came first with the emotion: Nash isn't going to leave me.

No, in fact, Nash has drawn closer to me, literally, than he ever has before.

It's like he has taken into account the extent of my stress and my unspoken emotions and without speaking followed through with equal force in the opposite direction, as if to say: *I will not leave you. I will never abandon you. You are safe with me.*

"Hey, Nash?" I say.

He looks down at me. Which isn't easy to do, as a matter of fact, since my face is directly beneath his, buried in his side. "Hmm?"

"I'm sorry for . . . what happened back there."

"What, you being human? Don't apologize, Pip. I got you."

He smiles down at me, his blue eyes crinkling at the temples in what I do believe is the most thrilling smile I have ever experienced.

And the sturdiness behind his eyes is the secret sauce that throws my heart into full gear.

I can be human, I can screw up, and nothing changes.

He's a rock to stand on in a sea of changing tides.

It's almost . . . well, it's almost enough to lose your composure over.

"And for the record, I'm the one who's sorry," he adds. "All I was trying to say is that you're special, Pip. And you deserve someone who's aware of that every single day."

"Well," I say, taking a quick, steadying breath to force myself specifically *not* to become the girl weeping on his jacket right now, "if we're going to start interviewing, let's go with Neena. She's the only one here who looks like she won't accidentally stab me."

"To Neena," he announces, and together we begin striding her way.

CHAPTER 13

"YOU DON'T MIND IF WE SIT HERE, DO YOU, CHICKA-
dee? It's just vitamin D is so important for our mental well-
being."

Carefree Neena has stripped off her purple outer layer
and is now basking on a lounge chair beside the rippling
Mediterranean pool. A group of women are doing water
aerobics with little colorful foam weights across the way.
Neena's hand is outstretched with a crystal goblet, and a
waiter rushes over with more foamy pink drink. Sunlight
stretches across the length of the deck, so much so I pull
down my sunglasses to keep from squinting at the glossy,
blinding marble statuettes at every corner. At the far end of
the boat, a group is clustered around the helm, each standing at an easel, each with a paintbrush in hand.

I'm not gonna lie.

It's a weird place to conduct an investigation.

This was *never* a setting in any of Hugh's books.

Nash, in true bodyguard fashion, stands a few feet away,
his eyes cautiously bouncing from one person to the next, as

if expecting to see some elderly woman pull a gun out of her foam noodle.

"How are you feeling, Neena?" I say.

My phone is quietly beside me, the Notes app open and ready for typing.

Surreptitious is the plan.

Although to be honest, I can only appear so casual when I'm stretched out in black work leggings on a lounge chair.

"Awful, of course. Thank you, young man," she says to the waiter, winking at him as he tops off her glass. "Just awful."

I purse my lips.

"Who was it—Ricky perhaps?—who said you've been taking some pills to help your nerves?" I say casually.

"Yes. Quite the stuff indeed," she replies, then takes a sip of her drink.

I frown. I'm not so sure alcohol plus medicine is a good idea, but now is not the time.

"Why?" she says, turning to look at me. "You need some? I have a wonderful tele-visit doctor—"

"Oh no," I say quickly. "Appreciate the offer. I'm good. So."

"So," she says back.

How do I do this again?

How did Hugh have his detectives start off?

I'm having a case of too many bookish examples running through my head.

"I guess . . . we should start at the beginning."

"It's a very good place to start," she replies, then giggles at herself. "*Sound of Music*."

"I'm aware. Okay." A pause. "Right."

I'm floundering here.

It's a little bit of a unique situation.

I'm not exactly a detective off the streets.

How do you start an interview with someone you've already known for years?

"So. I guess . . . we'll just pretend I don't know you to get this going."

"Fine by me," she says patiently, and gives a little wave to a lady she chatted with at breakfast who walks by.

She's settled back in her chair like she is perfectly happy. Like this is just another day in paradise.

I cast a glance to Nash, my eyes saying, *Are you seeing this? What is wrong with this woman?*

He shrugs back as if to say, *What is ever right with Neena?*

And for a moment, it feels like old times.

"Okay," I say for the zillionth time. *C'mon, Pip. Business.*

I grab for my phone. Forget it.

I can't possibly try to figure out how to be a detective while pretending I'm not trying to be a detective.

That's too sleuth for a beginner like me.

"Where were you when the night of the murder happened?"

"Which one, dearie? You're going to have to be more specific."

"Hugh's," I say. "Let's just, for the time being, assume all of my questions unless specified are about Hugh."

"I was in my bed, same as you and everyone else. Well, minus one of us, of course." She laughs a little to herself and takes another sip.

My eyes go wide and shoot over to Nash again. *Are you hearing her?*

He takes my cue and steps closer to listen.

"And the morning he was found . . ." I say, typing into my phone.

"Oh, you know that, dearie. Where was I? Where do you know I was?"

She sounds teacherly.

"In . . . the library," I say.

"Spot on," she says, tapping her nose and then pointing at me proudly. "Very good. Jot that one down."

After a few furtive looks in her direction, I begin typing into my phone, only to realize she has quietly scooted herself over and is now hunched over, hovering over my shoulder, reading the screen.

"Now, I'm only a humble writer and no great sleuth, but I'd type a header for that one, dearie. Something like . . ."

I purse my lips together.

Pause.

And after several moments, give in and begin typing *Location.*

"Very nice. Very specific." Her flowery-perfumed hand pats my shoulder, and she drops herself back in her chair.

Honestly, is someone drugging Neena? Is that a thing?

"I don't think you ought to take those pills anymore, Neena," I say as an aside.

"As you wish," she says with a little carefree smile, and sips again on her pink drink.

She may go back to being an absolute wreck tomorrow morning, but better a wreck than this completely insensitive, dreamland woman.

Moving on.

"Did you notice anything unusual the night he died? Did you go out of your room in the middle of the night? Have you ever, for that matter"—I pause, casting another furtive glance her way—"left your room in the night for any reason?"

She takes a strong inhaling breath as though this was a deep question worth working through, then shakes her head. "No. Not that I can recall."

"Which, of course, would be easy to recall. Given we are talking about the last seventy-two hours."

"No. All I did the first night was what I always do—take my sleeping pill and fall asleep to a soundtrack of Stevie Wonder. Oh. And the night after, I stayed up wallowing in despair, of course."

"Of course."

"A casual self-wallow before bedtime is a must," I say, typing down her strange account. It takes several minutes, and I tell her at least twice that no, she cannot take a break and join the ladies for water aerobics "real quick."

Maybe she's sleepwalking, I realize.

Maybe she's actually talking to herself and the pills have made her sleepwalk.

I need to see the bottle and look up a list of side effects.

That would be a relieving realization. On the one hand, I'm driven to figure this out, but on the other . . . it *can't* be Neena. Eccentric, grandmotherly Neena. It just can't.

(You're a terrible detective, Pip. You're supposed to be unbiased.)

"And what was your relationship with Hugh?" I say.

"I think you know that, chicky."

"Yes, but tell me anyway. How long have you known each other?"

"A little over forty years. I was twenty-five when we first met. He was quite the catch back then, if you catch my drift."

My brows shoot up. "You dated Hugh?"

"I was engaged to Hugh, honey. But that was a lifetime ago."

"That wasn't a *lifetime* ago, Neena. This is your life. How did I not know this?"

It's ridiculous, but I feel a sense of betrayal here.

I mean, they knew everything about me. Everything. And to not share *this*?

She waves a hand. "What's there to share? I've been engaged to a dozen men over the years. I barely remembered it until you told me just now." She laughs.

But it feels . . . a little forced?

"And who broke it off?" I say into her laughter.

I can't be sure, but I could swear there's a millimeter pause in her laughter—a break in the cadence before she forces the laughter to hit a natural end.

"He did," she says at last.

Her tone is airy, but the way she reaches to the ground to set down her drink is unusual. Her face purposefully turning away. No witty, flighty quips that are so . . . her.

"That must've hurt," I say, setting my phone down.

She sees me set it down and draws up a smile. "Oh honey, what is love if there's not risk of hurt? I've written 106 books now, and if there's one thing every good romance story needs, every single one, it's a heart that's willing to risk getting hurt. Those are the stakes of love."

She grips my hand in a moment of clarity. "And listen to me, Pip. Anyone who risks their heart for love *is* a winner. It doesn't make you any less of one if it turns out the one you trusted has pulled the wool over your eyes. It just means you gotta pick yourself up and nobly try again." She lets go of my hand. Sits back again as the air clears. "Just in case you didn't know."

"I know."

"You know who I'm talking about."

"I know," I say tightly.

"I'm talking about *him*."

"Yes. I caught that."

"And The Incident."

"Oookay," I say.

"And The Breakthrough."

"Alright, Neena. I got it."

"And the celebratory life you get to lead now. Without *him*."

I purse my lips. Maybe it's best just not to answer.

"Well, I think that's all, isn't it?" she says brightly with a slap of her thighs. "I think I will take that quick dip. Unless you have anything else to ask?"

"No," I say with a shake of my head. "That's enough to go on for now. Thank you." *You totally loopy, grandmotherly love-doctor nutcase.*

She nods and shuffles herself to standing.

"I'll see you at lunch then, dearie," she says, giving me a little kiss on the cheek, the smell of peppermint leaving with her. "Try not to take yourself too seriously."

When she's just dipping her toe into the pool's edge, I remember something.

"Hey, Neena?"

"Hmm?" she says, turning.

"Did he hurt you? Hugh? When he broke it off?"

She looks at me through the purple haze and the bedazzled sunglasses and the heavy flowery, pepperminty perfume cloaked around her. And in that moment, I see something dark. Something entirely out of place amid all the happiness she has clothed herself with.

"Hurt doesn't begin to describe it."

And as she turns, I see a bright smile shimmy onto her face.

With mask firmly in place, she calls with a wave to the ladies in the pool and wades into the water.

CHAPTER 14

I'M NOT GOING TO SAY I *MISS* THE ROLLER-COASTER ride of Neena from yesterday, but I'm not even seated before Jackie begins to complain.

"This chair is revolting," Jackie snaps, all the while wiping her lacy handkerchief over the imaginary dust on the pristine tan-and-white-striped lounge chair.

It's 10 a.m. There are seven more days on this ship before we dock. Yesterday I managed to squeeze in a Neena interview and a Neena interview only. What with group panels and packed cruise schedules, there was hardly time to breathe before Nash and I found ourselves back in the room heading for lights-out. To his credit, he stayed closer to me than my shadow all day. It was reassuring. Comforting. And I found that even in stretches of silence, we were comfortable. Not to mention, there was something quite bolstering about walking out of the bathroom this morning with my hair freshly dried (and down), a new billowy black blouse on, and freshly applied blush into a room where a man looked up from his computer, halted, and after an *eternally gratifying* five-second stare said, "Wow. You look"—(a cough)—"very beautiful, Pip. You're going to make the sunrise jealous."

I mean, he's a man of words, yes. Lyrics are a part of his nature.

I think I'm still blushing off that one.

At any rate, I'm going to have to do without my friendly shadow for a couple of hours.

It took some convincing, but Nash finally agreed to leave me for his own morning workshop session. He had to, really. It was one thing to announce everyone needed to stay in pairs, but the reality is, we also have our sessions and the public's expectations.

So, after making me promise to stay in public view among loungers, waders, and, least relieving, Neena, who is now fully immersed in water aerobics, he left me to interview Jackie.

The sky looks a buttery gold this late morning, with clear skies overhead and an abundance of golden inner tubes glittering in the pool ahead. The deck is unusually packed today, most likely because Neena tends to draw a crowd wherever she goes. People, as it turns out, love Nerve-Pill Neena. She's a regular fun bus.

Jackie, on the other hand . . .

When she does finally sit, she's stiff as a board.

You know, there was a leaflet I referred to when booking this place. On the cover of the ad was a big picture of a model sitting in this exact place, pool behind her. A woman in a flirty yellow polka-dot swimsuit leaning back slightly, laughing with her huge, bright smile toward the sky, like it'd just told her the best joke and all the world was happy and gay.

Meanwhile, Jackie's back is rail straight, her hands grip

each knee firmly, her feet are planted on the ground, and the toes of her brown loafers face directly north.

Jackie, let's just say, is not the kind of person you can use to market a vacation. She's more of a Zoloft-before-it-starts-working ad gal. The person you bring in to film the real doom and gloom before the antidepressant kicks in.

She glares at my barely slumped shoulders.

I know she's glaring to make a point about my barely slumped shoulders, because her exact words to me once were, "And how could you expect to find a husband, Penelope, when you are flying down life's highway toward hunchback land?"

I straighten.

And part of me automatically moves to look back to Nash, so used to having him, when I stop myself.

"How was breakfast, Jackie?" I say politely, holding my phone at my side.

"Don't waste my time with twaddle. Get to it."

"Please don't take this personally. This is just protocol," I say, turning back to Jackie. "I'm going to interview everyone to see what we can get figured out here."

"And your little cowboy boyfriend? What about him?"

My head jolts up from my phone. "What?"

"Or perhaps you prefer to believe the frailest of our group are the likeliest to commit the most gruesome of crimes," she continues, squinching up her little nose. "Seems you are picking favorites to me."

"Play nice, Jackie," Neena trills from the center of the pool, holding two bright pink fans overhead with the others while partaking in some kind of flamingo walk. "Just because your tea wasn't a perfect 180 degrees this morning—"

"People were *murdered*," Jackie snaps back loudly. "This is no time to sit around drinking *mojitos*."

Several ladies turn to Neena, who puts a flamingo fan to her mouth and says in a hushed tone, "Her only daughter turned thirty and told her she doesn't want children."

Several sympathetic heads nod.

Neena begins what looks like a conga line now, and the ladies follow in line, pink fans raised high.

Amazing.

Celebrity-ish folk can get away with just about anything.

"I'll just jump to it then," I say hastily, lifting up my phone. "We'll zip right through this and then you can be on your way. Where were you the night of the murder?"

"You know that."

"Pretend I don't."

Even her annoyed sighs are crisp and efficient. "In my bed like everyone else."

"How long have you known Hugh?"

"You know that answer too."

"Pretend I don't."

"Forty years."

"And how long have you been *working* with Hugh?"

"You know."

I grit my teeth. "Pretend I don't."

Jackie sighs in exasperation. "Forty years."

"And would you say your relationship with Hugh has been . . ." I hesitate. *Shoot.* I've boxed myself in with a yes-or-no question. Rookie mistake. "A . . . good one?"

"Obviously."

"You . . ." *Shoot. I've done it again.* "Like him?"

"*Obviously.*"

"How would you describe, in one word, your relationship with Hugh over the years?"

The little crease between her eyes deepens, and she purses her lips while she thinks. "Trying," she says at last.

Both ways, I'm sure.

I type it down while saying, "Why stay a part of The Seven then? Why not leave?"

"For obvious reasons."

I look up. "Jackie, anytime you find yourself wanting to say the word *obviously*, let's just go ahead and use that moment for you to explain precisely what is obvious, alright? Let's just assume that nothing is obvious to me."

She drops her head back, as though I have just asked her to do something incredibly demanding.

"When Hugh found himself on that elevator with myself and the others, I was a twenty-six-year-old woman with two meager books behind me. I went to that writing event to meet my agent. To my chagrin, over lunch, that agent let me go. I wasn't worth the invested time."

Jackie rubs her nose.

"I got on that elevator with every intention of leaving writing—my dream—behind. And when it halted halfway down, there I found myself, trapped with six other authors. Packed like sardines. But"—she shrugs—"turns out I was packed with none other than Gordon Pesque and Hugh Griffin, and that wasn't a bad place to be. Far less so six hours later when Hugh hatched his grand plan. I went into an elevator at the worst moment of my life and emerged at its peak."

Well. It's both sweet and sad to announce the happiest day of your life was forty years ago.

"What about Neena, Ricky, and the other two—"

"Patricia and Mark—"

"—who've retired now? Were they successful too?"

"Everyone except me on that elevator could have stood under the definition of successful. But even Neena's sixty thousand copies sold on a book is a far cry from two million. Gordon and Hugh were the lions of the group."

Fascinating. I knew Hugh was always right up there with having his face on a cereal box, but not Gordon.

"And why do you think he wanted you to join The Magnificent Seven?" I say. "If it wasn't for the sales."

"I had a bag of toffees in my purse."

I tilt my head. "I'm sorry. What?"

"I had a bag of toffees in my purse. I shared them at some point."

I must have looked dubious, because she adds, "What? I'm not a monster. At any rate, he said he was forever in my gratitude." Jackie sniffs a little longer now and reaches for her hankie. "At least that's the way the story goes. The reality is, I was just in the right place at the right time. Hugh, unlike others in my life, had no problem sweeping me along despite who"—she sniffs again—"who I was. Trying as he may have been sometimes, he also . . . is the kind of friend few are lucky enough to experience in their life."

Emotion fills her throat as she speaks, and I catch the double meaning in her words, the self-awareness as she quietly admits how difficult she can be.

She's never admitted it.

Hugh loved her through it all.

As should I.

"*That's* why he called you Toffee sometimes?" I exclaim. "I thought it was to annoy you."

"Particularly remarkable people can draw up feelings of reminiscence and annoyance simultaneously."

Jackie gives a sniff as she puts her handkerchief to her nose.

"Oh, Jackie." I can't help it. I reach out and give the hand gripping her knee a sympathetic squeeze.

For anybody else, any normal person, you would've heard those words and thought nothing of them. But in half a decade, I can honestly say this is as emotional as Jackie has ever been. And that includes the time everyone surprised her for her Historical Lifetime Achievement Award *in London* three months after her husband had passed (which, for the record, included a twelve-hour flight) and she gave us in turn a very connected eye glance from the podium during her speech.

Which of course sent Neena into tears and drew Crystal—who had completely missed the moment by hovering over the cheese table—back to her seat begging to know what she'd missed. (The real question: What *doesn't* she miss?)

Jackie pulls her hand away from mine.

That was enough human contact to keep her fueled for the next ten years, easy.

"Right. Well. Let's move on," I say, taking her cue and looking to my list of questions. "You are among the closest companions of Hugh." I quickly add, "Aside from the pool of support in being a part of The Seven, have you ever gained direct monetary resources from Hugh or will you in the future?"

Jackie purses her lips. "If you're not so subtly asking if I was greedy for money, no. I didn't *need* Hugh for financial gain, or any gain for that matter, five years after the commencement of our social contract. I could have stepped away and published successfully onward forever. The choice to stay was and is entirely mine. And if you're trying to ask if I'm in his will, how would I know? He never told me if I was, and I don't care about his stuff either way. I don't need money. I don't *need* anything. It's quite obvious who the killer is." She shakes her head. "Stupid man. I always told him he would get himself into trouble."

My slowly retracting shoulders shoot up. "Who do you think it is?"

She frowns as if I'm the stupid one now.

Her nose creases.

She waves a hand. "It's obvious, isn't it? I must've told him a thousand times what a foolish game it was to play the hero, skipping down to the station in his free time just to solve the unsolvable crimes. Shuffleboard, I told him. A good hobby for a man his age was shuffleboard. But did he listen? Noooo. Determined to pore over all those old crimes, making a gruesome game out of gruesome events. Well, now he's had what's come to him, hasn't he, and we're all stuck in this mess."

"Yes, but the whole wing was locked off. And none of us lost a key. And Carragan said there was no sign of forced entry."

"Unless you are just determined enough to steal a key from one of the staff."

Of course.

The wind sucks right out of my chest as I sit back in my lounge chair.

Of course.

How had I not seen it? How, in all these hours, had the fact that Hugh dabbled in detective work for his former police unit not dawned on me? How many angry, unhinged people had he set off?

I guess Carragan had guided us early on to assume it was one of The Seven. And when he said he knew who it was after interviewing everyone, it was so clearly inferred that it was one of us . . .

But if we widen the possibilities . . .

Jackie's alarm goes off on her phone and she jumps up with the words, "Time for a break."

My head pops up. By the time I get my feet planted on the ground, she's already several yards ahead.

Arms tucked into her sides, legs briskly sweeping her away.

"Where are you going?" I call out.

"Ambulatory recess," she says over her shoulder.

"What?"

She turns her head a little more sternly my way. "A *walk*, Pip," she says, eyeing me like an unintelligent child who is proof that the education system of our government has let all of society down. "I'm taking my *walk*."

"*Now?*"

"Every hour on the hour from dawn to dusk. A turn around the boat for circulatory health."

"But we're in the middle of an interview!" I call out.

Several heads turn.

"Circulatory *health!*" she repeats.

Amazing.

The woman can manage to hiss at you while yelling at the same time.

Now the heads bobbing in the pool turn their curious eyes on me, and I'm forced to put up a smile.

"For . . . a magazine," I say. "A . . . very elite . . . *League of Luxury Cruise Liners* interview."

I have no idea what I'm saying. I just threw out a bunch of random words. Nevertheless, attention drifts away from me.

And the watery swirl of the flamingo water dance continues.

Fine.

Jackie's taking a recess from the interview halfway through for the sake of *circulatory health*. How long will it take her to circle back? Ten minutes? Twenty? Surely not twenty. The woman walks like she's in Olympic training.

"A refreshment, ma'am?"

An older gentleman has glided over in his coattails and elegant peacock bow tie and is now standing over me poised for an order.

I realize how out of place I look in my fully clothed, mostly-in-black self—I'm probably the person they put on a poster during hospitality training as an example of being "a veritable cry for relaxation help."

"Something more tasteful, perhaps?" he inquires, casting a subtle eye at my ensemble. Neena and the others have now picked up Hula Hoops in the water and are twirling. "Something a little more . . . *elevated*? A nice red blend from the esteemed Château Calon-Ségur?"

"No, thank you."

"A cup of coffee?" he says, shifting quickly. "Some still water in a chilled glass?"

"I'm probably fine. Thanks—"

My words cut off at a curious sound and I jump-start to standing. To his ears, and to everyone else around no doubt, the sound is nothing more than the caw of a passing seagull. Swift. High-pitched. Not lasting more than a heartbeat.

But to me, having been sitting on the edge of a knife the past few days, eyes and ears on high alert, the sound was undeniable.

Jackie.

I jump up and begin a brisk walk in the direction Jackie went.

"Will you return, miss? May I raise your umbrella?" the man calls out.

At this point it's just rude to deny him. "Oh yes!" I call back. "Thank you. That'd be terrific."

And then I turn the corner.

The stretch of deck ahead of me is long and narrow. The ship railing lies to the right, with a stretch of ocean beyond. A dozen doors stand stoically to the left, quiet and waiting.

A few strollers dot the deck, floppy hats and bright tops whipping in the breeze.

There is no sign of Jackie as far as the eye can see, and I would spot her, given she was dressed like she was prepping for a funeral just as much as me.

It should be as easy as spotting a penguin in a crowd of flamingos.

I never should have let her go. What was the rule we all agreed on?

Groups of two or more.

Ambulatory recess or not.

Swiftly I pull open the first door to my left.

A carpeted hallway running the length of the boat.

Empty.

Next.

I stride on, yanking open door after door.

By the time I'm on my eighth door, my certainty about hearing Jackie's cry is waning, and a part of me is starting to consider turning back.

Perhaps she's walked the circle by now and is waiting for me, foot tapping, sighing exasperatedly.

She's probably dusting off her lounge chair right now, scowling at the server trying to offer her an umbrella in a drink.

Just one more door.

I dart a look inside the door ahead of me. Just as I'm about to move on, however, my eye is drawn to the only—and unusually—dark room to the right.

A gilded sign hangs on the wall beside the entry. GREETING LOUNGE.

A greeting lounge for the hallway, just like in every other hall on the ship, and yet this one is dark.

Intentionally dark.

I take a step forward.

Feel my nerves shoot through my body.

Hesitate to walk another step.

"Jackie?" I call out, arm holding open the door.

Sea-salt air mingles with trace orangey scents of room perfume, the thick Atlantic mixing with the crisp thin oxygen of manufactured air-conditioning.

Childhood me feels incredibly guilty as I hear my mother's voice telling me not to let the air out and *shut the door.*

"Jackie?" I call again.

The pause before she responds is a lifetime.

"*What?*" she snaps at last, and I can honestly say I have never been more relieved to hear her irritated voice.

I let go of the door.

Step forward as the door swings shut.

Turn the corner.

Halt.

"Jackie? What are you . . . doing?"

I cast my eyes around, gathering in the surroundings.

Jackie is standing in the center of the room, in the dark. The heavy drapes on the wall of windows are drawn. A coffee table is beside her, alongside half a dozen wingback chairs.

Nobody is in the room.

Jackie herself looks . . . in a word . . . *rigid.* As in, *more* rigid. (Has she ever *not* looked rigid? I bet the woman sleeps like a statue.)

"I'm . . ." She looks to the ceiling, directing her scowl there for several seconds. "I'm . . . stretching."

"Here?"

"Yes." With minimal effort, she draws her left foot backward, then leans her weight on her right thigh.

"In the dark?"

"It's calming."

My brows furrow. "With a knife in your pocket?"

"Obviously not."

I point at the handle of the steak knife at the hip of her tweed pants.

"Except . . . for that one," she says, pulling it out by the gleaming white handle.

What . . . in the Sam Hill?

She takes a breath.

Looks up at the ceiling one more time.

Squeezes her eyes shut.

And opens them.

When she looks at me again, there's a certainty in her expression.

Something surprising. Something decided.

It sends a chill up my spine.

"Fine. You caught me. You no doubt find it suspicious. But *obviously* I keep personal protection on me, Pip. I'm not a fool who would walk anywhere around this ship *alone* when two people have been *murdered*. Luck favors the prepared."

"Right." I take a step backward, because for the first time I see something in Jackie's expression that leaves me truly unsettled. It's a moment when you think you know everything about a person, and then they take you by surprise.

Her eyes flashed at the word *murdered*.

Flashed.

Gleefully.

I cast a glance down the empty carpeted hallway and the bizarre thought *I can outrun this woman, right?* enters my mind. But surely I could, right, in a worst-case scenario?

I know I'm not exactly the *most* athletic person, but surely a twenty-seven-year-old can outrun a sixty-six-year-old woman in a pinch—even if she's an award-winning ambulator?

"Let's finish with that interview of yours," she snaps.

"That's what you're after, isn't it? You didn't have to hunt me down. You'd think you wouldn't be so impatient as to cut off my walk. We'll do it here."

"No," I say quickly. The last thing I want right now is to be alone with her.

Pairs. Forget pairs.

We need to be in groups of four or more.

Why did I leave Neena again?

Look at me.

Am I not a walking case of secondary character bound to get herself killed?

I left the safety net of the passel of people. I raced after what I believed was a cry for help. And now I'm standing with a suspect with a knife, in the dark, away from the public eye.

Just. Perfect.

"You can finish your walk," I say, taking two quick steps backward.

"Too late now. You've ruined the mood."

The mood for the walk. Sure. One must have a mood. Just a minute ago it was all "we must have ambulatory walks for our health in the middle of interviews, rain or shine," but now, apparently, one also needs to be in the mood.

"We'll finish it up outside then," I say quickly. "Healthy sea air and all that."

The silence stretches a mile long between us.

"Fine," she says at last.

My eyes can't help it. I'm drawn to staring at the gleaming white handle and sleek silver body of the knife. Perfectly clean. Perfectly ready.

She looks from me to it.

"Well, if you're going to obsess . . ." Jackie says.

Then she does the unthinkable.

She drops the knife on the floor. Casually. Tip of the blade face down. Like it's of no more significance than a tissue.

It rests on the dark red carpet like in a pool of blood.

Who is this woman?!

I'm gaping at her when she starts after me, and when she makes that first step, I call out, "Terrific. I'll meet you there" and dash for the door.

The door resists my attempts to open it because of the wind but, with a frenetic yank with both hands, finally releases.

I practically leap for the promenade deck and don't look back until I'm in the safety of the wading ladies.

The scene has shifted with the change of the hour. The clock reads 11:05 a.m. A live band has set themselves up in the corner now, testing their instruments, and a group of ladies has settled by the bow of the ship, large blank canvases set on easels before them. A man in a hat stands in front of them, holding up a palette of paints, instructing as he points at the horizon.

Sure enough, an umbrella is open over the lounge chairs where I left them, and I note two glasses of sparkling water on a little silver tray between them, the frost on the glasses still visible. The man in the peacock bow tie stands over by the bar, and our eyes meet.

I feel compelled toward the glass, drawn by his gaze.

When at last I take a sip, he smiles, satisfied.

There's comfort in knowing this highly attendant man isn't far off. He looks like the rescuing type, doesn't he? Saves the day via drinks with umbrellas, ergo saves the day via restraining the knife-wielding, ambulatory woman?

Jackie walks just as strict and composed as she always is toward the chair.

Dusts it for a particularly long period of time.

Sits.

I look over at her body. Nowhere as far as I can see is there a steak knife.

"Now where were we?" she says.

"Okay. Yes," I say, taking a breath as I open my notes. The stream of words I was typing earlier breaks off abruptly. Notes about the murderer acting out of revenge over one of his previous solved crimes. "You were saying you thought the murderer is someone from the outside. Someone, perhaps, who had faced jail time and had gotten out and was ready to get revenge. Care to elaborate?"

"I'm wrong. Stupid idea. All his solved murders were men, no doubt, and look around. It's a women-filled ship."

True, there are a lot of floppy hats.

"Well," I say slowly, "women *can* commit murder."

"Of course," she snaps. "They just aren't so stupid as to get caught."

I stifle a smile. Seems even under the threat of death I find things funny.

"So you retract your idea then?" I say. "You *don't* think it was some irate criminal seeking revenge?"

"I never retract anything, dear. I'm just elaborating on my supplied response."

Sounds a lot like a retraction to me, but I don't fight her on it.

There's a peace in thinking the crime was committed by an outsider, even if it also is a little scary to have the net of suspects widened by several hundred. Still. I'd take that over the possibility of it being one of The Seven any day.

I switch over to text message and type in the name of young Cedar Pogache, who has taken over the case.

Do you have the names of everyone on the ship? Are there background checks for everyone on the ship?

I doubt he would allow me to have access to the names, and if I press too hard, I wouldn't be surprised if he gets irritated with me even trying to have these little interviews with my working peers. But he's young and impressionable. Less confident and demanding than Carragan. Perhaps he will be willing to share some information.

"I don't have all day."

I look up from my text to see Jackie's bitter glare.

Quickly switch back over to my notes.

How do I jump in again? I think, racking my brain. The goal is to ask, "Are you by chance the murderer?" without exactly saying, "Are you the murderer?" To hedge around the question without saying outright, "So . . . were you just hanging over his bed with the knife, or what?"

How did Hugh do it in his books again?

A perennial favorite book of Hugh's comes to mind—*A Game of Hot Seat*—and I cling to that thought. Ask as many questions as you can at a rapid pace, take a stab at every subject possible as quickly as you can, and see what suspicions come out.

"So I have to say," I bring up quickly and casually, "it was a little surprising seeing you back there with a knife."

"I don't see why. Neena's been carrying one around in her purse two of the past three days."

"Do you always carry around a knife?"

"Obviously not."

"But you carry one around now."

"Given the situation, yes."

"And you and Hugh have never had any trouble getting along."

"Nothing beyond the typical."

"Have you ever had any arguments?"

"I didn't say that."

"What have you argued about?"

"The usual. Transportation services. Publicity plans. The weather."

"Have you ever killed off anyone in your books?"

"I write historical. Death is abundant."

"But murder?"

She pauses.

Purses her lips so deep I wonder if she's going to make herself bleed.

"No." She pauses again. "I mean yes."

I lift a brow. There's at least one that I know of. *The House of Claire.* But I haven't read all of her works. "No, but maybe yes?"

"I . . . I can't be responsible for remembering every little detail in my books."

"It's a pretty big detail to include," I say. "It's a pretty major premise."

"Unlike people and their one-hit wonders, I've written a lot of books."

"What?" I say. Is she really insinuating that she can't be expected to remember those kinds of details from her books? I was planning to use this quick-pace style of interview to guide her toward talking about murder in her books and how she feels about the motivational factors for her killing characters. Hoping to catch her resonating with them. Figure out why.

But *this*?

I've talked to Hugh plenty of times over the years. The man may forget what he just bought in a bag in his hand, but he never forgets his books. Any of them.

The plotlines are a part of his core memory.

When you're a reader, you forget details. You forget scenes. But when you have poured your heart and soul into a story you've created in your mind and spend a year editing, followed by another year of meticulous edits, you don't forget.

I know as close to firsthand while not actually firsthand as anyone can get.

And what Jackie has said is just not true.

"How many books have you written now, Jackie?"

And to my surprise, she frowns deeper. "Why? What does that have to do with anything?"

A thought is forming, but it's too vague to see any clear shapes yet.

"Just answer the question."

"Thirty-six."

"Thirty-six," I say, typing it down. "Half the number of Hugh's books, and yet he can recall every single one."

"He had a sharp memory."

"As do you," I reply. "In fact, you often pride yourself on that sharp memory."

She does. We can't have a conversation in the group without her informing us who wore exactly what on which day.

"You're simply wrong. Perhaps *your* memory isn't as sharp as you think," she retorts.

"Tell me, what is the premise of *The Black Portrait?*" I say, throwing out a book of hers from a few years back. I've read it. It's your typical Jackie Ann work: depressing plotline, multiple tragedies, war nurse who gets the guy briefly before he dies in battle, that kind of thing.

"A young nurse defies her isolated, dying father and joins the war force, finding love and ultimately death in Okinawa," she spouts back.

It sounds rehearsed. The elevator pitch, a perfect twenty words.

"And the plot to *The Coal Sisters*?" I say.

"Two widowed sisters fight to keep their farm running during the most devastating fire to engulf their Appalachian mountain town," she says automatically.

And there it is again. That elevator-pitch response.

I switch it up.

"You say that your first two books were less than successful. But after you teamed up with The Seven, sales grew. Was it right away?"

"Alliance with the group gave my books immediate results. Yes."

"Which, I assume, led to higher and higher advances. Royalties."

"And?"

"Remind me, Jackie," I say, tapping my head. "What happened again in that scene in *Where the Jasmine Grows*? Did Jasmine tell Hunter she was a Confederate supporter or keep the secret to the end?"

And to my surprise, she does exactly what I found myself wanting her to do, what I suspected, and yet at a deeper level, what I didn't really expect at all.

Jackie squints at me.

Her mouth opens; she's poised to answer.

Wanting to answer.

And yet . . . doesn't.

Turns her attention to the water glass beside us.

Takes a sip.

"I don't *know*," she says at last.

I'm already two steps ahead of her now, though. I've already gotten into my email, found the file, opened the pdf document of one of her former books, scrolled down to a random place, read a few lines.

"What about when Joetta meets Emsley's grandmother?" I say. I hardly remember this scene myself, but it's at the tip of my memory. "What happened just before that again?"

Her blue eyes are ice as she furiously sets her glass down.

Skirts her eyes around her surroundings, cautious that no one is close enough to hear.

Through her clenched teeth she elucidates slowly, "I. Don't. Remember."

Incredible.

This really *can't* be possible.

"Jackie? Did you . . . *write* these books?" I say.

And as if this is the last straw, she stands. "I am frankly *appalled* you would ask. I have done *nothing* illegal and built my career *on my own*. To insinuate something so . . . well, I'm done. Play your little sleuthing game if you like. I have a session to attend to."

But then, just before she begins to move, she leans down and says under her breath, "*But*. If I *didn't* write them on my own, that is *not affiliated* with the murder and *no concern* of yours. And if you tell *anyone*, mark my words, I will sue you for defamation of character faster than you can type the words on your little phone."

And as the band strikes the first note of their cheery song, she strides away.

CHAPTER 15

I CAN'T BRING MYSELF TO CALL FORWARD ANYONE
else for the rest of the morning.

I'm so unsettled by the turn things took with Jackie that
my guardian angel, the server in the peacock bow tie, brings
over a silver platter laden with seasickness medication options arranged in a neat little circle.

I'm so startled by his sudden presence over my shoulder,
however, that I scream and push the platter over, and all the
bottles of pills scatter onto the floor (which turns into one
long circuitous round of us both apologizing back and forth
while gathering pills on our hands and knees).

Eventually Nash comes back and—seeing my white
face—immediately vows to stick around from then on,
peanut butter on jelly style, and I can't say I complain.
Enough independence from me.

The rest of the day is one big buzz of activities, filled
mostly with me racing around the ship from one speaking
space to another, solving problems.

Gordon getting lost on the ship and not being able to

find his session meeting place. Gordon not knowing how to work the projector screen.

Crystal being MIA for her session.

Gordon finally getting the projector sorted out, only to realize when a giant heart pops on the wall that he somehow opened Neena's presentation.

Mostly Gordon problems.

Nash tags along as I move from problem to problem, which I highly appreciate. His company is reassuring, and the comment about me being his *lucky star* rings in my ears whether I mean it to or not.

It feels . . . I don't know . . . immature even to think about it at a time like this, but I can't help it. And of course, there's the whiplash of the interview thoughts.

Did he mean it?

Or did it mean something more?

And also . . . is Jackie a murderer?

Or was Nash just looking out for me? As a friend?

It's a challenging thing to analyze, simply because he's the best human being I know.

Other, lesser human beings would make it easier to tell if they liked you.

Am I just a small, frail friend he realizes he needs to look after in these dire circumstances?

The man missed his own award ceremony to head out to the Appalachian Mountains, riding his horses up and down the mountains providing hurricane relief after the Helene storm.

Am I just another recipient of his far-reaching goodwill?

How is it possible that Jackie has used a ghostwriter all this time? *Really?* You think you know someone . . .

At three, I stick around for Nash's session.

And believe me, he took his vow to stick close by seriously.

I tried at one point to step out the door to answer a call and he broke off his lecture to say, in essence, *seize her.*

(They did in fact seize me.)

So. Staying wasn't really a choice.

"How did it go?" Nash says, shutting the workshop door behind him.

We're the last ones to leave the session room. Fifty or so of the readers from the workshop have stayed to linger just ahead of us, each, I notice, keeping their steps slow and bodies as close to Nash as possible. Waiting for a moment to strike up a conversation.

I've seen it at the other workshops too.

One person tripped and fell to the carpet, faking a massive knee injury, to get Ricky's attention from the crowd two hours ago. The medics came and everything.

"Jackie did say something, I don't know, *freaky* to me this morning."

"Oh? Which was?"

"Well, for one thing she said I'm probably not supposed to be telling you. What with you being a suspect and all. She said I'm showing favoritism."

"But I'm not the killer."

"A good thing for a killer to say."

"Well," he says, "if we're really going to go down that road, you're as much a suspect as any one of us. Maybe more."

"Me?" I say in a *how dare you* tone. "How so?"

"You do have more to gain."

"Like what? His nonexistent crown jewels? I'm out of a job now."

"You still have managing The Seven. Now Six."

"Fine. I'm out of a job *except* for managing this unruly group of The Seven. Now Six. Still. It's not like he put me in his will or anything. I know. I've seen it. I've memorized it."

Nash's brows shoot up. Somebody casts a glance back-ward, and he says under his breath. "You . . . memorized it?"

"Yep. In my first month with him he showed me the two locations for his will and asked me to read it. You know how he was. I think he was always coming up with creative ways to worry about someone doing something criminal to him and getting away with it, so he always was thinking five steps ahead. I guess you can't be thinking about devious ways to get away with murder and theft for a living with-out getting a little paranoid. I always took his paranoia as a funny little part of the job. Until"—I shrug—"of course, he was right."

"What does the will say?"

"I'm actually not sure I should tell you, if you are a true suspect. It's stupid, but . . . Jackie did have a point."

Nash lowers his voice. Leans closer. "Pip, I'm not your killer," he says, his words tickling my ear. "And you know it."

I ignore the hairs that have raised on my arm for entirely different reasons than fear. "Oh yeah?"

"Yeah."

"How do you know?"

"Well, for starters, we share a room."

"Subsistence reasons only," I say (lie). "I had to go with my best odds of survival."

"And you knit me a scarf when I went to Point Barrow for research."

"The Arctic Coast gets chilly. It's just common sense to keep your employers alive when they get stupid ideas."

"It wasn't a stupid idea."

"YouTube exists. One need not camp alone in negative-thirty-degree weather with the polar bears just to see if"—insert air quotes—"'my character can do it.'"

"And you wouldn't have let me get this close."

I look forward and realize everyone has turned a corner. It's just us in the hall.

Alone.

And . . . okay, fine. I love it.

Somehow I've drawn myself toward him in the past five minutes.

I don't know who is really in charge of my arm, because *I* don't consciously recall setting it on his shoulder.

Heat immediately floods my cheeks.

He has a point.

Like a bunch of seagulls following a piece of shrimp dangling from a fisherman's hand, the group seems to have noticed their shrimp (i.e., Nash) has disappeared from view and rushes back. Several heads peek around the corner, then nonchalantly-but-extremely-chalantly walk back to us, wait until we are right with them, and then start walking again.

A woman in a brown T-shirt of Nash's head on a sandwich smiles at us.

I smile back politely and pretend not to notice.

"Right. Well, I know," I whisper back. "But the fact is, I would've assumed *none* of The Seven were either. And it's gotta be someone. *Someone's* killed them."

My arm, I've realized, has not moved off him. It's still playfully hanging there, holding on to his bicep. Gripping the flannel.

His eyes crinkle as a smile plays on his lips.

He ducks his head a little as he tips himself closer.

"Interview me next then," he says in a hush. "Cross me off your list. Then we'll trade secrets."

I raise a brow. "You have secrets you can share with me?"

"I have one."

"Death secrets?"

"Not death secrets."

"Secrets I'll actually care about? Something worth trading will information for?"

"Something worth trading information about a will for. I hope."

I take a breath.

Who are we kidding?

I was going to say yes all along.

"Fine," I say at last. "I interview you, clear you from suspicion, and then we'll swap secrets."

"Deal." He's grinning as he leans back, and I feel the void, the cold air where his arm used to be.

He points at my back pocket.

"Plus, to be fair, if I'm going to be sleeping on the floor of your bedroom, I probably ought to be cleared of murder. It's just the right thing to do."

Two people directly ahead throw glances back at us. The lady with the Nash-head T-shirt sizes me up with a frown.

I elbow him, although my elbow against his layer of flannel does little.

"Fine," I say pulling the phone from my pocket. I type down his name. "We'll get this over with. Where were you—"

The ladies directly ahead of us squeeze in closer.

"The night . . ."

I pause. I'm about to trip on them, honestly.

I stand on tiptoe to reach him.

"*Hugh*," I whisper in his ear, at such a hush a mouse wouldn't hear it, "was—"

"Hold tight," Nash says.

"Why?"

But before I know it, he reaches around my waist, swings me into his arms like a maiden in distress, and turns down another hall.

And then *tears down it.*

"Nash!" I scream in shock.

I'm supposed to say *Put me down* and *We are in the middle of a book cruise here* and *This is NOT professional* and of course *I am in mourning!* but the words just aren't coming.

Instead my arms are wrapped around his neck and I look back, seeing the group pour into the end of the hall and stare at us as Nash carries me farther and farther away. He carefully keeps my feet from whacking the wallpaper and gilded paintings as we pass.

A woman steps out of her room. "Excuse us, ma'am," he calls, turning us sideways to squeeze past but not slowing.

"They're trying to video this!" I say, my nose peeking over his collar.

"Sorry, everyone! Late for a meeting!" he calls over his shoulder.

I laugh outright—my first real burst of laughter in what feels like forever—and then duck my head into the neck of his shirt to hide my face. "This is going to end up everywhere on social media. Conspiracy theories will abound. Headlines running: 'Did We Really Go to the Moon?' and 'Nash Eyre Steals a Faceless Woman off a Ship.'"

"You think?"

"Yes. I think."

He doesn't put me down, though, which I halfway feared, halfway really needed.

Instead he takes a couple more steps and then suddenly swings me around to face them head-on. "I'm taking this here lady with me!" he drawls in a most countrified, ne'er-do-well voice. "A Miss Penelope Mae Dupont, and I claim her. She's-a-mine!"

He waits as people take several pictures, then swings me around, and we carry on down the hall.

"There," Nash says. "No more faceless women here."

That's it. I can't help myself now. I shriek with laughter, bouncing in his arms all the way down the hall. The group of ladies who all have their phones out now gets smaller and smaller, until they are out of sight entirely as we turn another corner.

"You know, it's a little unsettling," Nash says when the laughter subsides and I can breathe again. "Not one of them even considered coming to your rescue."

"Why would they? They were too busy wishing they were me."

The words pop out of my mouth in the spontaneity of the moment, and as soon as I say them, I feel myself flush and bite my lip. Well, it's true, isn't it? Everyone has a little crush on Nash Eyre.

The five o'clock shadow on Nash's jaw tightens, and while looking straight ahead, I see the tiniest flicker of a smile on his lips that makes my stomach churn.

"So. Where do you intend on stealing me away to, then?" I say, trying to change subjects and direct attention elsewhere, but finding even that question a little too on point.

"To a place where we can finish the interview. Clear my name."

We reach the end of the hall and he presses a button.

The door opens.

We step—he steps—inside.

As the golden doors shut, and we—or rather, he—stands in silence, he presses the button for the ground floor. We begin to move.

I hesitate, seeing that glowing button 1, and fight a flip in my stomach.

It's fine. Focus on this moment.

It's fine.

One last person steps in front of the elevator doors just as they close and snaps a picture.

"Congratulations. I just went from faceless to the envy of every woman on this ship. If I go missing, check that lady with your head T-shirt first."

To which Nash cocks a brow.

He shakes his head. "Have you met yourself? Nothing about you, Pip, is faceless. Nothing about you is unoriginal. At all."

CHAPTER 16

WHAT DID I SAY ABOUT AUTHORS BEING ABLE TO GET away with just about anything?

Well, they are.

Because that was one of the sweetest things anyone has ever said to me, packaged in a glaring double negative. And it worked.

Gently, I unwind myself out of his arms and set my feet unsteadily back on the ground. The elevator draws us downward to the bottom floor, then dings.

"I think you've made your point," I say, smoothing my hairs back in place. "In more ways than one. Thank you."

I realize Nash still has his arm clamped around me, his face awfully close.

Does he realize it too?

"Anytime," he says quietly.

And for a moment that lasts forever, it's just him and me on a flashy elevator in the bottom of the ocean. We stand like a couple in those moments just before the music turns on and they begin to tango. His face close over mine. Arm wrapped around me. Me looking up. Both of us frozen.

When I can't bear it any longer, I murmur, "So."

"So," he repeats.

Then, out of nowhere, a blast of music plays from somebody's phone. I turn and to my shock see a woman has squeezed herself as tightly as she can into the corner of the elevator, her arms tucked to her sides as she clearly tries to make herself invisible.

"Oh, so sorry," she says in a hush to no one—a.k.a. us—as she swiftly turns the ringer off. And with a little squeak of her shoes against the porcelain tile, she pulls herself another inch toward the wall as if trying to melt into it.

I take a *wide* step back from Nash and the rest of the ride passes in silence.

When the elevator doors slide open, a whole new world emerges.

The carpet on the lower level is much more vibrant than upstairs, with playful swirls of gold dancing over red and blue and green. The walls are covered in a textured wallpaper of horses and their stables, and in the distance I can hear music coming from multiple different restaurants and bars. People teem in the halls, carrying drinks and shopping bags as they go out from one door and into the next.

So *this* is where everyone's been. Dining and shopping and who knows what else.

Nash's arm has gently come behind me and quietly urges me out of the elevator.

I hesitate.

Feel one foot step onto the plush carpet as the doors close behind us.

Sinking in.

I look around in vain for any windows.

We're just . . . down here.

Encapsulated.

"Take your pick," Nash says. "We can stow away in any of these."

There's a tiny pinch in my chest that I steadily ignore. I look to the place closest to the elevator. "The piano bar," I say, and he nods, gently stepping us around a woman holding an actual coconut in her hand with a green-and-white-striped straw popping out of a little hole inside.

Together we go in.

"Two, please. Is there a wait?" Nash says to the hostess.

My eyes scan the bar. There are two pianos back-to-back on a stage in the center of the room, a little pink glow lighting up the ebony keys and empty black seats. Thirty or so black tables surround the pianos, each holding a single white rose in a small vase. Crystal twinkles in the dark space beneath the dim light of one enormous chandelier above. The room smells of red wine and meat.

No windows in sight.

Her eyes flick to a poster with Nash's face on it announcing the activities for The Book Cruise. She looks at the laminated room overview below her and wipes a dry-erase marked note off a two-top table with her thumb.

"You're in luck, a two-top just left," she says, gathering the menus in hand. And in her cheeriest tone, "If you'll follow me."

She leads us to a table directly by one of the pianos, swiftly picks up a little golden *Reserved* placard, and sets the menus down.

I shake my head as she leaves.

"What?" Nash says.

"Nothing. It's just, you'd think after five years I'd get used to this."

"What?"

"You authors, casually getting away with anything."

Nash lifts a brow. "It's not because we're authors, Pip. It's because we're the cruise entertainment. If the highlight of the cruise was a magician, she'd have done the same thing for the guy and his rabbit."

I smile a little. "Do you think they'd give the rabbit his own seat?"

"On a ship like this? They'd give the rabbit its own menu."

After we're seated and some water is brought, I pull out my phone.

I'm anxious being alone with him here. Nash and I have always been friends, but never before would I have agreed to go so far (and he never asked) as having a meal alone together, whatever the pretext. Here? I have no excuse. No clear borders. But here we are.

I don't quite know how to proceed when we don't have The Seven hanging around as foils.

"So. I guess we ought to do the interview then."

"Guess so."

I pull out the Notes app on my phone. At this point, it's a crutch, a baby blanket, but I need it. I need something else to look at every once in a while. Something to shift my attention to when this conversation feels too intense. I clear my throat. "As I was saying, where were you the night Hugh was murdered?"

"With you."

I frown.

"Watching the meteor shower," he continues.

"Wow. That was only a few days ago. Feels like a lifetime. After you dropped me off, though, did you notice anything unusual?"

"No, I just went to bed."

"And what was your relationship with Hugh? How long have you known each other?"

"Four years. Hugh is . . . interesting. I appreciated my time with the man and the network he built up."

I raise a brow. "But you weren't close."

"Not like the others, no."

"Why is that, you think?"

Nash shrugs. "Some people are just not your type. Hugh was not my type."

"He's not Jackie's type either, and yet they formed a close"—although, I note mentally, quite complicated and possibly backstabbing—"bond."

"Everyone else had four decades with the man. I think that length of time with anyone will make you love them or hate them. And he provided something they all wanted, which wasn't the case with me."

"Which was?"

"Fame."

I raise a brow. "And you're telling me"—I lift up my phone—"on this very serious and official record, that wasn't the case for you? You *don't* want the fame?"

"No."

"The sales?"

"No."

"Why?"

Nash shrugs. "Everybody tries to hate on being in the middle of the list, but it has its perks. Success without notoriety. Success without the pressure."

"Really?" I've never heard it put that way.

"Four years ago, I had my tenth book out. My sales were fine, nothing that left the publisher bragging, but not so low that I had to fear being cut loose. They weren't thrilled with me. There wasn't energy around my books like there was with Hugh's. No adrenaline. But they were . . . content enough. And that sums up how I felt too. I had a rhythm; I kept to a pace. I got a contract and I began writing. I finished that book, got another contract, and kept writing. For a less-than-peaceful type of work, it was about as peaceful as it came."

I set the phone down. "You know, I don't think any author I've ever met has held the same view. It's always *more, more, more*. The publisher wants more. The author wants more. That must feel kind of . . . freeing. Relaxing, not having to put that kind of stress on yourself."

Nash shook his head. "Writing as a career is inherently competitive. I don't blame them for pushing for the top to keep themselves from sinking to the bottom. I just can't live that way. I figured, if it wasn't meant to be for me, and sales dropped and I got cut loose, I'd go another way. There's more than one way to make a living."

My brows rise. "Whereas to everyone else, it's write or die." I swallow, then take a sip of water. "Writing is their everything. Not yours, though?"

"It's work, like any other work. There are benefits to it, and things you wish you could avoid."

"And the benefits?"

"I make my hours. I work for myself. I can write anywhere."

"And the cons?"

"Being noticed."

I laugh. "Being noticed, if you'll recall, is what got us at this table right now."

Nash grins. "Anonymity, I've found, is worth a fifteen-minute wait."

"Fine. If it wasn't for the money and it wasn't for the fame, why did you join the group? What was so tempting about the group that you just couldn't resist?"

For a long moment, there's silence between us.

Just Nash looking at me.

And me back.

"You."

The thought is so outrageous, so absurd and impossible to take to heart, that I lean back in my chair and laugh. "Me."

But Nash leans forward, the flannel of his shirt rubbing against the table between us, a little dimple peeking out from the corner of his lips. "Yes," he says with all the sincerity in the world. "You."

"Stop teasing."

"I would never."

"C'mon."

"I am."

Oh my *gosh*—he *is* serious.

Nash is *serious*.

I feel a little bump as somebody grazes the back of my chair in passing and hops onstage.

I look around. More people are gathering in by the moment.

The man onstage is wearing sneakers but also coattails, jeans but also that telltale peacock bow tie. He's younger—mid-twenties or so—but as he slides onto the piano bench, I notice the classic swirl to his hair and swagger to his style that speak of a golden era long ago.

People begin to clap, the noise like thunder in my ears.

My chest tightens another notch.

Focus, Pip. This is *not* the time.

I force myself to stay calm. Tuck my hands under my legs on my seat.

The feeling of being even more constricted makes me panic a little more and I quickly untuck them.

"Do you remember the first time we met?" Nash continues.

"Sure I do," I say. "But nothing happened. It was just an ordinary day."

"It's funny, isn't it, how two people can see life in extraordinarily different ways? Mark had asked me to come to lunch with him on the heels of news of his retirement. He wanted me to meet some of his friends. I didn't want to, but he insisted, and he'd been a mentor to me for some time. Of course I had to say yes."

I nod, remembering that day quite clearly.

In my memory, I was actually pretty distracted at that lunch. Hugh was two weeks out from his latest release and the publisher had lost their minds, going with a mere thirty thousand copies for the first printing. Consequently, and to no one's surprise, stores had already sold out of whatever they'd been given, leaving frustrated bookstores with readers who wanted to pay good money, a frustrated publisher working to get a second printing underway as quickly as possible, frustrated readers trying to hunt the book down, and of course a completely oblivious Hugh going about his business and asking the waiter if he could order every single type of olive in the house and five glasses to perform a little test to see which exactly *is* the best in a dirty martini.

I was on the phone nonstop.

Oh, and it was my birthday.

Michael had promised to come home for it but ultimately decided (hindsight really is 20/20) it wasn't worth the nine-hour drive and he was messaging me relentlessly, each time with a new reason it would be better to back out. Which was truly worse than just saying the inevitable bluntly, and a thousand times worse than choosing the mature route and apologizing for being a selfish pig and taking responsibility.

But no. Instead, he spent the entire day ruining my day by backing out.

Texting me about the horrible traffic on I-75.

Texting about how he had practice on Monday, and how he hated how painfully short the trip was going to have to be.

Texting about the horrible timing with him starting to feel sick.

Working his way to backing out instead of facing me directly and just saying, "Hey, I know this is a crap move, but I'm not going to come after all and I'm really sorry."

Essentially pushing the move into my court until it sounded like *I* was selfish and a demanding girlfriend if I didn't call it off.

And given I had told my roommates *not* to throw me a party they had initially insisted on, and had made reservations *four months ahead of time* to The Palm upon Michael's insistence that the trendy new restaurant far out of my budget and frankly interest was our "must-do" for my birthday . . . let's just say, it was a day of many, many distracting calls and texts swirled into the general emotions of angst and disappointment.

I wasn't exactly at my best.

There's a *swoosh* by my head and a flash of rhinestones as a woman glides past me and goes up the steps, the train of her black-rhinestone-studded dress following behind her. She stops at the second piano bench, tips her rhinestone hat to the applause of the crowd around us—a crowd getting larger by the minute—and swings her knees beneath the piano as she slides onto the bench.

I look around for multiple exits. My chest restricts further.

Ignore it, Penelope.

Tamp it down.

Tamp.

It.

Down.

Nash is oblivious. "You remember it?"

"I remember the restaurant staff getting way too invested in Hugh's weird new conquest to determine the best olives," I say, "and then of course Ricky totally freaking the waitress out when he grabbed her ankle underneath the table just to see what it would feel like in a scene he was writing—"

"I thought she was going to sue," Nash says with a reminiscing grin.

"To his credit, he was aiming for Neena—and honestly, that would have been hilarious. And then Crystal tried to order chicken wings—"

"Of which there were none on the menu, naturally—"

"And Jackie called the hostess aside to ask her to 'inform the owner of the establishment that the sign saying *Des oreilles en chou-fleur* is actually a taunt to readers that our ears are the size of cauliflowers, as anyone with even an amateur level of French would understand.'"

"And Gordon was still wearing his Gandalf hat," I say. "So. Basically you saw a normal day at the office."

"And everyone was twice as bad as the rumors that preceded them. But then there was you."

I purse my lips.

"I wasn't even sitting down yet and had already all but called the case closed from whatever Mark had planned. It wasn't hard to put two and two together—he'd hinted before at wanting me to be his replacement. I'd never given him much support on that front, but I never pushed against him either. I realized when I got there to lunch and saw his 'friends' what he was aiming at. And I knew what my answer was going to be before I even sat down."

"You actually planned on saying no?" I say incredulously. "No writer on the planet would've said no."

But I guess that really sums up what this group is about.

A group of eccentric writers thinking uniquely and wholly in their own ways. I never thought about it that way, but maybe Nash truly fit in after all.

Nash shrugs as someone stops by our table and tops up our waters. "My work was hard enough at the time, and like I say, I wasn't particularly driven to want anything besides what I already had. Problem is, at the time I was having trouble with just that: my work."

"Which book was that one now?" I ask, thinking aloud. I mentally run through the titles, seeing all the covers in my mind. "*Highway to Haven?*"

Nash lets out a breathy chuckle. "Of course you recall it. It's incredible how you juggle all of our books in your brain. Anyway, yes, it was. I may not have remembered the title, but I do know where I was stuck at the time: forty thousand words."

"Everybody's stuck at forty thousand words."

"Not like this. I was *stuck-in-the-mud* stuck. Knee-deep-in-quicksand stuck. I wasn't going anywhere, and hadn't been, for five months."

"*Five* months?" I say, giving a low whistle. "When was the book due?"

"Two months later."

I shake my head. I'd heard all the author woes over the years. Two months to write half a book while in the middle of a creative freeze was no place to be.

"And you'd tried it all, I'm assuming."

"Drafting poorly to throw words on the page. Setting alarms. New scenery. Morning work. Evening work. Reinforcement therapy. Punishment style. Everything. All it got me was twenty thousand words in the wrong direction that needed deleting."

I wince.

"Twice," he adds.

I wince again. "Ouch. So how'd you get out of your slump?"

"I'm getting to it," he says with a twinkle, his blue eyes flickering in the dim light. He rubs his hands together as if he's warming himself over a hot fire. He can say what he wants, claim he could switch careers at a snap, but Nash is a true writer at heart, a man who delights in telling stories—even the true ones.

"So I'm sitting there at the table with this group of people who are acting like they've escaped the mental ward, next to Neena currently asking me out—"

"She *didn't*."

"She did. And then you stalk in."

I rub my face. "You mean glide, I'm sure."

"Oh, I mean stalk." He grins. "You stalked right in just like you always do"—he waves a hand at me—"the little five-foot twenty-four-year-old surrounded by a bunch of literary giants in one of your bookish cardigans and ballet shoes, and you take one look around, snap that phone of yours into your back pocket, and slam your hand on the table.

"Took you no more than ten seconds before Ricky was back in his seat, the table stopped shaking, Neena let go of my collar, Jackie had apologized to the owner of the establishment while providing only two more offensive remarks in the process, Crystal was satisfied with an order of some sort of breaded fish, and Gordon put away his hat. Even Hugh popped all the olives into his mouth at once and slid away the glasses like he didn't know where they came from.

"Then next thing I knew you were sitting next to me, snapping a napkin and setting it on your lap like this was just another day in the life. I'm not even sure you realized just how much of an impact you made on everyone."

"Oh, I did," I say, recalling. "It was a particularly trying day. I did."

"But then you really shocked me."

My brain is flying through that day, but nothing comes to mind.

"You were talking to the waiter and said something to the effect of, 'I'll take the fish, and oh, by the way, Hugh, I've been thinking about it and I think you need to reveal the secret about the Roman dodecahedrons on page one hundred sixty-two. I think, but I'm not certain, that might give you the final *zip* you're after.'"

I laugh.

It's nice to be reminded of small victories.

"You remember that?" Nash continues.

"I do," I say, nodding. It was a good moment in a bad day.

"Hugh dropped his napkin so fast. He spent the rest of the meal over his laptop like a toddler tapping at an iPad, and bought—"

"A dirty martini for the whole restaurant to celebrate," I finish. It was a victory indeed.

"You saved his book."

I shake my head, but the kindness was a bright spot in an otherwise miserable day. "He was stuck. It was my job to help him with his research."

"Your *research*, sure. But the creative punch? To give him the thing that made that book outshine the market? You were far more than an assistant. You were a writer."

I open my mouth to interject, but he beats me to it. "And then not thirty minutes later, you fixed me."

"What?" I say incredulously. "No. How?"

"I saw what you did, and I did something I'd never done before. Not even with my editor. I told somebody about my book. I told you."

I remember that. I remember him breaking it down for me, first meeting.

It was the distraction I needed at the time, actually. The thing that mellowed me from my skyrocketed blood pressure of a day with Michael. Something to listen to. Something to weigh in on.

Nash continues, "I told you all about it, which was no big deal to you, but to me, it was everything. And it was . . . well, it was such a different feeling. Sharing about something I habitually keep close to my chest until the very end, and how you responded. You seemed interested. You *looked* genuinely interested."

"I was interested."

"But enough to listen to me talk like that, sharing the entire plot's breakdown—"

"Again. My job," I say.

"Maybe. But still. Listening, I've learned in my lifetime, is not a skill regularly practiced. To be a good listener is to be . . . amazing."

I take in a breath.

A pinched breath, true, as the darkness of the room around me raises my anxiety to a level hard to keep in line.

But still a nearly happy, honored-by-his-attention breath.

"Anyway," Nash continues, "I went right up to where I envisioned the book ending, then backed up over the hole where I was stuck, and I hadn't even had time to ask you what you'd recommend when you swirled your salmon in lemon aioli sauce extremely casually and said, 'Have you considered adding sky-liners to the plot? It'd be a bear to change in those early chapters, but if a few sky-liners crossed paths with the brothers as they guide their herds through the Rockies, they could face a showdown in the hole you're stuck at and give the readers a climax they're hoping for. I think it would be something worth thinking about.'

"And then the cake came. Hugh had ordered, and everyone was singing happy birthday to you, and I didn't even get a chance to say thank you. And your face, as they brought out that cake and everyone was singing all around us, was something else."

"What did I look like?"

"Like a person surrounded by a family who loved them."

I nod. Rub my nose.

"And that's when I decided to join the ragtag group. It was solely because of you."

The idea is mind-blowing. I backtrack as I raise a finger. "I'm sorry. We're going to need to back up here. You're saying I helped you in your book—"

"And every book ever since. You know I don't send it to my editor without your vote."

"And you joined the group," I say for clarification, "*not* because of the all-star cast. Or the fame. Or the glory. But because of me."

"Yes."

"And you . . ."

Suddenly there is a thunderous pounding on the piano directly behind me, two dozen keys launching into a fiery war.

For a hundred reasons now my heart feels like it's about to jump out of my chest.

"You decided to tell me this now to . . ."

"To clear myself of murder."

I nod briskly. "Right. Yes."

"And to let you know *XY ABJASD KGJ$EH.*"

The words that come from his lips are halfway muted by the pounding on the second piano adjacent to the first.

"What?" I yell.

He gives me a full-charm smile, the kind that says *you are adorable and I'm being patient.* "*XJEDBJWEHIBDFB,*" he says louder.

It feels embarrassing, a point against me and my pathetic ears for having the audacity to not hear. But the pianos are in a full-on war right behind me.

I scoot the chair over until I'm but two inches away from his face.

Mark my words, I will *not* miss it this time. "One more time," I say.

And with a smile that creases the corners of his eyes, he grabs my shoulders and draws me in until his breath tickles my ear.

"I'm in love with you."

I don't move.

I'm frozen.

People are moving around me, trickling closer to the stage behind my head. Grins on. Cameras out to capture the dueling pianists.

The bright light of the cruise hall is dimming with the influx of bodies, the room getting darker by the moment.

People are blocking the path to the entrance of the bar.

The only entrance.

The only exit.

Closing us in.

Flashes of underwater scenes come to mind as another pound on the piano roars in my ears.

Did Nash just tell me he loved me?

Did I hear that correctly?

Or am I in the middle of a panic attack and every sense in my body is overstimulated and I'm only hearing what I want to?

It's terrible timing.

Surely he didn't say . . .

"You are . . ." I breathe.

"In love with you," he says again.

My heart is pounding.

My ears are pounding.

"And I'm telling you now . . . at the worst time . . . because I've been the unlucky soul knowing you were the right one at the wrong time for the past four years, and now you're free, and I can't let another minute pass without letting you know."

Michael.

He never told me because of Michael?

A flipbook of memories from the past four years comes to mind, of dinners and events and coffees and conferences and meetings. Of emails and text messages and phone calls. A mix of Michael and Nash side by side in the timeline of my life, but never touching. Never overlapping. Of course, Michael was hardly in the city, and when he was, on those rare occasions when he was going to go with me to events, Nash always stepped into the corner of my periphery.

Or ended up not attending at all.

Or ended up not attending at all.

Was that . . . *why?*

On those mysterious days when he suddenly went from a firm yes to can't attend, *that was why?*

Little . . . old . . . me?

I never thought anything about it.

To be more exact, I knew I wasn't worthy of being thought of like that.

Correction: *thought.*

I thought I wasn't worthy of being thought of like that.

I guess that's what happens when the person you're already with continually makes you feel like you are not enough. Why would you be special to anybody else if you can hardly measure up to the one you're with?

Nash was and is wildly independent, and whenever he didn't make it to something, it could be chalked up to him racing away to the wilderness.

Never once did I think there was a correlation between the times he skipped out on events and the times I brought Michael.

Nash never brought up Michael in conversation, I remember.

Ever.

It was like . . . Michael didn't exist to him.

And all of this . . . is why.

Nash dips his head, his face overshadowed by the brim of his hat. When he looks up again, his eyes are soft. A rare moment of vulnerability.

"Look. I know it's a terrible time. An insensitive time. But if I have to wait one more day to tell you how I feel—and worse, if I risk not telling you before something else gets in the way—I just won't be able to live with myself. It's just . . . the day you walked into my life, I started thinking about you. And I haven't been able to get you out of my mind since." His smile twists. "No matter how many trips I take out into the wilderness to try to shake you. You're just . . . unshakable."

I truly can't breathe now. My breaths are coming in short spurts. "That's why you went off-grid? Part of it . . . was me?"

His steady gaze is my answer.

"But . . . but you could've told me," I say. "You could've said something. This wasn't *marriage* with Michael." I cringe even saying his name. Bringing him into the purity of this conversation—it's like dragging a dirty wet rag over a white wall. "You could've . . ."

"Pip," he says. He shakes his head. "I didn't resist because of honor. I resisted because you wouldn't have listened. I saw that from the beginning. You were all in. He got you to lock yourself in and throw away the key a long time ago and nobody could get you out. Even if we pried the door open ourselves, you would've stayed. Right. There."

He was right.

Michael had so twisted me up over all the years, flipped rights and wrongs upside down, shaken up my certainties until they were so confused I couldn't see through the glass, convinced me that clouds were concrete and the air was sea.

I didn't have eyes to see anymore.

I didn't have ears to hear.

It would've taken nothing less than watching the whole thing unfold at a gas pump on public television in front of the whole world to open just a crack in the door for me to see.

I've always admired Nash.

Always cared for him.

But never in the past have I let the thought linger even that far.

Was it . . . love . . . all that time, hidden under covers?

But of course it was.

There are things the heart knows even when the mind won't acknowledge them.

And as if the pianos couldn't have escalated any louder, they do, and people begin to whoop and clap. A hundred crystals on the chandelier quake above the windowless tomb where I sit, deep underwater.

I feel the press of Nash's hands over mine.

They're warm.

Encapsulating.

Suffocating my hands, just as the crowds are stealing the air.

Nash frowns. "Pip, you're sweating."

"Yeah," I say. "That'll be the oncoming panic attack."

"The—what?" He inches back, inspecting me closely for a blink, and then quickly moves to standing. "Come on."

Swiftly he gathers me up and takes me by the hand as he snakes me around people, making a way with his broad chest where there was no way, the sound of the pianos dimming to a mere loud throb as we work to exit the restaurant.

When he breaks through the last of the crowd and jams his finger over the elevator door, the breathing comes a little more easily.

It isn't until the elevator opens at the very top and I step into the humid sea-salt air of the observation deck that I take my first full breath.

I've sweated through my cardigan.

I'd be embarrassed, except that there are bigger things to deal with at the moment.

A flood of things.

Too many things.

"Let me get you a water." Nash starts to walk off in the direction of one of the several water stations dotting the halls and then turns back as if remembering himself, grabs hold of my hand, and takes me with him. Even twenty feet is too much distance for him.

Gently he sets the cup in my hands. His hands linger on mine, the warmth of his palms set against the cool water in mine.

"Listen, Pip. Don't . . . don't answer me now. Everything is just . . . crazy right now and I know you have a hundred things you're going through. I don't even want to know your thoughts until everything settles down. Just . . . just do me a favor, will you?"

"What's that?" I whisper.

"Just don't fall in love with anyone else before you give me a chance."

It takes another five minutes before my heartbeats slow.

But my head is now throbbing, a sizable migraine coming on in a hurry. I feel swept up in intense moment after intense moment, with only one anchor to cling to: Nash loves me.

Nash, after all, loves me.

The absurd thought has become the dazzling reality.

"Just take your time. I'm not going anywhere."

His words are a shower of rain on desert ground, instantly soothing the dry and cracked wounds of a past life I didn't even realize were there.

I nod.

That's it.

That's all I can do right now.

I *know* what I want, I *know* how I feel, but then, I thought I knew what I wanted for the past eight years and it turned out I couldn't have been more wrong.

Because as it turned out, persevering in one direction for the sake of perseverance doesn't make you successful or mean you're doing the right thing.

Being loyal for the sake of loyalty doesn't make you wise.

Doing everything you thought was right with a blind eye to all the red flags around you, believing "the strongest relationships are those that persevere to the end," doesn't make your life everything you were promised it would be.

I needed time.

And Nash just gave me the one thing Michael never would: the gift of time.

Michael was always rushing me.

Filling my head with ultimatums.

Telling me to choose him or miss out forever.

To let go of that wrong he did or else he'd walk away and I'd regret it for the rest of my life.

To drop everything and cancel every appointment to be with him at a moment's notice, or lose his trust and ultimately him forever.

Living with that underlying stress had broken me more than anyone, including myself, could ever know.

I throw my arms around Nash, water cup sloshing and all.

His arms don't hesitate in wrapping around me back.

In the silence, my face deep within his flannel, I speak. "Thanks."

He exhales a little.

I've surprised him, I think.

But not in a bad way.

Not in a way that makes him angry.

"Of course."

We stand like that long enough that the lady with the Nash-face T-shirt stops and offers to take our picture.

Several ladies walk by holding plates and settle themselves in lounge chairs as the sun sets.

Steaming broccoli.

Ruby-red lobster on a bed of macaroni and cheese.

"Hungry?" Nash says.

"Headache." Stars are starting to flash in my vision now. It's time to lie down in utter darkness *immediately*. "Correction. Migraine. I'm going to take some medicine and lie down."

"I'll come with you."

"No. It's fine. Really. I can make it twenty feet to an elevator."

But my protest is useless, as I knew (and appreciated) it would be.

I don't put up a fight.

It's not pretty, or even remotely romantic, him seeing me

this way—blundering around with my eyes nearly shut—nauseously making gentle steps inside the room and urgently hunting through my unorganized clothes for some Excedrin.

The migraines only started after the research dives.

I only brought medicine on this trip in case I ended up in the lower caverns of the ship and something like this happened—and it precisely did.

And I know my meds are *somewhere* in here, jumbled in the pile of clothes I keep unfolding and tossing like a fabric volcano.

Somewhere.

I feel Nash reach for my hands. Still me.

"I've got it. You just lie down."

I don't fight him or his arms guiding me to the bed.

It takes approximately thirty-two seconds for a knock on the door to come and a waiter to drop off an entire silver platter with ten various brand-new, unopened bottles.

"Geez, Pip, you really picked the Ritz here. This one?"

"Whichever knocks me out."

He picks one and hands me a glass of water.

"They tried to give me a cooler of bottled water options," he says with a touch of humor.

And I would crack a joke about it, if I could laugh without my brain exploding.

Instead, I manage a tiny smile before I set the pill on my tongue and chase it with water.

I tuck myself under the covers as soon as possible afterward, pulling the thick white comforter up to my eyes.

I'm otherwise entirely hidden beneath blankets.

I look like a dead snowman.

"Go on to dinner," I say, my voice muffled through the blankets.

"No."

"I'll feel terrible if you don't go. Go on."

"No."

"It hurts to talk," I say. "And I don't want to talk. But I will to save you from hunger if I have to. Go."

"No."

"Go."

"No."

"Go go go go go—"

"*Fine.* I'll go."

I hear footsteps.

The door opening.

The lights flick off, and I hear the door shutting.

A minute goes by.

"You didn't go," I say.

"No."

I can't fight him on this.

I'm not going to win.

And frankly, as he knows, and I know, it's too painful to do anything much besides what I'm doing right now. Lying as still as possible in a room as dark as possible with as little noise as possible until the nausea and head banging subside.

So I don't try.

At some point, some time later, I think of a wet washcloth. And then once I've thought of it, I can't think of anything *besides* it.

Wet washcloth.

Wet washcloth.

Wet washcloth.

At last I groan.

Move to stand up.

He stops me before I make it all the way up.

"What do you need?"

I purse my lips, trying to decide if I want to fight him on this, to be a capable and independent woman, or give in to the offer of help and show my weakness.

Weakness wins.

I slump back. "A wet washcloth. If you don't mind."

"I don't mind."

He comes back, and I feel the press of the warm cloth against my head—the first moment of *something* to help.

I purse my lips.

"What's wrong?" he says.

"Nothing."

"What's wrong?"

"Nothing."

"What's wrong?"

"I was itching for it to be cold."

He grunts. "Itching, huh?"

A little while later he returns. Replaces the warm with cold.

After a few seconds, I give a blind little chuckle, all tucked up now, nothing more of me to see.

"You ready to take back your words?" I say.

And as soon as I say them, I instantly regret it.

A fear takes over.

Rational or irrational, it's there, and I'm just not confident that I'm quite the catch he says I am. And a part of me suddenly waits to hear his words: *"Yeah, actually. I am. You're not the girl I was hoping for, after all."*

What I get instead, however, is a cold tingle that runs all the way up my spine. That tingle your body gets when it senses somebody hovering just over your shoulder. Right behind your ear.

Or in my case, a hair's breadth above me.

And the brush of his lips against my cheek. *"Never."*

↶

I fall asleep.

When I wake the headache is gone and the room is utterly black—now not just from the drawn curtains but from the dark of night outside the patio doors. The clock on the bedside table reads 11:16 p.m.

Nash is seated on the chair in the corner.

His laptop is open on his lap, dimly lighting up the flannel on his chest.

Still working on that book.

Still working on that ending.

The brim of his hat is down over his face, and he's slumped over in his chair.

Sleeping.

Or . . .

My feet hit the floor so fast it sounds like cattle racing.

The second I grab his shoulder and give a firm shake, he jumps to standing and shoots his head around, ready to fight.

"Where?" he says.

His head swings automatically toward the door and he throws me back, one arm stretched behind, the other out toward the door. His body serving as a middleman between me and the unknown threat.

"Sorry," I say weakly. I rub my forehead. "Sorry, I just . . . I saw you slumped over in the chair and . . . for a second . . ."

"Don't worry about it. We're all on edge." He rubs his face with his hands. Waking himself back up. Looking back at his computer.

I run a hand over my matted hair, embarrassed.

Nash has done so much, *been* so much, and what have I done?

What have I helped?

Nothing.

He's carried me down the hall. He's taken me—or attempted to take me—to dinner. He's announced he loves me, a wreck such as myself.

And so far I've had a migraine and made him sit in the dark.

I have brought a total sum of *nothing* to the table.

Per usual.

I look out toward the lamp.

Stride over, anxious to turn it on and get some light in here.

To find *something* productive to do with my hands.

My eyes land on the curtains. The entryway to the little balcony, where one table and two chairs sit.

And I have an idea.

CHAPTER 17

LET'S START BY SAYING: NASH WAS UP ANYWAY.

My little flash of terror moment jolted him awake. He wasn't planning to fall back asleep anytime soon.

Which was perfect for letting me try out my idea.

I'm not going to say I *forced* Nash into the bathroom to take a shower while I prepped, but he was forbidden to come out of there until I got everything set up.

Turns out, having a slew of personal staff available on a gold-star ship *can* come in handy at midnight in a pinch.

One call to the front office, with only half a ring before they answered, and five minutes later three staff members were lined up at my door, each with arms laden.

I took the silver platters.

And the armful of candles.

And the rolling three-tier carts.

Nobody asked questions. Nobody showed any expression on their face.

I have no idea what other people do or ask for on this

ship at midnight, but it was plain as day that they have seen weirder.

Now, as Nash emerges, hatless with hair dewy and fresh flannel, I'm waiting.

His brows pinch together.

He looks around the room, puzzled.

"Oookay. What am I looking at?"

I wave my arms toward the drawn curtains.

I'm grinning despite myself.

I'm bad at surprises, or at least I've been told by Michael that I'm bad at surprises.

Shake it off, Pip. You did good.

"Follow me." I draw the curtains open.

The small balcony overlooks the orb of the full moon.

It glows brightly in the distance.

Stars twinkle.

A white latticework bistro table rests there with two petite chairs on either side.

Two black-and-white-striped cushions sit on the seats, while bundles of glowing votive candles light up the balcony.

They are flickering on the ground; flickering on the table; flickering in every little corner I could possibly and without threat of serious fire arrange them.

A covered silver platter sits at one seat.

A laptop at the other.

The whole landscape consists of two colors: brilliant white and a deep, inky black.

It's terrifying, quite frankly, and under no circumstance but this one would I be caught dead walking onto a balcony over the ocean in the dead of night.

But . . . the landscape is also beautiful.

The light and dark enriching the other.

Spotlighting the other.

Showing off each other's beauty, each other's strengths.

Like Nash and me, maybe.

I hope.

"I read the last chapters of your work in progress while you were in the shower," I say, carefully (and I mean *carefully*) tiptoeing onto the balcony and sitting down.

I open the laptop. "You had sent me up to chapter 22 before the cruise. Now I'm up-to-date. Chapter 26. And I see what you mean about being stuck. I've made some notes."

I gesture for him to sit.

"What?"

Nash looks dazed, but he follows.

When he does, I lift the top from the platter.

Steam blows up in his face as he looks down at the little feast.

I can see immediately from his reaction that it was a good call.

"You missed dinner to watch me sleep, so . . ."

"This is *great*." He says it like I slaved away for hours.

"I mean . . . let's be honest. I only made a *call*—"

"You mixed the dressings," he murmurs, looking at the two tiny silver cups beside the salad, which for the record is sitting beside the biggest steak I maybe have ever seen (when you say you want a steak as big as a stop sign . . . they *really* follow through).

I shrug. "I know you like the blue cheese and the honey mustard mixed, so. There you go."

"Aren't you going to eat?"

I wave him off. "My stomach's too upset. It'll settle down by breakfast. So here's what I'm thinking . . . I have a part two for my thank-you-for-sticking-with-me-while-I'm-down-and-out plan."

"You don't need to thank me for being with you, Pip."

But I shush him, and for the next twenty minutes I go over my notes.

And the hour after that, we brainstorm.

After my third yawn, Nash stops me. Puts a hand over mine as I'm in mid-type.

"Pip, I think we've done enough for one night. This is amazing. But it's probably time we called it a night."

"*This* is what I have to offer you, Nash. You've said it yourself. It's not much, it's just my brain, but here it is. It's the least I can do for all you've done for me."

He frowns. "What have I done for you? Nothing."

"Not true. You're here," I say, "insisting on keeping me safe."

He tilts his head. "Not exactly a sacrifice, Pip."

"On the *floor*," I add. "Which, by the way, the staff saw and freaked out and apologized a hundred times as though they were responsible and brought in a cot."

I point over to a little folded-up cot in the corner. "They were very upset."

He shakes his head. "Again. All that is just being with you. Not a sacrifice. The *opposite* of a sacrifice."

"And you . . . helped me when I had a migraine. You gave me medicine."

Nash's face is starting to look a little disbelieving. "You do realize these are things average people do for one another. Total strangers, in fact."

"And you . . ." I venture, fishing in my brain. "You just . . . you're you, okay? Just let me do something nice in return and get over it. I can't take you looking out for me without doing *something* in return, and seeing as how I can't exactly look over *your* life with incredible strength and the ability to knock down a door with my bare hands—"

"Do you think I do that? Just go around knocking down doors with my bare hands?"

I shrug. "I mean. That's what you were doing on that lady's T-shirt today, so dare I question it? If it's on a T-shirt?

"The point is," I continue, "this is what I've got. *This* is all I can contribute. So let me contribute it."

The unspoken words sit there.

The reality as I tell him: *I fear you are superior to me in every way, and I need to feel a little less like that right now. Please.*

Nash shakes his head.

It's clear he doesn't agree with me. It's clear he doesn't agree with my methods or madness. But he gives in.

"Alright, Pip," he says in a low murmur. "Solve my book for me. Finish up this puzzle and I'll be forever in your gratitude."

"Thank *you*," I say a little sarcastically (but totally not sarcastically) and look back to the computer.

It takes two more hours to get there.

We brainstorm long enough to a eureka moment, at which point Nash takes over the computer.

Meanwhile, with phase one of "help Nash finish his book" complete, I move on to phase two.

I order refreshments to the room (I honestly don't know how I'm going to go back to normal society after this) and have begun to imagine a man on the other line in coattails and a peacock bow tie crying out the second we hang up and a flurry of people in coattails and peacock bow ties sprinting down the halls, when there's that polite knock on the door.

I've hardly had time to set the phone back on the receiver.

It's incredible.

With a glance back to Nash—who truly does look quite contented surrounded by the flickering candles, typing on his laptop with zeroed-in focus—I look through the peephole, see the bow tie, and open the door.

"Hello," I say.

"Your dessert, ma'am."

I take it from him, squinting as I look for some sign that would give him away.

A pulse bouncing at his neck.

Sweat building up at his temple.

Anything.

"Anything else, ma'am?" he says politely, like it's not two in the morning but a sensible hour in the middle of the day.

"No, that's all for now. Thanks . . . again," I say and hand him a bit of cash (which in itself is stressful—you feel like an idiot handing over an old wadded-up ten-dollar bill when it seems pretty clear fresh-off-the-mint hundred-dollar bills are the only acceptable form of payment).

He gives a sincere little bow and slips the bill somewhere out of sight on his body.

I'm still almost certain he will disinfect the bill the second he gets to some back room. There's probably a whole bin dedicated to disinfecting crumpled less-than-one-hundred-dollar bills.

I move to shut the door with my two plates of cheesecake in hand, but upon second thought open it again and look out.

Perhaps I will catch him sprinting down the hallway now, off to another errand.

He's stepping lightly but is no speeding bullet.

I watch in silence for him to suddenly leap like a deer or something, but he just glides through the locked door for the wing and over to the elevator doors. Presses the button. Waits in silence.

How deflating.

The elevator dings, and as the doors slide open and he slips in, I hear a latch turn to my left. My head turns without really thinking, and a moment later I suck in my breath and duck my head back in.

At two in the morning, there is *Crystal*, alone.

Walking out her door.

Her face says it all.

This is a woman who couldn't care *less* that a man was murdered.

Ten seconds later, she comes into view. Strides past without stopping.

What is Crystal doing going out, alone, at two in the morning?

And who, precisely, is she supposed to be bunking with now?

Is she bunking with anyone?

There's really only one way to find out.

I tap Nash on the shoulder.

"I'm going to do a little sleuthing."

CHAPTER 18

"I FIND YOU CONCERNINGLY GOOD AT THAT. WHAT other secrets have you not told me about?"

We are standing just inside Crystal's room.

I've just shut the door behind us.

The room is pitch black but for the dim light of a muted television screen.

And yes, I did just use a variety of household goods to break into the room in under a minute.

"I've practiced breaking into everything for Hugh," I say. "I can pick 90 percent of the locks in New York City in under fifteen minutes. Ninety-five percent if you give me an hour." I pocket the pin I pulled from the hair dryer and wind up the cord.

"And this is your party trick?" Nash says. "Something that really wins the guys over? Your ability to break into things."

"Hey, apparently I won you over, didn't I?" I say, tossing my head back.

A little slip of a smile moves up his lips. "I will say, watching you know your way around a lock was oddly attractive."

"Weird, but I'll take it." I grin, flick on a light, and cast my eyes around the room. "You man the door," I say. "I'm going to check for clues."

"Which are?"

"I'm not sure yet. Hence the vague term *clues*. Now make sure not to *touch anything*."

"Okay, Edward Scissorhands. Noted."

I give him a sarcastic thumbs-up—though at the moment, my thumb, like the rest of my fingers, is tied up in an elaborate twist of elastic bands and a plain T-shirt. It took me a couple of minutes (longer than the lock, if I wanted to brag, and I don't mind if I do) to get the makeshift gloves in place, but once they were all together, my fingers fit snugly, and except for the excessive number of rubber bands, they're a pretty decent pair of gloves. Nothing to see the opera in, but here in the silence of this suspect's room (a.k.a. little old Crystal . . . which is super weird, but I gotta stay focused), there are no fingerprints to be found.

I slip off my shoes and begin my light step on tiptoe in my socks around the room.

"What are you doing?"

"Leave no trace," I say, moving around a lamp. "It's not just a motto for the woods."

The room is in disarray (no surprise there). Clothes are dumped from her massive backpack suitcase and are strewn about the room in various piles. Multiple hair appliances clutter the desk. The remote rests on the unmade bed around a pile of open chip bags. At least three little gummy men litter the formerly perfectly white sheets, staining the white in colors of blue, green, and red.

I clench my teeth.

I'm going to be the one who hears about this.

A woman holding a stinky sock in her hands goes on

elaborately about the power of her laundry softener in a commercial on the television inside her mirror. *Her mirror. I had no idea we had a television inside the gold frame of our mirrors.*

I look at the ring on the desk made by a coffee mug.

Oh, I'm *definitely* going to hear about this.

I tread lightly around stacks of her books. A few Sharpies (one notably open) sit inside and around the books. What is she even doing with all of these in here?

I purse my lips, trying not to be *really ticked* now.

I told everyone to sign five hundred copies in the conference room, at the *book table.*

If I wanted them to drag five hundred copies of their books to their *rooms* to be stained by *gummy worms*, I would've said *that*, now, wouldn't I?

I bend down and shut the open Sharpie.

Fine.

So I'm going to leave a trace.

I can't help myself.

The thought of the slowly drying out Sharpie staining her sheets will be running through my mind all night if I don't. (And honestly, does Crystal ever notice anything?)

"Find anything yet?" Nash whispers.

"No," I say.

"How much longer?" he says, looking through the peep-hole.

"Not much." I tiptoe around beside tables and look through piles of clutter. "You'd think for a two-hundred-square-foot room, we'd see anything in a second, but there's a lot of stuff here. Honestly, how can she *live* this way? How did she fit this much *stuff* in that backpack suitcase?"

"You think she went out for ice or something?"

"Do people go out for ice at two in the morning?"

He shrugs. "I don't know. It's Crystal. You never can tell what she's off to do."

"She probably went skinny-dipping. You know she told me *just* before we got on this ship that she was going to go skinny-dipping."

"She wouldn't get away with it."

"She taunted me with the plan." I look over my shoulder. "How much do you think all this is going to cost me?"

"In fines? Nothing for you. But she's going to be handing over her next check to the ship . . ."

I quicken my step, sensing the urgency to hurry up.

"What is even open right now? Nothing on the deck," I say.

"All the entertainment on the lower floor. We could . . ."—he hesitates, then says with less certainty—"go down again."

"I'm not going down there. You can go down there."

"I'm not leaving *you*."

"Then *who* is going to find out what she's doing?" I say, squatting down, opening the bottom drawer of a dresser. "Better to find out she's partying and is a total narcissist in the face of murder"—Note: I hear it. I hear how hypocritical that sounds given my romantic patio dinner just now—"than the alternative." I pause, looking at a wound-up cloth covered in red.

Gingerly, I pick up the long, heavy, stained bulk of fabric.

My hands are already starting to tremble.

I unwind the fabric slowly.

And there is the knife.

Covered in blood.

CHAPTER 19

APPARENTLY, I'VE PASSED OUT.

Because that's what you do when you're a sleep-deprived, adrenaline-electrified amateur sleuth trying to get herself killed by finding crucial clues in a murderer's lair.

Pass out until they find you.

Thankfully, in my case, I have Nash.

And next thing I know, I'm in Nash's arms and he's opening the door.

"Wait!" I cry, flinging my arm out.

I wouldn't say he screamed exactly, but whatever it was, it was clear I just went from dead asleep to life in his arms, and the sudden scream made him leap two feet off the floor.

I push his hand away from the knob and turn it myself. "Did you get my shoes?"

"Geez, Pip!" he says. "Yes, I got your shoes!"

I see them dangling from his hand.

"Did you put the weapon back?"

"Was I supposed to?" he says, frowning.

"Yes!" I cry out. "Yes! Leave it here and we'll get the detective so he can see for himself. It doesn't do us any favors to hand him a weapon from *our hands* and claim it's from her."

"Breaking and entering and then claiming we found the weapon looks a little suspicious, you're saying," he says, moving my entire body into one arm and throwing open the drawer in a move of extreme strength, dropping the knife inside, and slamming it shut.

He adjusts to hold me with both arms. "But running back to the room and then calling him telling him to look for a bloody knife in a drawer won't? I'll be honest, Pip, I'm starting to wonder if we didn't think this through."

"Time was of the essence. I saw her leave and had to do *something*," I say in a rush. "C'mon."

I bounce my useless dangling legs like I'm trying to *giddy up, horsey* him.

"Let's brainstorm back in the room. I can call him from the room. Or . . . or whatever. But we'll figure it out *there*."

As he races us back to the room (why doesn't he put me down? I don't know. You don't do things that make sense when you're under the knife, turns out), I feel an intense adrenaline rush in the settling reality: Crystal is the killer.

Crystal, turns out, *is the killer*.

I'm supposed to say there's something terribly sad about that, but the truth is, I'm nothing but relieved. Relieved it's not love-revenge Neena. Relieved it's not ghostwriter-secret Jackie. Or sweet Gordon. Or Nash, obviously. Or even . . . in my own way, Ricky.

We've only known Crystal now, what? A year? Two?

She's but a blip in the memories of our lives. Good memories, sure. But there are just a few of them. And quite frankly, Crystal and I have never quite clicked. Maybe it's all the tracking down I've had to do for her. Regardless, she doesn't take up the same amount of space in my heart as the others.

It feels like less of a betrayal. So she betrayed us. But anyone can fake a personality for one year. It's truly horrifying to fake it over five.

Mostly, I feel an adrenaline-pumped relief. It's over. *We figured out the killer.*

I pull out my phone, even as Nash is running.

Begin to type Cedar's name.

Stop.

Start again.

Scenarios from a dozen of Hugh's books fly through my mind simultaneously, fighting for attention.

The Quiet Cuban where Bembe tells the detective about the weapon. Doesn't go well. He dies.

Murder on the I-95 where Stieg runs to the detective and leaves the weapon at the door for him to find. Doesn't go well. Again: death.

Race Against Time. Monroe keeps the fact to herself. Doesn't go well. Dies.

Man.

There's just no good way to be an amateur sleuth here.

Doomed if you do. Doomed if you don't.

The struggle is being a suspect and detective at the same time, isn't it? It's a little more challenging to clear yourself while announcing someone else's guilt simultaneously.

Hence why the detective in the novel *always* says more or less, in the same gruff way, *Stay out of it, puny civilian.*

It's not just because we tend to be clueless in matters of violence and causation.

It's because there's no easy way to clear ourselves of guilt.

Well, hang on. There's one way.

One sliver of a chance.

Follow the book *Ode*.

Point Cedar to the weapon without him knowing we're pointing him to the weapon. Something dramatic enough to catch his attention.

And *fast*.

Once Nash sets me down, I look around the room for possibilities.

Run to the patio.

Snatch up a votive.

Race back out the door, pause, backpedal, and open the little closet by the front door.

Nash frowns at the candle in my hand. "Pip, what are you doing?"

"I have a plan." I reach for the fire extinguisher.

"I see that. And we need the fire extinguisher on our floating wooden vessel because . . ."

"In case my plan goes terribly awry. Let's go."

I tiptoe-race back down the hall, unlock the door (even quicker this time, *thank you very much*), and step inside. The question is, what can I light on fire that won't go up in *immediate* flames?

Nash is slower behind me.

"I think there is another way," he says cautiously.

"I'm sure there is. But what if she's planning to throw the weapon overboard the second she gets back and we never see it again? All the evidence is gone."

For that matter, *why hasn't* she thrown it overboard? That's the first thing I'd do if I were a killer. The great wide sea, and nobody would ever see it again.

I feel the distinct crunch of a Frito chip underfoot.

Maybe that's one clue.

This is Crystal we're talking about.

I move toward the glow of the television screen.

Something near wires.

My eyes land on the curling iron resting among the other hair appliances.

Bingo.

Flipping the iron to high, I hold the candle over one of her books. Flames begin to grow.

Perfect.

I wait as the fire gathers, swivel round, then push Nash out the door.

Once in the hall with the door wide open, revealing the smoke and orange glow of the flames, I look at Nash. "Ready?" I whisper.

"For what *now?*" he whispers back.

I stride next door to Gordon's room and bang on it twice.

"Fire!" I cry in a low, mangled voice through my elbow. It sounds like someone else entirely. "Call someone! Fire!"

I run and do the same at two more doors, yelling the same thing in the low voice.

Ten seconds later Nash and I have made it back to our room and shut the door.

"You sounded like Elmo," Nash murmurs behind my shoulder as we both look through the peephole.

I lift my chin up. Our eyes inches apart. The tips of our noses touch.

"A very cute . . . Elmo," he whispers, and for a moment we say nothing.

Then the first scream comes.

"Oh my—fire!" Neena cries out.

I look through the peephole and see her in her bathrobe, barefoot as she runs in front of Crystal's room, looks in, and wheels around. "Call security!" she cries, her voice trembling. "Fire!"

It doesn't take much longer for everyone to emerge from their rooms, wide-eyed in their pajamas.

And frankly, for as quick as the waitstaff is about delivering cheesecake at 2 a.m., they sure take their sweet time over a legitimate emergency.

Probably because of all the guests who were calling out for cheesecake.

Ultimately, it's Jackie who puts out the fire.

After a "What in the—" cry, she elbows her way between the useless group with a fire extinguisher and flings herself into the smoky abyss. In silence everyone watches, no one saying a word. At this point Nash and I are both in the group watching, taking pains to look tired and in panic at the scene before us like the rest.

All of us in a fair bit of Jackie awe.

Through the smoke Jackie emerges, triumphant, a frown on her face. The fire extinguisher hangs limply at her side.

She looks absolutely irate for a hero.

"Where is she?" she growls at us, searching each of our eyes. "Where's Crystal?"

Ooooob, she's in trouble now, a childish singsong voice plays in my head.

"She was in her room, right?" I say. "Has anyone . . . else seen her? Who was her buddy?"

"What's the problem here?" a staff member, the same kind-eyed, silver-haired man who helped me prop up my umbrella the other day, says, as two others in uniform rush to inspect the room.

"Nothing. Just our author-child trying to burn down our ship in the middle of the Atlantic," Jackie snaps.

"Crystal, sweetheart?" Neena says, her hand curled around her phone.

All eyes shoot to her, and she spins around for privacy.

"You better get up here," she says in a hushed voice. "Seems we've had a little fire in your room."

"Where is she?" I say.

"Can you hurry, darling?" Neena says.

"Found the problem," a woman says, emerging with the crisp black cover of a partially fire-eaten book in one gloved hand. "Curling iron left on. Seems it caught on some . . . belongings."

"Is Pogache coming?" I say.

"I'll call," Neena says swiftly and begins dialing.

It takes a full fifteen minutes for Pogache to make his way to us, which is simply shocking given the circumstances.

Crystal has already come and apologized through every *how-could-you-do-something-so-stupid?* snap of Jackie's. Even the staff members have finished cleaning up and moved on. Adrenaline is slowly giving way to exhaustion on everyone's faces and the desire to return to our beds.

I never got a clear word on who Crystal's latest partner was. At first it was Gordon, but then Neena, then Jackie, then at the very last both Gordon and Neena claimed her as their own. So clearly, no one.

Though, given Crystal is the *killer*, was it such a bad thing to have been absolutely terrible at being buddies with her?

At last, Pogache makes his way down the hall. Gone are his official blue jacket and name tag; on is a pair of basketball shorts I'm assuming he wears for pajama bottoms. He wears a plain gray sweatshirt. He looks exhausted.

"Where have you been?!" I say, throwing my hands out. I mean, *honestly.* "We're in crisis here and it takes you half an hour to show up?"

I fling my hand toward the door.

Pogache peeks inside. Pointedly ignores me as he addresses

the group. "I've been appraised on everything that happened tonight."

"Apprised," I say, frowning.

"You all can get back to bed."

"Are you going to inspect it?!" I say, motioning to the room.

Easy now, Pip. Easy.

"It's already been inspected," Pogache says. "The source of the fire was found."

"Yes, but was it by *accident*?" I press. My eyes dart around. "I mean, given the circumstances here, I think it's pretty obvious that it would be unwise to assume *anything* about *anyone*."

My eyes land on Neena, who jumps in. "I hate to say it, but she has a point."

Gordon nods as well.

Pogache looks uneasily around the group.

"Fine," he says. "Fine. I'm going to inspect the room just to make sure we're all clear"—he gives me a pointed look—"*again*."

He walks inside Crystal's room.

Shuts the door.

I feel a tingle of adrenaline prick up my neck and just barely let my pinky finger graze against Nash's.

This is it.

He's left us alone with Crystal in the hallway, and any moment Pogache is going to find the knife and the whole thing will be given up.

I eye Crystal.

Now's the time to plan next steps.

What is she going to do?

Make a run for it?

But where could she go?

Hide inside a crate of lemons for the next week until we get off this ship?

She'd be stupid to give herself up like that.

Better to pretend it isn't hers.

Better to have some fighting chance by feigning ignorance.

And yet . . . my hand grips Nash's and squeezes tightly before releasing. Sending a little signal. *Prepare yourself.*

We have no idea what's about to happen next.

I inch closer to Crystal, Nash beside me, and Crystal catches my eye.

Her smooth forehead creases into tiny furrows.

She gives me a queer look.

Almost a . . . a loathing look.

"Funny how the fire just started out of nowhere, isn't it, *Pip?*" she says.

My heart pounds in my chest. "I heard you left your iron on."

"And yet . . . if I'm not mistaken"—she takes a strand of her long brown hair and winds it round her finger, inspecting—"I didn't curl my hair today."

She flashes a smile I've never seen before, and my blood runs cold.

It's absolutely shocking seeing her like this.

I mean, we haven't been the best of friends, sure.

I might have thought her a bit too flighty, sure.

A little too reckless.

Careless.

Unstable.

The kind of person you like enough at a distance but don't invite over to dinner at your place because, well, you just never know what kind of chaos you might end up in.

But . . . this look.

This *murderous* look.

I mean, it's shocking.

Just when you think you know someone . . .

I'm really going to have trouble trusting anyone. Ever. Again.

Suddenly, Crystal's door swings open.

Pogache steps out, arms behind his back. "I've finished my search."

"Yes?" Nash says, frowning.

"And I did find something . . . *quite* . . . concerning."

I lean forward in anticipation.

"And . . . ?" I say, unable to help myself. "And? What is it?"

"And *this*," he says, whipping it out, "is not allowed on board. I'm going to have to take it."

Crystal flings out a hand. "No, dude. Not the board."

He's holding out a hoverboard with a long flame down the center. And he's looking at it like he's fully intending to use it the second he gets down the hall and out of sight.

"Code 7375. No hoverboards, Airwheels, or drones allowed on the craft. Do you"—he looks up curiously—"have a drone in there too?"

Crystal glares. "No."

She grabs for the board.

Swiftly, he puts up a hand. "Code 6828. No physical contact with an officer. Get your hands off me before I cuff you for physical aggression with security."

And while they continue to scuffle like schoolchildren at a playground, I loudly clap my hands. "Hey! Kids!" I call out. "Anything *else* in there worth noting?" I wave my hand around at the others. "Because if you haven't noticed, we're a little stressed."

"Miss Dupont." Pogache looks me straight in the eye. "You would do well not to stereotype people. *Me* included."

It's a little hard to take him seriously with a hoverboard tucked under his arm.

"Rest assured," he continues, "I am taking this all very seriously. Very seriously indeed."

"So you didn't see any evidence inside?"

He moves to lift up the heinous hoverboard to show it to me, and I add, "Any *real* evidence that would help with this case?"

"The man says *no*," Crystal puts in.

He looks to her. "Thank you."

I squeeze the back of my neck. Working with this guy is a nightmare. This whole situation *is a nightmare*. I throw my hand out toward her hand, which is now reaching gently for the hoverboard, and he, idiot that he is, is unconsciously handing it over. "She just wants the hoverboard back. Please. For the love of all, *focus*."

But it's no use.

Pogache orders us all back to our rooms.

Nash and I are both exhausted. Absolutely and totally exhausted. To the point of making mistakes if we're not careful.

Nash pushes the rolling chair to the door.

Drops down into it.

Crosses his arms one over the other.

"What are you doing?"

He tilts his head. "Pip, you weren't exactly discreet."

I open my mouth to protest, but he beats me to it. He raises a hand. "I'm not saying you did any less or more than you had to do. That Pogache kid is incompetent, as has been made abundantly clear."

"Do you think he really missed the knife?"

"Of course. I think he took one look around, ate some Fritos off the floor, and stole a hoverboard. Because he's *twelve*.

"But regardless," Nash continues, "if Crystal is the killer and saw you hinting as much, and if we really have this situation on our hands to deal with on our own, then I'm going to park here and personally make sure we don't have any visitors in the middle of the night."

That's it.

Nash has summed it up nicely, unfortunately.

It *is* up to us now.

Not just "could be up to us" but definitely *is* up to us to figure this out, and soon, because the second we get on land, there's no doubt the killer is going to make a beeline out and we'll never see them again.

Or worse, I'll spend the rest of my life looking over my shoulder for crazy lunatic Crystal to come at me with a knife.

Just. Super.

No pressure, Pip, at *all*.

I look over at Nash.

Good, unbelievably good, Nash.

His hat is tipped over his face again, boots on. One leg crossed over the other at his ankle. Leaning back in the chair. Chin dipped to his chest. Arms crossed. Pocketknife, I note, resting in his hand.

"Do you really think she did it?" Nash murmurs.

My cheeks flush, leaving me feeling spotted for staring at him in the dim light.

"She must have. I guess," I add with less certainty. "We all know Crystal is unreliable. And emotionally irresponsible. And spends way too much money on ridiculous things—"

"I think she has a whole wall of those hoverboards," Nash says.

"And who knows?" I say with a shrug. "Maybe that's it. Maybe somehow money had a part in it. Usually does, somehow. Anyway, I think I'll have a better guess after I interview her tomorrow."

"After you *what*?" He tips his hat up. Gives me a look that absolutely should *not* make me feel a thrill inside, but there it is. It can't be helped. Concern for someone is entirely attractive. Especially when tipping up a cowboy hat is involved. "You can't be serious."

"I have to. What better way to get a good read on the situation than by interviewing her, just as I have the others? Everyone's agreed to it. She'll look suspicious if she denies my request to interview her. And what is she going to do? Kill me in plain sight?"

"Yes, that's exactly what she could do. Kill you in plain sight."

"She wouldn't."

"And how do you know that? You have an inside track into the minds of murderers?"

"She likes to hoverboard. She *wants* to keep the hoverboard. And nobody who has a death wish of being tossed overboard in your wrath, Nash, has an active hobby of hoverboarding. The girl wants to live. She *wants* to get away with it."

"I don't like it. I saw the way she looked at you. She suspects you now—"

"I couldn't help it. I had to *try* to get Pogache to use his brain. He's the one with the handcuffs after all."

"Let's hope that's all he has on him. I'd hate to think he's walking around with a gun."

"Hovering around, you mean. The point is, I have to interview her. Because the problem is, *everybody* is starting to look like a killer on this ship. *Every* interview has been weird. I think it's Crystal *now* with a knife in her bedroom, but then, who knows? Tomorrow a waiter could be poisoning Neena's water for all I know, and I'll be thrown again. Frankly, I wish it *was* someone else entirely on this boat. Someone we don't know to make this all easier. Speaking of—"

I pull out my phone, dial Pogache's number. He doesn't answer.

I tap to call him again.

Pogache picks up on the third ring.

"What now?" he says.

"I'm calling about the checks. Did you have that information?"

"Checks?" Pogache says.

"*Background* checks," I say. I hear a familiar song on the other end and frown. "Are you seriously leaving a *crime scene* and moving on to a restaurant right now?"

The music immediately stops.

He's muted me.

Muffled me.

"If you must know, I'm in *bed*. With the television on. Like *you* should be."

He's trying to sound authoritative. It falls flat.

"Did you do the background checks?" I repeat.

There's a massive sigh. It goes on . . . and on . . . and on.

"It's none of your business," he says at last. "But they're all clear."

I feel a drop in my stomach. I didn't even realize how much hope I had in this theory, treacherous as it was, and now it's slipping away. "*Everyone* on board?" I say. "There are, what, three hundred people—"

"Two hundred ninety-seven," he corrects, and I'll give him that. For the first time he sounds a *little* like he knows what he's doing. "And they were all checked before we even boarded."

I nod sullenly.

I had background checked many of the people myself be-fore they came on this cruise. Not a legitimate background check, of course, but I looked up their social media handles before adding them to the list of people coming on this trip.

Everybody looked about the same. Pictures of their Christmas trees in their living rooms. Pictures of their new wainscoting in their hallways. Pictures of grandchildren dressed up in matching blue gingham for Easter.

Nobody looked like they were secretly hoarding hate and planning murder.

But of course, I guess, the good killers never do.

"And the staff?" I venture hopefully.

"All checked. The cruise ship, as you can imagine, keeps close tabs on their staff."

"Not even for money?" I say. "Maybe somebody offered them a lot of money—"

"The job's competitive. They make good salaries and travel the world thirty weeks out of the year. For free." I open my mouth, and he adds, "While eating the same food they feed us."

"So . . . free lobster."

"Free lobster," Pogache repeats. "Nobody, I can assure you, Miss Dupont, is killing on this ship for money. They're all happier than we are."

"And . . . none of the guests for sure—"

"Stop it. Stop it right there. I'm done talking about this. I am the professional. Now if you'll excuse me, it's late. I have to go to bed."

"I thought you were in bed."

Pogache pauses. "Again."

He hangs up and I hang my head.

Silence weighs heavy in the air. Nash breaks it.

"So?"

"That's it. I can't trust myself. I *am* going crazy," I say, putting the phone back on the bedside table. "There's not *one* person here who looks like they aren't covering up murder. Even Pogache seems off."

"Except for me."

I smile lightly. "Yes. Except you. But everyone else seems absolutely sinister," I say, waving a hand in the air. "Jackie's harboring the secret that she uses a ghostwriter to make her books a success."

"Really?" Nash says, looking as startled as I was at the news.

"Crystal's got the *weapon* in her dresser. Ricky screams of psychopath hiding behind curtains writing thrillers. And did you know that Neena and Hugh were engaged at one point? And then he broke it off with her?"

"Neena?" Nash rubs his face. "I know Neena has always been flirtatious with Hugh, but . . ."

"And apparently holding it against him. *Everybody* has a motive, Nash."

"Except Gordon."

"Nope." I shake my head. "Even Gordon."

"Why?"

"Gordon's in the will."

"So?"

"Gordon's the *only* one in the will. Gordon gets it all."

CHAPTER 20

"WHY WOULD HUGH DO SOMETHING SO STUPID? He must have millions."

Nash, at last, has moved to standing from his seat at the door. Too many questions are running through both of our minds. Too many ideas gnawing at us. Too many problems with those ideas.

Dead-end trails.

"I'm telling you, this is tough," I say. "*Everyone's* suspicious."

The coffee maker gurgles in assent as Nash stands over the little golden coffee bar in the corner of the room.

Seems we're going to have another long night. Both of us too frazzled, both of us feeling the weight of anxiety hanging over us.

He has taken off his hat entirely now. It rests hooked on the golden cart.

The coffee maker gives a merry little (and ultimately very expensive-sounding) ding.

He rubs his weary face and proceeds to pour.

"Dozens of millions," I say.

"And all of it . . . ?"

"Some of it will go to charities. But yeah, the rest—"

"His property?"

"To Gordon."

"His investments?"

I laugh. "It's Hugh. What investments? We're lucky he didn't bury his money in gold under a sewer cap on Thirty-Third Street."

"Or unlucky . . . depending on how you want to see it," Nash murmurs.

He hands me a steaming cup of coffee.

Gold-rimmed teacups in a hotel room. That's a first.

I grip the cup of coffee in my hands, knees pulled up beneath the covers to my chin.

"How many interviews do you have left?"

"Three."

Nash sits on the end of the bed. "Okay, Pip. Break this down for me. All the way."

And I do.

For the next two hours, I go moment by moment, detail by detail over every single conversation, look, and gesture I've experienced over the past three days. Eventually I take to referencing Hugh's books, and I go from mentioning the way suspicious things parallel certain scenes to pulling up said scenes on my laptop and sharing them out loud. Soon enough I'm taking a page from *This Side of Destiny* and typing up a brain dump of instances, both noteworthy and not. Just getting everything down.

Nash eventually nods off.

While Nash sleeps, I break down the brain dump into categories in an Excel sheet, organizing things into lists and those lists into other lists and those lists into more lists.

Then, against Pogache's wishes, I go back again through

every single reader who joined the book cruise, searching through their email confirmations and hunting down each of the cruisers in more detail one by one.

By the hum of Nash's deeply sleeping chest, I write it all out in meticulous fashion, color coding anything fishy with mild yellow, medium orange, or highly suspicious red, and when my hand aches and my eyes refuse to stay open and my head eventually sinks onto my chest, the alarm clock reads 5 a.m.

To say it was tough to wake up is an understatement.

Nash had to shake me like a level 4 earthquake to get me moving.

"I'm up, I'm up," I murmur, my head sandwiched between two pillows.

Soft pillows too.

"Pip," Nash whispers, shaking my shoulder again. "You can sleep in and I'll message the group. Or you can get up. But I'm going to miss my session, and you seem to care about that—"

"I'm up," I say, jolting up with the realization I was drifting asleep again.

I look around, disoriented.

I'm sitting on top of my bed, surrounded by papers and my computer and tablet. My hair is in a high bun flat on top of my head. My glasses are crooked since I slept in them. I look like I was plotting a heist. An Ivy League law student who forgot to study for the final exam. A corporate executive in one of those movies who ends up leaving the life of the city to find her huntsman in the woods.

I reach up.

Nash, quite unjustly, looks remarkably well.

He stands in front of me holding out a cup of coffee.

"Thank you," I say, which, unfortunately for me, comes out far more like a croak than in the sultry tone I would have preferred.

Let's just say, it would be very nice to be more put together than I am right now.

"No problem, Kermit," he says with a smile. He gestures to the pile surrounding me. "So. Are you . . . pulling off a heist?"

"I kept brainstorming after you fell asleep," I say, adjusting my glasses.

"And this is the method to your madness?"

"Little bit, yeah."

He picks up one of the handwritten pages I obliterated with haphazard writing.

Turns the page horizontal.

Turns it another ninety degrees.

"Hugh always said you were a mad author waiting to happen. This is definitely mad author behavior." He looks to his right. "Did you pin notes *to the wall*?"

"I'll tag it to Crystal's bill." I take a restorative sip of my coffee.

"Did you"—he squints at a sheet on the wall—"make up your own personalized background check for the guests on board? 'Donna Richardson. Fifty-eight. Two dogs. Questionable son. Could be link. Martin Richardson, son of Donna Richardson. Twenty-nine. Norton, Indiana. Second DUI in 2007 . . .'"

His voice fades as he looks at me.

It's the face of someone who saw their crush pick a lock with a dryer pin the night before and then woke up to said person hanging stalker-level research on the walls.

Like I say, it's good Nash knew me through my more composed season of life.

I shrug. "I realized something fully last night. I can't trust Pogache as far as I can throw him. So I'm going to do my best myself."

"How many people have you gone through?"

"One hundred and seventy-three. Twenty-two are on the highly suspicious list. I'm going to dig deeper into them today when I'm not interviewing."

He drops the page from his fingers and it flutters to the top of the bed. Picks up another.

"Hugh has gotten at me plenty of times for how much I research. But *this*—"

"That's why Hugh needed me. At least, that's why he said he needed me. I like to see things up close and personal, from every angle, before making a decision. And once I make it"—I swallow, remembering the years dedicated blindly to Michael—"it's final. For better or worse. So. I like research."

I look around the room that yes, more so than usual, looks like the science laboratory for Frankenstein.

"Did you find new suspects?" he says.

"Only about a hundred."

"A *hundred*? And you found new motives?"

"Only about a thousand." I hold out my coffee cup. "Alright, hold this. I'm going to try to get out of my bed of papers," I say, unwinding my legs from beneath the covers.

Ten minutes later, we head into the library, where everyone is already gathered. The rising sun shines bright over the glassy sea out the windows. It's bizarre, actually, seeing everyone sitting so near each other, looking for just a moment like the old team I knew, and with a heart swell, I taste the bitter sensation of old times gone.

WITHOUT A CLUE 227

I shut the door behind me.

Neena stops talking as everyone turns momentarily and looks at me, then back at each other.

"You're going mad over those pills," Jackie says with a sniff. "There's no whale out the window."

"I saw what I saw," Neena says, wiggling through the crowd to get a closer view through the window. "There *was* a whale, and it was beautiful. It leapt right out of the water."

Jackie throws back her head with a *phff*. "A one-hundred-thousand-pound whale. Jumping right out of the water."

"It can be done."

"A pod of killer whales," Ricky says slowly. There's a monumental pause. "Attacked and sank a fifty-foot yacht." The clock on the wall ticks. "In the Strait of Gibraltar. Seems . . . plausible . . . that with enough collaborative effort . . . they could take this ship down."

Reliably grim as always.

"It could be pirates," Crystal says.

Gordon perks up, squints out the window.

Jackie folds her arms. Shifts her attention with the perma-scowl of hers on me. "Enough wasting the day. Let's get on with it. I want breakfast."

"Okay," I say and tap on my tablet for the day's schedule. "Obviously we've had a rough patch lately."

"Did you figure out the killer yet?" Jackie says, scowling pointedly at me.

"I . . ." I begin.

"Because my nerves are running on thin ice here," she says. "I can't express enough how much *I want this to be over*."

"I have a few more people to interview."

"We're going to be on land in a matter of four days," Jackie says, throwing her hands in the air. "And I don't care what *anyone* says—I'm getting off this thing when we get there, heading straight for the airport, and flying myself home. This entire experience has been *unbearable*."

"Something to take the heat off?" Neena says, opening up her purse.

Jackie pushes her away.

"So we're continuing with our morning workshops today," I say, "followed by lunch and an afternoon all-group event in the ballroom. I will help however you need, and plan"—I give a pointed look to Jackie—"to squeeze in the last interviews as I can. It's a tight schedule, though, people. The itinerary is only getting busier and busier as we near the end of the trip. Please stick to groups. Three if you can. Anybody else need help with anything for this morning session?"

Gordon raises a hand meekly. "I was trying to get my computer to open today . . ."

Neena pats his hand. "You and technology, darling. It's agonizing."

⌒

In good news, it was just a stomach virus that took hold of me the next seventy-two hours and gave me the shakedown of my life. Not attempted murder. And when I'm back on my feet, I go straight to Crystal.

"Does he really think I'm going to pound your head with an eight ball while you're in here with me? Does he really think I'm that stupid? For Pete's sake, Nash, *shut the door*. Let the girls *talk*."

Crystal, standing on a hoverboard no less (her "backup," she says), pulls back on the pool stick as she eyes the white ball down the line of the pool table. We're in some kind of game room I didn't know existed.

Apparently there's a lot of the ship I didn't realize existed.

But then again, that's how it goes when your boss is murdered while on vacation, I guess.

She shoots.

I jump.

The sound of balls rocking against each other as they pound the sides of the expansive pool table rattles me.

Two balls roll into the pocket.

Crystal smiles.

I can't tell if it's about her ill-timed "joke" or about the fact that she got some balls in.

Either way, it's creepy.

For the record, I don't recall Crystal being this . . . obviously *insane* is the word I'm hunting for . . . in the past. Forgetful? Absolutely. Immature? Yes. The kind of girl who stumbled into insanely good fortune with career success and yet still manages to *forget* that adults pay taxes? Yup.

"Can you turn off your phone for this, Crystal?" I say, pointing to the phone video she has propped up on the table recording herself. It's going to end up as a TikTok in about twelve seconds.

"What's the magic word?" she says in a singsong voice.

"Please."

"Can you get your boyfriend to get his foot out the door?"

I grind my teeth. I'm not emotionally equipped yet for her to talk like that about Nash and me. "Yeah. Fine."

"No," I hear Nash say, without seeing him. "I'm staying here, Crystal."

"Is this because of the little incident the other night?" Crystal says, holding her pool stick at her side. "Because, correct me if I'm wrong, but I was almost certain somebody *else* lit that fire. And I'm awfully convinced it might have been *you.*"

She shoots me a look.

"Door's staying open," Nash says, taking another step toward us.

I don't dare hold out my phone to take notes with her.

She's so intense—far more intense than any of the group I've interviewed so far. I'm afraid she'd snap her mouth shut. This new, brash Crystal seems like just the type to put her foot in it because she's too hotheaded and conceited to look where she's going.

"What was in the room?" I say.

"Tsk, tsk, tsk," she says, wagging her finger at me. As she hoverboards to the other side of the table, she says, "Do you really think I'm that stupid?"

"Depends. How stupid?"

"Stupid enough that if there *was* something in my room, and there was *not*, I'd tell you. All I can say is that I'm disappointed in you, Pip. I thought we were closer than that."

Yeah.

Tell me about it.

She leans over with her pool stick for another shot. "Of course, some would say life is full of disappointing people. Fathers, for instance."

"Fathers? What . . . so your father disappointed you?"

She laughs, one of those humorless, heartless laughs.

Takes a shot with the pool stick.

The balls go rolling.

"You could say that. He was a *reeeeeal* piece of work."

Well. At least she doesn't have a problem with dispensing information. "How so?"

"You know how people don't have secret daughters anymore? How that's one of those old-fashioned things only terrible people did in high positions hundreds of years ago because they sucked and reputation went with money? Yeah.

Well, sometimes it still happens. Or perhaps you haven't heard my real name before."

"You're Crystal Murrell," I say automatically. I've seen everything on her. All of her social account names. All the contracts she's signed with us. Everything. I pause. "But you're saying it's a pen name?"

"Yep."

"And your real name?"

She frowns. "Try this mouthful on for size. Mary Alice Givens Griffin. I know. It's awful, isn't it? My parents had no chill." The seven ball drops in and she moves around the table.

"Griffin?" I say, my brows rising. My eyes link with Nash's. His hands are stuffed in his pockets. He's leaning back and forth on the heels of his boots as if poised for action at any moment. "Crystal. Mary." I shake my head. "Are you telling me you are Hugh's daughter?"

She raises her pool stick. Grins.

"Secret daughter," she corrects. "Secret daughter he was so bent on teaching to raise herself up by her own bootstraps that he only allowed me to join this ridiculous little group of his if I changed my name."

"Wait. But you're not in the will—"

She laughs.

"Don't I *know* that?" she says with an edge in her voice. "Don't I know how *ridiculous* it is for him to go on and on about how I need to learn self-sufficiency and how 'it doesn't do you any favors to take the shortcut,' but then I join this little parade and realize that all this time he was not helping me, he was doing everything he could to try to help *you*? His special Penelope Dupont princess. The little administrative genius. He was willing to do more to jump-start *you* into a writing career than *me*."

I grip the pool table. "But . . . but . . . I've met your dad. At the July Fourth party—"

"Yeah, you mean my portfolio manager, Frank?" She laughs callously. "You're so stupid. You've always been so gullible, Pip. You'd believe anything. Explains a lot about why you stayed forever with that loser Michael—"

"Hey!" Nash takes a step toward her. "That's enough, Crystal."

Crystal immediately puts her hands up. "Alright, alright. *Geez*. Pip, call your bodyguard off."

Nash looks to me and his eyes say it all. Pure fire. *Give me the word and I'll kick her out myself.*

I'm good. It's fine.

It's more than fine, actually.

Nash standing there, putting himself on the line without a second thought. That face. That fury.

It could melt metal, that look.

"And the name's *Mary*," Crystal calls out to him as I wave him off. She smiles again at me. "Horrible name. Bland as it gets. You got a real keeper, though, haven't you there? Man, if I had a man like that tearing down the rainforest to make my way—"

"Why did you tell me that?" I interrupt. "What purpose does it serve you to tell me you're Hugh's daughter?"

"You'd figure it out soon enough. Might as well beat you to it."

"And put yourself on the prime suspect list?"

"Over what? That he's my less-than-average father? Oh, honey, you have far more interesting suspects to consider than me."

"I don't know. Jealousy is a solid reason for revenge."

"Oh, I've been watching him dote on you for years now with that stupid smile on his face, but I didn't kill him."

"Then who do you think did it? Who's a better suspect than you?"

She laughs. "Only *everyone* else here? Neena was jilted at the altar, and between you and me, I think she's been a little cuckoo since. And of course Jackie . . . well, you know."

I raise a brow. "What do you know?"

"Let's just say, Jackie hated when I found out she didn't write her own stuff. Hated me enough to try to frame me with that knife you found in my dresser. Yeah, I know you found it. Welcome to my world. I found it there too and didn't know what to do."

"So you did nothing?"

"Should I have put it somewhere else and gotten myself caught?" She shrugs. "The reality is, just because it was found in my room doesn't mean I put it there." She looks me up and down. "We all *clearly* can get into each other's rooms if we want to badly enough. At any rate, if Jackie would frame me for knowing, I can't imagine what she actually did to the man who said he was going to tell the world. Oh wait. I can."

I raise a finger. "So . . . you think Jackie killed Hugh for letting out her secret, and you think Jackie is trying to frame you for knowing as well? What does that make me then? Now that I know?"

"Easy, I should think," she says. She pops a ball down the line. "Her next target."

CHAPTER 21

THERE'S NO WAY JACKIE IS THAT CRAZY.

To murder one person is undeniably insane.

But to proceed to go on a rampage trying to knock off *every. Single. Person* who ends up hearing her little secret? Absolutely unhinged.

Beyond unhinged.

Impossible.

I shake my head. No. It can't be.

It just . . . can't . . . be.

Crystal spouts out other names and dates and facts as I ask about them, but nothing is quite so interesting, or confusing, as her announcement at the very beginning of our conversation. And she was so *lackadaisical* about it. That's what was so concerning.

And so . . . so full of hate.

Crystal—or Mary, I should say—once brought me a crazily mangled croissant from my favorite bakery. It was awful. The elaborate story of how the croissant traveled via electric scooter through wind and rain and passing taxis—even lore of a snatching tourist she beat down to get it back—became famously known in our little group.

Hugh laughed and laughed and made her tell it to us all again. I'll never forget the boom of his laugh as it rattled through the chambers of his belly and filled the room.

I can still hear it now.

It's just so wild to imagine her as anything but precisely that—and yet the woman I saw today—she *delighted* in showing off her true self.

She *delighted* in hurting me.

Even down to the Michael comment.

It was a side of her I'd never seen, and yet another fact to chuck into the bucket to make me realize: It's really possible you don't know anyone.

People who choose to lie, can lie fabulously.

People who choose to deceive, can deceive famously.

For long periods of time.

There's never any true way to know who and when to trust, is there? Both in love and in hate.

"Well, that was . . . enlightening," Nash says, standing in the doorway.

His eyes hold the same *What on earth was that?* expression as mine, and I nod to say, *Right? See what I mean?*

"Who's up next?" Nash says.

"Ricky. Although he's not answering his phone. I'm just going to have to hunt the ship to find him."

There's a squeak of a chair behind me.

"I'm . . . right . . . here."

I scream.

Nash automatically reaches for a pool stick.

And out of the wingback chair in the corner rises none other than Ricky.

"How did you get in here?" I point. "How long have you *been* here?"

"I didn't know . . ." he says slowly, "it was a confidential . . . meeting."

"Of course it's confidential!" I cry, moving my hands to my hips. Heart pounding. "You listened to our whole interview with Crystal?"

"You mean . . . Mary."

I nod. "Yes. Yes. Obviously, that's who I mean. So you listened in."

"Nash listened as well. I didn't know"—his fingers run slowly over the top edge of a paperback book in his hands— "you wanted a . . . select audience."

How is he doing that?

He looks like his fingers are going to slice into papercuts any second.

It's too creepy to watch.

"Alright, let's get this over with. I'll come to you."

The power of mind talk is so strong between me and Nash that I don't even need to look at him without knowing we both *absolutely* agree that this conversation is a keep-the-door-open-in-case-he-pulls-out-an-envelope-opener situation.

I move over to the second wingback chair in the corner.

"Penelope," Ricky says in his low, formidable tone.

I wait.

I wait, as it turns out, for an eternity.

Ricky, if it's possible, looks even more tired than usual. He's always had hollow eyes that give off an *I'm Dracula* vibe. But clearly this trip has thrown him even more. He's as pale as his white linen shirt.

"You're not particularly . . . perceptive . . . are you?" he says, sitting back down. He's crossed one knee over the other now and is looking at me like . . . well, like someone who wants to eat you for lunch. His knuckles are pearly white, strained with pressure as they clasp his knees. "I would avoid dark alleyways . . . if I were you."

My knees pinch together. Jackie should just see me now; I have no trouble sitting rail straight at the moment. How many times have I sat alone with Ricky? Truly alone? Does the eternal sixty-eight seconds together in the cab while waiting for Hugh count? "What does that mean?"

"Just that it would be such a pity if you were killed due to your own incapacity to . . . be aware of your . . . surroundings."

He looks downtrodden, as though I've died already.

"Such," he continues, "a pity."

Stop doing that! I want to cry while waving at his face. *Stop thinking about me dead.*

"Is this some kind of threat?" I say.

"Of course. Threats are"—he sighs—"everywhere. We could fall off this ship . . . perish by the teeth of a hundred sharks . . . get stuck in a wheel . . . poisoned by stale potatoes . . . all . . . in an instant."

He sucks in a breath, shaking his head as though wondering how we could be so stupid as to have flipped ourselves off the ship. "We could . . . eat some broccoli with . . . E. coli . . . We could—"

"I get it," I interject, putting up a hand. "The world's very scary and we're all gonna die. Let's just get this over with. How long did you know Hugh?"

"Forty-two years."

"Two years longer than everyone else," I note.

"We are in a similar line . . . of work. Mystery . . . intrigue . . . murder . . . We were meant to find . . . each other . . . and we did."

"And you two became friends," I finish.

Ricky gives a unique little pause, saying at last, "You could say that."

I look up from my notes. "*Can* I say that?"

"You . . . could."

"But can I?"

"I suppose."

I purse my lips.

I can't tell if he's speaking sarcastically or sincerely. I can't tell anything if there's some darker underlayer to everything he says.

Ricky could be talking about picking up laundry detergent and it would sound like it was code for *gun*.

"Right . . ." I say, trying to be exceedingly slow and clear. "So *were* you and Hugh friends all along?"

He gives me a look. "Forty years is a long time for friendship."

Okay, but what does *that* mean?

Was he ready to throw him off the ledge?

Let's change tactics.

Shoot for yes-or-no answers. "Do you think Hugh had people with the goal and intent to kill him?"

"Don't we all?"

No, Ricky. We don't *all*.

"Do you think . . . Hugh," I say, changing course, "had a more than *average* number of people incentivized to kill him?"

"All the good ones do."

"And *you* think that?"

"What do my thoughts . . . matter? What do . . . anyone's . . . for that matter?"

Amazing. I am totally and sincerely at a loss.

Let's be blunt.

I set the phone down.

"Did you murder Hugh, Ricky?"

"Ah. Oh dear." Sure enough, one of Ricky's white finger-tips has slit on the corner of the book, and now a thick drop of blood is leaking from it. "No. Although, has anyone ever . . . at this stage . . . said yes?"

"No, but . . ."

"Would be foolish . . . I assume . . . to finally get away with . . . the murder of your dreams . . . only to tell some-one . . . now."

Yes, yes. I *know*. But I'm clueless here. I need to stick to the basics: securing a motive, means, and opportunity.

Problem is, we were all in our rooms the night Hugh was murdered.

We all had the means to slip in.

We all had access to a knife.

None of us have an alibi.

The only thing we don't all have—well, except on this crazy ship where *everyone has one*—is a motive.

Stick to that.

"Have you ever had disagreements with Hugh over the way he ran the group?"

He pauses, thinking, looking up, for an enormous amount of time.

"I didn't like the croissants," Ricky says at last.

"The . . . croissants."

"Yes."

"The croissants we got catered to the room for lunches," I say.

"Yes."

"You didn't like them."

"I prefer Asiago bagels."

"I get the croissants for the lunches," I say.

"Oh. Then . . . nothing."

So nothing.

I sigh.

"You've never disagreed with Hugh, over *anything*, in your entire life." The lady at the CVS checkout line has had more disagreements, according to this man, than Ricky.

"I guess not. But that's how . . . rage goes . . . isn't it? The deadly ones . . . we just hold . . . inside."

The grandfather clock opposite strikes three and begins to chime.

We stare at each other in silence.

"Are *you* harboring rage you aren't telling me about?"

"Aren't we all?"

"Well, yes, but that's not the point. Are *you*?"

"I've already . . . discussed . . . the croissant situation."

Okay.

It's time to move on.

I suck in my breath, staring at his hand and the fact that blood is now running down his finger, apparently unbeknownst to him.

Can he not feel that?

Is he not interested in *doing* anything about that?

"Why do you think someone would want to kill Hugh? Were you surprised when you heard the news?"

"I'm never surprised . . . by earthly death. It's the fate . . . of us all. I am . . . however . . . continuously surprised . . . that people are surprised . . . by it. Pip."

He beckons me closer.

I hesitate, not daring for a moment to move, but the opportunity of the moment gets me.

I move forward until we are a foot apart. "Yes?"

"Do you think . . . there will be . . . those grits at dinner again?"

My brow knots. "Your friend *died* and you're asking me about dinner choices?"

"Your friend also died . . . and you fell in love with the cowboy. Life stops . . . for no one."

"Well . . . I haven't said I love him."

"What's stopping you now?"

I look over to Nash, trying painfully not to blush right now. Is he hearing this? If he is, he's graciously pretending not to.

"They were . . . remarkable grits," Ricky says. "It is . . . curious timing, though."

I point to his finger. "Are you going to do something about that?"

"Nash falling so obviously smitten with you . . . now. Now that death is at our door and the buck must lie . . . with someone. Are you . . . truly going to consider . . . Nash's suspicious nature? Or, like my finger, will we both ignore . . . what is right . . . before us?"

Did he . . . did he *cut* himself on purpose to make a chilling *point*?

To try to say *Nash* is a murderer?

"I've interviewed him already," I say quickly.

Ricky lowers his voice to a mere whisper. "And yet . . . I fear . . . he hasn't mentioned . . . his criminal background . . . has he?"

I can't help myself.

My face has fallen.

I inch closer.

"Nash doesn't have a criminal history," I say lowly. I glance up. Nash drops his eyes on me every once in a while, but true to his word, he has given me space to talk privately without hearing.

"Do you know that?"

Ricky ever so slowly pulls a crisp white napkin from his pocket. Which he has waited precisely until this moment to use. "I rescind my statement . . ." he says, wiping the napkin round his finger. "Hugh liked to . . . see the best in peo- ple . . . despite their faults. I . . . on the other hand . . . prefer to see people . . . as they are. Four years ago . . . we disagreed on precisely . . . that."

"And what . . . precisely . . . is that?" I say.

His eyes move silently to stop at Nash.

That?

Ricky and Hugh disagreed four years ago about Nash joining the group? *That* kind of that?

"I would . . . consider your friend . . . again. Now . . . I am . . . finished."

Ricky has ended the interview, not me, and with a sober look, I find myself compelled to stand.

He doesn't.

Just goes on back to staring at the wall from his wingback chair, in total silence.

I don't know if he's counting the books or determining his blood count, but either way, of all the interviews so far, I am all too willing to get out of here now.

I make for the door.

"Oh, and Pip. I almost forgot," he calls out.

I turn at the door.

I can't even see his head beneath the height of the wing- back chair.

I return to him.

I don't want to talk to him. I don't want to have this conversation anymore. I feel cold, the kind of cold you get from being outside in twenty-degree weather for too long. A brittle cold laced over your bones, the kind that takes an hour-long shower of pure heat to try to soak through to your insides, and even then you feel a lingering chill for days.

It's not a desirable feeling.

Ricky holds out an envelope, sealed in red wax with the monogram *H*. I recognize the seal immediately. I've sent a thousand letters on Hugh's behalf, but he never let me use that seal. He held on to the integrity of it, saying a letter with the seal of his ring meant it was truly and wholly from him.

Hugh.

It's my turn now to have my sentences drift off. "Is that . . ." I begin.

"He wrote it to me the night of his . . . murder. Told me to only open it . . . if something went terribly . . . wrong."

I flip it over. Frown. "But it's still sealed."

"You have become the investigator."

"Not me, Pogache—"

"And I trust that in matters of life or death . . . it's wisest to put a letter like this in the hands of the true decision maker."

A pure, unopened letter from Hugh.

A wax seal.

I know this handwriting.

Perhaps Ricky is tricking me now; perhaps there is some way he has counterfeited all of this. Perhaps he's just trying to convince me the suspect is someone else; either way, I find myself carefully putting the envelope in the inside pocket of my navy blazer.

Because the fact is, I know this handwriting.

I know this seal.

It's Hugh's through and through.

"Why didn't you come show me sooner?" I say.

"I have never moved, Pip," Ricky says lowly. "I was always waiting . . . for you."

Creepy.

As I pull Nash out to the hall and shut the door behind me, as one shuts a tomb, there is silence on the other side.

The hallway is full of warmth, the golden sconces lighting the cheerful carpet and the lively faces of passersby. Instantly lighter.

"How was it?" Nash says.

"It was just as you'd expect. Thoroughly creepy." I give a half-hearted laugh but find myself wrapping my arms tighter around me, the edges of the envelope poking my ribs in secret.

Secrets.

I find it hard to look at Nash.

"You look like you've seen a ghost," Nash says and puts an arm lightly to my back. It jump-starts me, a little too much, I realize.

"Sorry," I say. "I think this whole place is starting to get to me. I might go up and get some fresh air." I make the mistake of casting a look at Nash and feel a fresh chill run through my body. "And maybe some tea."

"He really did get to you, didn't he? What did he say?"

I shrug. "The same thing they all say. 'I'm nothing like you expected and absolutely capable of murder.' I just . . . I think I need to sit down privately and work through everything. Sort it out in my mind."

He casts me a puzzled look.

Calm down, Pip. You've got to chill out.

"If you don't mind, though," I say, "could you run to get me some tea? I like the kind they keep at the tea bar in the Magnolia room. It's the loose-leaf cinnamon."

To be fair, it's the really good kind.

A cup of that actually does sound good.

I mean, as long as he doesn't poison me along the way.

There's an instant pounding in my temples at the thought that dared enter my head.

Oh my GOSH. Pull it TOGETHER.

This is Nash we are talking about.

The man who volunteers in hurricane relief with horses.

The man who stays up with you to watch the stars.

Cling to that reminder.

Cling to that fact.

The midday sun hits on the surface of the saltwater pool, Mediterranean tiles shimmering green in the sunlight. A few ladies cluster at tables at the other end of the pool, playing some sort of card game at the instructor's guidance. In my periphery, Crystal (now Mary) flies by on her hoverboard, laughing maniacally, while several staff with untucked shirts and flying bow ties race down the hall after her, fruitlessly pleading with her to stop.

I slip down into the same lounge chair I used for Jackie's interview and for Neena's. Immediately the same friendly butler pops up, offering to open the umbrella.

I assent.

"And something to drink, miss?" he says. "Perhaps something to keep up your spirits?"

I must look like death rolled over. I can only imagine after these days of living off stress and no sleep. "How bad do I look? Is it that bad?"

"Oh, miss . . ." He trails off.

"It's that bad, isn't it? I'm braced for the truth."

"Perhaps a double shot of espresso. We don't typically allow triple shots given the number of pacemakers on board, but just this once, I could slip you a third upon request."

I squeeze the bridge of my nose.

"I'll take that," he says after a long pause, "as a request for a third. You also may consider removing the . . . for lack of a better term . . . debris from your hair. If I may . . ."

Before I know it, he's gently removing something from the top of my head. Swiftly and with a polished air, whatever it is vanishes from his fingers and into his pocket before I can look.

I drop my head. But of course I'm walking around with "debris."

"You know, miss, we do have a salon available," he continues, whipping out a tablet before I can interject. "If I may, I can slip you into a quick appointment—"

"No, no," I say, smoothing a hand over my hair and running into quite a few unfortunately unknown objects and bumps along the way. "I appreciate that. But I'm busy—"

"Oh, madam." His eyes crinkle in a soft, fatherly way. "If you cannot allow yourself to relax here, I daresay you will spend the rest of your life wishing for relaxation but never finding any. Please, allow others to help you."

"Unfortunately in my case, if I relax now, I just may never get the opportunity to relax again." His look is so concerned at my dark comment, I add, "I'm working."

His face clears.

He waves a hand out at Neena at one of the bridge tables, holding her cards like she's having the time of her life. She elbows Jackie beside her, who frowns deeply at her cards. "Ah, but, madam, they are too."

"It's freakish, isn't it?" I say. "Almost like they didn't care about him at all."

"Miss?"

I turn my attention back to him and sigh. "What is your name?"

Out of everything I've said, he looks the most taken aback by this. He pauses. Bows as he speaks. "Oliver, miss."

"Well, Oliver. It's nice to meet you. Officially. Do you have good friends?"

"Of course."

"Friends who are there for you through thick and thin?"

"Naturally."

"Consider yourself blessed. Because unfortunately, what I think I'm learning through all this is that I've never had real friends after all."

"Oh, miss, but I'm sure you do—I myself have witnessed their companionship with you."

"Money, jealousy, and ambition are powerful motivators. And with enough motivation, you could quite possibly mask your entire life."

Because no matter how this all shakes out, one thing is certain.

The fact that the members of this "Magnificent Seven" have all shown their true colors, their lack of devastation, their willingness to so easily move on, and their sole concern for themselves just shows that they aren't so "magnificent" after all. They're just writers—some of them, at least—who happened to cling to the coattails of someone famous and used him until he was all used up.

This time it's Oliver who doesn't speak, and after a long enough wait, I rub my brow. "You know, Oliver, I think I will take that espresso after all. Double or triple. Surprise me."

Oliver's brow immediately smooths now that he's tasked with something far more manageable than solving life crises, and with a bow, he glides out of view.

I take a breath.

Sit back in my chair.

Fight a rising headache.

And looking left then right, behind and in front, I lift my legs up and tuck my feet under me, forming a little wall with my knees between me and everyone else. Quietly, I slip out the letter from my blazer.

I hesitate for a blink, momentarily consider bringing this straight to Pogache, and then carefully break the seal on the envelope.

I rub the thick ivory cardstock between my fingers and recognize it immediately as Hugh's. Not counterfeit.

The page is mostly blank.

For a man who made his career with words, he was always good at getting directly to the point:

If you're reading this, it's over for me.

Don't overlook the one who looks most innocent of all.

Nash Eyre

"Madam."

A voice behind me makes me scream.

I look up, clutching the letter to my chest.

It's Oliver, bowing deeply and looking entirely apologetic for startling me. "My biggest apologies," he says through at least another two bows. "I just wanted to inquire about your preferences. We have a quality dark, nutty Peruvian and a bold Costa Rican."

At least two more bows follow.

What is he asking?

"The Peruvian," I say quickly.

"Excellent choice. Tremendous. Excellent."

Three more bows, and he whisks himself away.

I look around. No Nash in sight.

Crystal is on her way through another loop around the ship.

Gordon's probably off at the movie theater.

Ricky's downstairs. I feel a chill run up my spine, remembering Ricky's freak appearance in the wingback chair, and add to myself, *I mean, of course he is. Vampires can't come up to the main decks during the day.*

Neena looks as unhinged and cheery as ever. But Jackie?

Jackie's eyes are like slits watching me above her cards. Our eyes catch and hers drop down.

What am I going to do?

Nash is going to be here any moment.

I need to go back to the room. I need to get there when Nash isn't, the *only* moment we're not together, and do a thorough look through his things for clues. It just . . . seems so impossible.

And there's a dread that hangs over me.

A thud deep in my chest.

It just . . . *can't* be true.

But what motive could he have had?

I flip over the note, hoping for some more words, some more clues, but there are none.

I gently slip it back into its envelope and tuck it into my blazer. This needs to get added for evidence.

I look around.

This is my moment, maybe my *only* moment, to sneak away.

Waders are still in the pool. Some people lie on lounge chairs, books in hand.

Crystal has just swung by again on her hoverboard, with a trail of pleading staff. Ladies are still at the card tables. Neena's still clutching her pearls, thrilled. Jackie, for the moment, at least, is distracted by a waiter's question.

I feel bad for bailing on Oliver's kind offer of espresso, but this is my moment.

Run.

I start slow until I make it to the hallway, and then I *fly*.

I dart down the hall, my steps ultralight, until I'm at my door.

Cautiously I unlock it and then, with one last look left and right, step inside.

I turn the lock.

Flick on the lights.

Look around the tattered mess of a room I left behind this morning.

Quickly, Penelope. The goal here isn't to find something. It's the hope you DON'T.

I only have moments here before I need to get back.

What will Nash do if he finds I'm gone?

What excuse will I give?

Do I have that much time? Can I check the room that quickly?

Nash's laptop bag is sitting by the floor lamp, and I crouch down. Carefully I pull back the leather flaps.

Nothing is out of the ordinary. A couple of pens in their pen holes. A thin sleeve of laptop. A small Moleskine notebook. A couple of well-worn paperbacks.

The notebook is mostly empty. The first few pages are riddled with book ideas of various locations, descriptions of the sky, descriptions of the plains. Random names of antique companies and random information about cattle. A mysterious phone number I type into the internet browser on my phone that leads to a dead end; it's just an auction company for horses out in Alvarado.

My eyes pause and hover over a journal entry dated just two weeks ago. I read:

> *The sun was slow setting on the horizon tonight, lingering as its golden sunbeams dallied on jagged mountain*

*peaks, like a child's cry of delight as he climbs up and slides
down, pleading for a few more minutes on the playground.*

It's a lovely thought.

A sunset playing on the swoops and ridges of mountains like a child does a slide on a playground.

The kind of thought lovers have, not killers.

And I both hate myself for even questioning him and feel the unwinding knot of relief.

Nash is innocent.

He's more than innocent.

He's giving and he's kind and he paints pictures of sunsets using playground imagery and a child's cry of delight.

He GETS the beauty of humanity.

And people who GET the beauty of humanity don't kill people.

You could make that point in court.

As I tuck the notebook back inside the bag, I slip out the laptop on principle. I open the lid and try a handful of password guesses. I even blush as I try my name. Nope. Let's pretend I never did that. Time to move on.

I check inside his coat pockets but get nothing but the scent of woods and the brush of leather on my fingertips.

I move at last to his bag. His weekender bag.

My bottom lip is pulsing from being clenched so fiercely through all of this. Which is better than passing out again, at least.

Do not pass out.

I summon my courage with the mental reminder that this is *not* betrayal (though it looks an awful lot like betrayal) but due diligence, and unsnap the straps of the bag.

Nash carries few items with him.

A couple of identical pairs of jeans.

A few folded flannel shirts.

He's the living picture of a man with a capsule wardrobe.

I slip my hand inside the various pockets around the bag.

Socks.

Deodorant.

I dig to the bottom of the bag and feel a bump under the flap at the bottom.

Freeze.

My fingers then curve slowly around the handle of something large and distinct.

Knife.

Slowly I pull it out, eyes widening until my fears are confirmed. A bloodied, caramel-colored cloth encapsulates a large knife. The type of hunting knife you might use to separate muscle from bone on a deer. The kind of knife that just might kill a person, or two, in the middle of the night.

It's plain to see.

One knife for Hugh. A second for Carragan.

Hugh's note directing us to beware of Nash. The knife in his room.

And it explains the Carragan murder. Perhaps he killed him and hid him under the bed while I slept. And then when he came back with me into the room, he stepped in first under the guise of "checking the place out," unrolled the body, and—*bam*—he has an alibi.

He just walked in with me, *practically* at the same time.

Airtight alibi.

And then throw a knife in Crystal's room for good measure and . . .

My heart feels like it lets out a deep, guttural groan of despair and I sink my head forward.

Despair for what was happening between us that will never happen. For a future together that will be no more.

And we were *so. Close.*

I was *so. So. So. Close* to such happiness.

I drop the knife in the bag rapidly, push it down until it's drowned in flannel, and snap the bag back exactly as it was before.

The whole way I'm running back upstairs, my hand is heavy at my side. An anchor at my side. Desperate to be scrubbed clean, but there's no time.

I skid to a stop as I near the corner and peek around it.

Nash is frowning, nervousness etched on his face, tea in hand. He scans the area.

And what I earlier assumed was worry for my safety shifts now as I see it with a pang of fear. What if he's nervous for other reasons? What's the saying? Keep your friends close and your enemies closer?

Quickly I move to the railing just out of view and drape my elbows over it. Staring out to sea and focusing everything in me on catching my breath.

Calming myself.

Settle down.

Calm.

My hand still pulses, and I look at it.

No sign of blood.

Yet still impure.

The salty wind whips at my face, quickly lapping up moisture that keeps rising in my tear ducts.

What are we going to do?

What can I do now?

I can't think about it.

Any thoughts just give way to a series of new fears, and those fears threaten to overwhelm me.

Don't. Think.

Just take it one step at a time.

Breathe.

Look at the horizon.

Breathe.

Focus solely on calming yourself down now, because you're about to give the most important lie of your life.

"Hey. There you are." Nash steps up to me. "Where did you go?"

I listen to the concern, bordering on frustration, in his voice.

Or is that anger?

Or is that . . . suspicion?

Focus, Pip.

I smile lightly as I turn to face him. He's holding out the tea for me. "I needed to walk. I needed to move around and clear my head."

"I searched the whole top floor for you."

"We must've been just missing each other." I motion to the circular loop around us and try to change the subject. "Did you run into Crystal on her hoverboard?"

"No."

I nod as though this sums it up then. "Yeah. Well, I was hoverboard side. You must've been on the opposite side as we went."

Nash's eyes are squinting at me, scrutinizing me as though he doesn't believe what I'm saying. "Okay," he says at last.

And it's over maybe.

The question is over.

This is my story.

He holds out the tea. "You want it?"

I feel myself hesitate, a foreign urge to resist taking anything from him at the moment. What if it's poisoned? What if . . . ?

But . . . to give him reason to have any more suspicion is unacceptable.

"Thank you." I take it and hold it to my chest.

The cup is warm, burning hot, I realize, against my fingers that are cold as ice.

"So. One more, then."

"Hmm?" I say.

"One more interview."

"Oh, right. Gordon. Yes." My eyes dance around as though expecting to land on him any moment. Suddenly the fact that Gordon is the sole beneficiary of Hugh's will matters little. It feels tedious to even talk to him now. But he's the last one on the list. "I probably ought to do that now before the evening session."

I hold the cup in one hand and pull out my phone with the other.

Nash frowns further. "Are you sure you have enough energy for this? Maybe you should go lie down—"

"*No*," I say, then feel a rush as I realize, *Nash sleeps in my room.*

How am I going to pretend I have no suspicions of him when I tell him I need to be alone in my room tonight?

Do I try to bunk with Neena?

Somehow the thought of her purple-sashed arms gives me a mental sense of warmth.

That's what I'll do.

I'll sleep on the floor of Neena's room. I don't know how a sixty-eight-year-old woman can protect me, but I have to believe her unbridled, temporarily insane joy will cover me.

Let's just focus on the *now*, Pip.

Those are trials to come.

Right now, it's time to talk to Gordon.

CHAPTER 22

"I DIDN'T KNOW SOMETHING LIKE THIS EXISTED ON this ship."

"Did you not?" Gordon says. His wizard hat is planted firmly on his head, and his hands are spinning at the retro-colored green and red buttons of the old arcade game. I can't be sure, but I believe he's winning. There are *quite* a few zeros beside his name.

"It's all so . . ." I scan the room. "Um . . ." How do I say this without offense exactly? "It just doesn't look like the kind of thing this type of cruise liner would have."

Let's just say, when booking, I was paying far more attention to the thread-count situation and free lobster than if it carried *Donkey Kong*.

But to be fair, the chaotically zigzagging golden, black, and red carpet looks like it is vacuumed every hour on the hour, and despite the thirty or so antiquated gaming machines around us, it's no challenge for the peacock bow-tie staff, who are roller-skating around all of us with silver trays in hand.

Someone drops a drink on a tray without looking away from their game, and the staff member doesn't even slow in gliding by.

There are sconces on the walls here, just like there are all around the ship, but these ones flicker ominously, purposefully, like we're in a dungeon.

And the wallpaper, most bizarre yet most fitting, is a deep maroon with figures of gold coins and dragons.

Hence the clever name to the place hanging over the door: The Dungeon.

"I like the one in The Hole better than this. It's bigger." Gordon makes a face. "But Hazel hogs the best machines."

"Who's Hazel?"

"Reader."

Ah. So we are now in petty wars with elderly guests we meet on a cruise ship. Nice.

"Have you not been there?" he says, finding this idea so preposterous that he's willing to break eye contact with the game to shoot me a glance.

I'm not sure of the goal still, but it looks like his game character is an elf who thoroughly enjoys bounding through a forest.

"No, I've only been down there once," I say, hedging the topic and the fact that the whole place gave me a panic attack.

One of his bushy salt-and-pepper brows rises as he looks me over. He shakes his head and returns his attention to the video game.

"What?" I say.

"You work too hard," Gordon says.

"Well, we've had a little *more* going on than just work."

He shakes his head, and it's silent between us but for

the manic tapping of his finger on the retro red and green buttons.

"You're too young and life is too short for you to be spending the whole holiday like this."

"Excuse me, but this is *serious*."

"It's somebody else's job."

"Who *isn't* doing his job."

"Do you know that with certainty?"

I swallow.

"You know, what's interesting to me is you can't help yourself, can you?" Gordon squints at me, seeing right through me. "You've got the investigator's heart. You can't leave things well enough alone. Hugh did too, you know."

I swallow.

The point is still too raw. "How can I possibly think of doing anything else at a time like this?"

Gordon waves a hand around us. "This is precisely what Hugh would've wanted us to be doing."

"This." My voice is flat as I look around. "Hugh would've wanted us to be doing . . . this."

"*Living.*"

He sighs. Pauses from the game (which promptly gets his character killed), fishes in his pocket, and pulls out a couple of quarters, which he hands to me.

"Here you go."

"What's this?"

"Play."

"I don't want to."

"Play a game."

"No."

"Trust me."

"How can I trust *anyone*?" I say, and dare a glance over

at Nash, who is standing guard beneath The Dungeon's entrance sign. To Gordon's credit, Nash looks the calmest and most distracted he's been in days.

Yes, Gordon has an entire inheritance and sum of who-knows-what being sent his way. But on the other hand, he's the least likely of us all and we all know it.

Or, of course, there's that horrible chance Nash is quietly writing his novel in the corner because, of course, he *knows* who the real murderer is.

It's himself.

Stop thinking about it.

Stop thinking or you're going to start passing out or crying or any of the things you need to NOT do right now.

Gordon pats my hand.

He draws my attention back to his eyes. They are soft. Gentle.

Wordlessly he guides me to the machine on the other side of him.

Wordlessly I follow.

"Tell me something, Penelope. Have you done *anything* relaxing in the nine days we've been on this ship?" He doesn't wait for me to answer. "You know, I'm a writer."

"I know that."

"As such, you know I firmly believe that our minds hold within them great capability to provide us with a dark or enchanted life. Not, in large part, our environments. Our brains. They can twist us up until we're in a cage and can't see our way out. Or they can make each day golden. The mind holds more power than our environment ever could. And the best part of all is that with great literature, we needn't leave the comfort of our own chairs to give our brains a jump start on great adventure. But in today's case . . ."

He takes the quarters from my hands and drops them into a machine.

"We'll take a shortcut."

A big yellow machine with a big yellow smiling ball staring at me.

Pac-Man.

I haven't played this in twenty years.

The *Pac-Man* game begins to ask for my attention.

"Go on," he says. "Just . . . let go."

Faintly I tap a button to answer the machine's question. Single player.

The game begins.

Gordon doesn't turn his attention back to his game until I'm racing the little yellow Pac-Man around the maze and I've gobbled up the second red cherry. I wouldn't say Gordon is right *entirely*, but there is something nice about having my attention on something else for a change.

It's as though my brain has been running an endurance marathon and finally gets a moment to rest.

With a decrescendo and confirming *beep beep* notifying me that the game is over, Gordon—without looking away from his own game—refuels my machine with quarters and I keep playing.

It's not until I'm five games in that he's willing to talk.

"Now," he says, giving me a brief look as his fingers play on, "I suspect it's my turn to be interviewed."

"That's correct," I say.

"And I'm . . . the last one, I hope?"

I nod.

"Well, I can tell you right now I didn't do it."

Maybe it's because it's been the longest week of my life, but I laugh. I'm getting fully delirious myself. "That's what everyone says."

"Is it?" he says, and raises not one but both of his bushy eyebrows over his blue eyes my way.

"Well . . . no," I say at last.

Now that I think of it, *nobody* has claimed innocence, have they?

Nobody, I guess, but Nash.

"Everybody has a clear motivation, means, and method. It's just that I assume they all would say they haven't done it."

"So I'm the only one who's really laid out that I'm innocent. Interesting." He whips the red ball around and his character spins over some kind of ogre. "So you think you know who it is?"

"I have no idea."

I have an idea.

But I'm deathly afraid to pursue it.

I'm deathly afraid . . . to pursue a reality where it's not Crystal. It's not Neena. It's not Ricky. It's not Jackie. No, it's Nash who's the perfect suspect.

What remarkable timing that after four years, he suddenly decides *now*, after a double murder, to tell me of his undying love for me.

What a remarkable instance that Carragan's body was found *in our room* in the middle of the night. And Nash? He was two minutes behind me in the hallway, wasn't he? How could a body get in our room like that so quickly? Unless . . . unless it was under the bed already. Next to Nash . . . as he waited for the perfect moment to dispose of it . . .

Maybe he'd planned to throw it overboard.

Maybe my waking him up, wanting to drag him down the hallway, was the perfect setup.

Easier to just roll it out a few feet in a matter of seconds.

Easier to look innocent with a sudden alibi when questioned.

*No, Officer, I was with Pip when we discovered the body in
our room. Right, Pip?*

Right, poor, gullible, love-dazed Pip?

Yes. For all but those two minutes.

Is everybody else terribly suspicious?

Yes.

But deep, deep down, it's Nash who fits the bill. You
can plant a weapon on someone. *Maybe* the knife made
it to his bag. But Hugh didn't leave a note telling me to
look into Nash for nothing. I need to dig deeper. Tonight,
in the silence, I *need* to look up everything I can about
Nash's life.

"If you were writing a book about all of this, who do you
think would be the murderer? How would you have master-
minded this plot?"

It's such a bizarre question, I find I have no prepared answer. "I'm not sure. I'd have to think about it."

"You wanted to write, did you not?"

"I . . . yes . . . for a time."

"And what's stopping you?"

I start to drop my hand from the *Pac-Man* game and he
gives a sharp look. I start playing again.

"If you're going to insist on trying to solve it yourself, at
least take yourself out of it," Gordon says. "Think like a nar-
rator. I always liked the omniscient POV myself."

"I . . . Gordon . . ." I'm so confused by all this, but the
reality is, he's taking over the interview. He's taking control
of the whole thing, and I need to grab the conversation back
by the reins. "Is it true you are the sole recipient in Hugh's
will?"

"I don't know," he says. "But I have a feeling you're about
to tell me."

"You are."

To my amazement, he seems completely unfazed. "Sounds about right."

"Do you *know* how much you're set to gain by Hugh's untimely death?"

"Millions, I suspect."

"Millions," I echo at the same time.

I wait in silence for him to respond.

He doesn't.

Just keeps playing his game.

"Well?" I say at last.

"Well, what?" he says back.

"Well, aren't you concerned that that makes you look extremely guilty in all of this?"

"Why should it? I'm not guilty."

"But you have a strong motivation. Money is a strong motivation."

"For the poor, the needy, and the perpetually discontent, yes. But I am none of those."

"Some people find they never have enough."

"Hence the term *perpetually discontent*. But I have learned to be content in all situations. Or at least in all situations I've come by in my time. I have everything I've ever needed."

I rub my eyes. "So you've never been jealous of Hugh?"

Gordon raises one bushy brow. "Why be jealous of someone else? What's the point? What's to gain? It's a gigantic waste of time."

"And you are financially in good straits?" I look at his game. "You don't . . . have . . . a gambling addiction or anything?"

That seems fitting.

We are here after all.

He chuckles. "We have a casino on board, Pip. Do you

think I'd be up here playing with quarters if I wanted that kind of trouble?"

Oh.

Right.

I have done what research I could on Gordon. As far as I know, he has no unique vices. Nothing, really. He's clean as a whistle.

I sigh. "Forgive me, Gordon, but I just can't get past this. Why *don't* you care? Hugh was among your best friends—"

"The best of the best."

"And yet here you are—not caring. At all."

"Who says that?" A flicker of a smile, one of those old, wise smiles, lifts his beard. "Who says there is only one way to grieve?"

That's all there is to it.

He didn't do it.

I take a breath.

"Gordon . . . what do you think of Nash?"

"Nash?" he says.

His brows rise as his gaze shifts to Nash and then back to me. I can see he understands the depth of the question. How I'm asking for *his* opinion, and his opinion only. There's weight to his words, and whatever he says next, well . . . it matters.

He purses his lips.

Pats my hand.

"I believe this is your interview, not mine."

"You won't tell me what you think?"

He shakes his head, easing my mind no more or less.

I sigh.

Gordon always has played by his own rules.

"Mind if I keep playing with you for a while?"

And at last, Gordon smiles.

Truly smiles and digs a handful of quarters out of his pocket.

His eyes twinkle. "I thought you'd never ask."

We spend the next couple of hours at that bizarre little dungeon of an arcade, watching each other play games and playing games ourselves. I'll never be a "gamer," but I will say, two hours and three fizzy Shirley Temples heavy on the cherries later, I'm feeling more refreshed than I have in a long time.

The world still doesn't make sense; nothing makes sense, but standing beside Gordon quietly cheering each other on as our players grab gold coins and eat imaginary cherries, well, it brings just a little fairy dust to the day. A little hope that not everything is going to stay dark forever.

"Well, I guess I gotta go back to the real world."

"It's the gamer's remorse. Probably wise to get out while you can."

"See you at dinner?" I say.

"I will. And before you go, Pip?" I feel the gentle press of his hand on mine. I turn.

His eyes are soft.

"Keep your chin up. I think we're nearer the end of this journey than we know."

⌒

"Six interviews down and done. Did you break through any mental walls back there?"

We are walking down the hall toward the dining room, and quite frankly, I hate myself for keeping a solid distance between myself and Nash.

Nash walks with his eyes alert but his hands in his pockets.
Afraid of something around the corner?

Or is he at peace knowing he's the only thing to fear on
board?

"Not yet," I say. I shake my head.

"Maybe it's as simple as someone else getting on the ship.
Some old criminal from Hugh's past. Revenge. That's the
most logical idea."

"They did know he'd be here," I say. "I publicized it enough
exactly where he'd be, sure. But"—I shake my head—"that's
not what Hugh alluded to."

"What?" Nash halts. "When he spoke with you the night
before he died?"

I flinch.

I'm guilty, aren't I?

He came to me, sharing his fears with *me*, and yet what
did I do?

Not take them seriously.

"He said he was afraid it was someone from the inside,"
I say.

"Yes, but did he know it for sure? He just felt threatened,"
he says. "It could've been anyone."

"Sure," I say, hedging around the fact that Hugh—or
possibly a skilled copycat—pinned the blame on Nash in
his letter.

A skilled copycat.

Could Ricky have . . .?

But surely even I could have copied that down . . . forged
his signature . . .

"I guess he could've been threatened by anyone. He wasn't
specific," I say.

"It absolutely would make sense if it was someone else.

What did he say again exactly?" Nash is keyed up about this direction.

He *likes* the attention being drawn away from any of The Six and spends the next five minutes breaking down, yet again, exactly why the most logical suspect is the one who got on board with an indirect relation to some handcuffed con man. Some elderly sister or mother or aunt of someone Hugh threw in jail.

Some elderly woman with the means, power, and motive to overtake two men when they least expected it and somehow slip one into my room when I wasn't looking.

I skirt away from the question and sit down at the same long table I've sat at the past several nights on this ship.

Darkness sweeps over the horizon outside the windows, and the glowing candles of the hanging chandeliers flicker with as much warmth and emotion as the ones in The Dungeon down the hall. White tablecloths have been replaced with deep red ones, each of the tables with its own set of flickering candlesticks dripping wax amid a cluster of votives.

Everybody else has come to this final feast on the ship in pearls and satin.

Emotions run high from nine long days at sea.

Tomorrow we set foot in Barcelona.

The trip is over.

A celloist plays solo in the corner, his bow sliding with long strokes against his instrument. The music swings between somber and sweet, I realize. I can hear both emotions in one tune.

A mood to be decided, I suppose, by your mind.

All the book cruise visitors are cheery, with cheeks sunburnt from days on deck with paintbrushes and salt water, minds energetic from daily workshops with favorite authors and new friends.

Everybody else is oblivious. And happy.

All in all (to their minds), the inaugural book cruise of The Magnificent Seven is a raging success.

As the meal is served, conversation buzzes around the room about evening activities in various venues all over the ship. A set of telescopes set up with a master astronomer. A slew of glowing bowling balls for a final tournament down in The Hole.

The Hole.

It was a horrid slang name for the bottom floor of the ship.

The rest of the musical ensemble joins in now, and a man who sounds an awful lot like Perry Como begins to croon across the room. It's not but a minute more before Neena is up and dragging Gordon along with her.

Our eyes connect as he walks to the center of the floor and takes her in his arms.

They begin to sweep along the dance floor.

He winks at me.

It's like he's saying wistfully, *See? See all that you can choose to live for? Go live.*

Slowly he dips her, and Neena, surrounded in a halo of shimmering purple, smiles like all is right in the world.

To everyone's surprise, several peacock bow-tie staff members walk to the tables and begin holding out gloved hands, and several ladies with broad smiles oblige.

Incredible.

Even the staff members dance.

"Want to dance, Pip?" I feel the press of Nash's hand on mine and look over.

There are approximately two male guests in a room of hundreds of ladies (not counting Ricky, who is currently inspecting an insect climbing up the wall), and one of them—the one who before all this I'd have wanted more than anything, more than Michael even, in my heart of hearts—is asking me to dance.

I feel his hand squeeze mine. "C'mon," he whispers, and I feel the heat creep up my spine.

"You don't dance," I say.

"When I'm in a room with the most beautiful woman in the world, I dance."

Nash Eyre is two people: a suspect on paper, and *this*.

The most wonderful man in the world.

And yet.

"It's a terrible time."

"Horrible," he agrees.

"We shouldn't be doing anything for ourselves at a time like this."

"Or ever again, most likely."

"But I guess . . ."

A tiny smile creeps up my lips.

Fine.

I'm the worst "investigator" in the world. I'm dancing quite possibly with the enemy. But I can't help myself.

"One dance."

Nash grins as his fingers curl around mine and he leads me to the dance floor.

He's quite a bit taller than me, pulling my posture straighter as I reach up and around his neck. His hand pulls around my waist, and for several seconds, we fall into a shuffling rhythm around the room.

Then suddenly his hand pushes me gently away at the

waist, his other hand holding tight to mine, and before I know it, I'm spinning and stepping sideways as we shuffle in the opposite direction.

His hands gently receive and release me a dozen times, this way and that in rhythm, and before I know it there are gentle swoops and smiles going around the room. Watching us.

It's effortless movement.

Somehow I step and glide around in ways I've never known before.

The tune drifts into a slower beat after one particularly energetic chorus, and Nash's hands receive me back into his arms one final time, and this time don't let go.

I'm breathless, I realize, with a mix of surprised euphoria and movement.

There's a little smile at the curve of his lips, put there, I'm guessing, by the feel of me clinging to the collar of his shirt with one hand and gripping his hand tightly in the other. His head dips toward me as we shuffle, his hat forming a sort of curtain separating us from the rest of the world.

I'm almost standing on tiptoes to be closer.

Him dipping down, me rising to meet him.

"I didn't know you danced," I whisper lowly.

"There was a girls' camp down the road. They always needed volunteers for the final ball. Let's just say, my mother was awfully generous with her five boys."

My laugh is warm, rich, and foreign to my own ears, it's been so long.

I feel his hand pull me in closer in response.

"What a kind mama," I say.

He smiles, and we spin again.

"They were all beautiful, I'm sure," I say. "Probably all quite smitten with you too."

"Who was?"

"All those pretty girls dancing with the charming and mysterious future writer in the cowboy hat."

"Them? Sure," he says, and I feel a twinge of heat despite myself. Don't ask a question if you can't bear the response. "But I have a type."

"Which is what? A penchant for girls in cardigans?"

"Sure. Who doesn't appreciate a good cardigan. And—"

"The kind who hates spiders?"

"A girl with survival skills. Very attractive."

"The helpless type high in self-loathing and poor self-esteem?"

His expression becomes puzzled. He pulls back to scan my face fully. "No, not that one. I've never met that one. I mean the brilliant, down-to-earth one who keeps an unruly group of literary fools in line and has a heart too big for her own good and makes me laugh and has an unnerving ability to break into places."

"Oh." I purse my lips. "That one."

"Yes. That one."

Nash's eyes are tender.

He doesn't pressure, doesn't pull.

There's never an urgency with him.

He just . . . waits, perfectly content to just be in this moment.

He has the self-assurance to look at me without wavering, to be confident in who he is and what he wants.

I grit my teeth.

It's painful.

It actually feels like my heart is *ripping* apart, longing so much to trust him with my whole person and yet forced to withhold.

On the one hand, to kiss him right here, right now, so

hard the chandelier falls, and on the other, to sleep at night with doors locked and both eyes open.

To fall in love with a potential murderer.

But who are we kidding? I fell in love with him a long time ago.

I can't live like this. I can't live like the others.

Like Neena beside me. Like Gordon.

How they can stand to drift together in and out, holding each other as partners while also considering each other a murder suspect . . . one would think it impossible.

The world swirls around them and they look like they're blissfully in the very center of it. Glittering chandelier overhead. Dozens of readers in their chiffon and satin, eating and making merry on all sides. Gordon and Neena twirling round and round in a rhythm of their own.

Gordon.

And Neena.

Cheek to cheek.

Nose to nose.

I slow.

Lean back and take a proper look at the two of them.

Neena's got her sheer purple scarf wrapped around the pair of them. Gordon's got his hand around her waist, fingers splayed, as they move in rhythm. His gaze is so intent on her, well, he looks at her like he looked at the game when he saved the princess and won the high score. He looks . . . well . . . if I didn't know better . . . in love himself.

"I've always had a weakness for a man in a good hat," I whisper.

"What?" Nash says, and I pull away, looking into his face.

"Neena said that when we got on the ship our first day. I thought at the time she was talking about the captain, but

Gordon. I never imagined . . . *Gordon.* He was right there all this time."

I remember the picture clearly. She was looking behind me just as the captain passed. The captain *and* Gordon wearing hats. I just assumed . . .

Nash follows my eyes toward the pair and together we watch.

"How long do you think it's been going on?" I say.

"I don't know," Nash says. "They didn't put up a fight when they were bumped from that flight to the German Book Festival."

"That's *right*," I say, remembering. They volunteered themselves to hop off the overbooked flight like it was nothing. Acting like taking a 3 a.m. flight was no big deal.

But of course it's a big deal.

Taking a red-eye is of course a big deal.

"You remember what she said?" I say. "He volunteered to step off the flight and she jumped up a moment later and said, 'Oh fine. I'll go. I wanted a Toblerone bar at the Duty Free anyway.' Who gives up eight hours for a Toblerone bar?"

"I love Toblerones."

"*Everybody* loves Toblerones. They're *delicious*. But the point is—" I wave a hand out at the two of them. "Hang on," I say suddenly, letting go.

I move toward our table.

"You want me to come?" he says.

"You want to stay here and dance alone?"

Together Nash and I make our way back to our table. Nobody notices or says anything, other than the occasional compliment offered our—mostly his—way.

I slide into Neena's old chair.

Nash slips down beside me.

"Help me look normal," I say. "Make conversation. Laugh."

I glance around. Everybody else is distracted.

Crystal is over by the bar chatting with the bartender.

Jackie's writing in her notebook, stiffly doing her best to push off a staff member trying to persuade her to dance.

Ricky's now in the corner reading with the spider climbing up the wall.

I wait for the perfect moment, casting my eyes around the room, then drop my hand below the table.

Neena's purse.

"What's the first thing you're going to do when you get off this ship?" I say, all the while carefully unzipping the purple pleather.

Nash warily assesses my hand digging under the table, while I urge him with my eyes to stay focused on my face. "I'm . . . uh . . . intending to step on land, grab you, and shoot a thousand miles in the opposite direction of here."

"Barring you aren't the murderer, I think that's an excellent plan."

"Should we grab a coffee in Barcelona first?"

"Can't imagine why we wouldn't."

"Want to swing by Ireland on the way home?"

"I can be persuaded."

My fingers tickle against a box of tissues, an unidentified number but seriously way too many tubes of lipstick, a sewing kit, two books, and a loose deodorant without any top. Then my fingers curl around the capsule and I pull it out.

Got it.

"Are they still preoccupied?" I say, eyes on him.

His eyes dance around while I unscrew the pill bottle. "Yes."

The bottle is half full, and as I tip it over into my hand, half a dozen pills spill out.

Six round white pills. Unidentified.

I bring them to my nose and sniff.

Then, to Nash's horror, I pop one in my mouth.

"What are you—?"

I grin.

Pop another one in and ruthlessly clamp it between my teeth.

Everything clicks into place.

Lightning strikes of clues now, and I decide to chase them.

I look over to Jackie, who is scribbling away in her notebook.

Then Ricky, who has somehow guided the spider into a glass.

Crystal, who is over at the bar, bragging to everyone now about one of her life stories.

It's a classic case.

Hugh's *The Last Detective*.

Everybody is guilty, ergo no one is.

"Kiss me," I say.

"*What?*" he says. He raises his brow, eyes dancing around for clues, gazing from me, to the pill between my teeth, to the air around us. "What happened? Why now?"

"Four reasons," I say. "Because you're not the killer. Because I love you. Because, I have realized in all this, I love myself. And you know what? I deserve this. I deserve good things. And lastly, because I've read about how smell is uniquely powerful in triggering vivid and emotional memories, and I for one will be drinking peppermint tea every day to remind me of this. Exact. Moment."

Nash's hands envelop mine. I can see him processing my words with each passing second he gets closer. A light reaches his eyes. Then a twinkle. Then a smile. "Peppermint kiss, you say?"

I grin. Crack the peppermint in my mouth. "A peppermint kiss," I repeat.

"That does sound refreshing." His eyes drift down to my nose, then lips. A smile tugs up his lips and I feel my heart race, the moment stretching.

I don't wait.

I can't.

I don't have another millisecond of patience in me.

I reach up, grab him by the collar, and pull him toward me. My breath catches as his hands gently cup my cheeks. His thumbs brush lightly over my skin, sending a shiver down my spine.

I draw his lips to mine, brushing lightly. His beard tickles my cheeks. He leans in further, his hands cupped around my face.

My fingers curl into his flannel.

Sparks fly.

Maybe it's on the outside. Maybe a transformer blew and the chandelier will fall down any moment. Maybe the candles have tipped over and the tablecloths are on fire. Maybe the world is in absolute chaos and the whole ship is about to go down.

Or maybe it's all just inside.

But whatever it is, I hold fast to Nash with the same ferocity as he holds fast to me, in the hope of never letting go.

I guess that's what happens when four years of waiting finally comes to an end.

When we break apart, the room is spinning, the dancers are spinning. My head is spinning. But Nash is still right here. His head bent over mine. Forehead to forehead. So close our noses graze.

"I love you, Pip," he whispers in a peppermint haze.

"I love you too," I whisper back.

I bite my bottom lip.

Inhale one more breath of this incredible moment.

Then stand. "Be right back," I say.

"Wait! Where are you going?" Nash says as I begin to stride off.

"To find the last clue and see if I'm right," I say and begin running. Over my shoulder I cry, "And if I am, to kill somebody myself."

CHAPTER 23

BREAKING INTO RICKY'S ROOM WAS EASY.

"Why are we breaking into Ricky's room now?"

And a bit to my pride, I notice Nash sounds a little winded from chasing me.

I cautiously step inside. Flip on the lights.

Part of me expected some random concrete gargoyle sitting on the desk.

Or a laser beam setting off sirens, letting him know we're here.

Or something in general to ease his ever-suspicious mind. But no, nothing.

The room is tidy, stacks of books neatly kept to one corner. A closed laptop on the desk. A neat row of fully sharpened pencils beside a notepad.

And, oh, there it is, a knife.

I throw my head back. "*Yesssss.*"

The relief is . . . well, let's just say I have *never* been more relieved *in my life*.

"Ah. Here it is," I say, stepping to it. "How thoughtful of him to keep it out for me."

"What?" Nash says, confused. "*Another* one?"

I pick up the knife and flip it over. Dried red stains streak across the stainless-steel shaft and dark handle. I bring it closer to my face.

If I'm not mistaken, this one's a little bigger than the others. And where is the cloth?

I look around Ricky's desk. Check the floor. The drawers.

I find it neatly folded into a red-stained square beside the remote. Naturally.

"It's one of them, yes," I say, setting the knife back where I found it.

"And you were expecting there to be more?"

"One in every room, to be precise."

Ah. And here comes the rage.

Relief is giving way, sure enough, to a level of anger I'm not sure I've quite experienced before. Relief-rage. It's a thing, a new thing, quite possibly, at least for me, and my fingers seem to be bursting with power as I swing back the door to Ricky's room and begin my charge down the hall.

"Want to do a job for me, Nash?" I call over my shoulder.

For once he's struggling to keep up.

He's scratching his head. "Sure. What?"

"Break into Neena's room while I'm gone. Let me know when you have confirmation you found the knife in her room too. Gordon's too, if you can. It'll be good for you. Practice your cat burglary skills."

"Where are you going? I'll come—"

I halt. Swivel round with my hand raised. "With all due respect, I'm in love with you, Nash."

He frowns. Crosses his arms over his broad chest. "Thank . . . you?"

"And I'd like you to stay in love with me."

"I don't think . . . you know how it works—"

"And right now, I'm about to put some hurting on somebody. And it won't be pretty. And it may get violent. And before you find me terrifying—"

Nash purses his lips. "You already are a little. Right now."

"I'm going to keep this happy dreamy daze going a little bit longer." I motion between the two of us. "Let's just keep this cotton candy vibe going for as long as we can."

"This relationship started in the middle of a murder investigation. So . . ."

"Well, the investigation ends now."

"I can't let you put yourself in danger."

I laugh. One of those very forceful, *I'm seriously going to get somebody as soon as I leave here* laughs. Maybe that type of laugh didn't exist in the world before this moment, but it sure does now. "Oh, believe me. The last person you need to be worrying about right now is me. And you're just going to have to trust me." I purse my lips, knowing full well that the next words that come out of my mouth will seal the deal. "Just like I trust you."

He raises a finger. "Now, that's not fair."

I smile. Smile like someone who has won. "Sure it is."

Nash frowns at me for some time, his lips pursed beneath that beard of his.

I stare him down right back.

Eventually he drops his head, his hat bowing to the ground as he waves a hand. "Fine. I'll call you when I finagle the lock and get into this next room. But I'm more accustomed to doing legal things."

"You'll be a natural, I'm sure of it."

I wheel around and race down the hall, hit my finger to the down button on the elevator, and step inside.

My heart is racing.

My chest is pounding.

Relief-rage.

It's a most fitting term.

And that relief-rage fills my senses and propels me forward with enough power that I don't even hesitate until I've stepped off the elevator to The Hole (*terrible name*), charged past the piano bar, and I'm two more shops down the hall.

I'm good mentally until I look back, and the exit (i.e., elevator) is so far away it's blocked by people.

You're fine.

You can do it.

I take a breath, trying not to focus on the zigzag pattern of the carpet or the growing noise.

Things are more neon down here, less antique gold and more glow, less the glissando of the harpist and more the loud speakers of the dance floor. It's darker, louder, and, overarchingly, far less charmed.

I hate it.

The growing tension gnaws at my stomach—the fight-or-flight reaction building for me suddenly to bowl people over and get out.

I urge myself on.

It's the worst of dreams, the kind where your feet feel like lead as you drag yourself forward. This is me inching forward while oblivious shoppers breeze by with their bags and takeaways.

At last, and with great mental endurance and emotional sacrifice, I stand beneath the large and glorious script of the last and final room: THE BLUE LAGOON LOUNGE.

"Hi, may I help you?" a host vaguely says to my left.

I don't look at him.

I don't have the capability, quite honestly, to look.

I'm zeroed in on my goal and, without wavering left or right, take steps toward the end in sight.

Everything around me is basked in an ethereal blue. It looks like we're in a shell, a white shell, with ribs of white sweeping this way and that without true purpose or order. Dozens of white tables and white chairs pop around the room; everything is white or a glowy blue. The place is packed. It looks like this is the hottest commodity on the ship.

Onstage somebody sings karaoke, following glowy blue words in a pitchy tune. I make the mistake of looking left and nearly fall to my knees.

A dozen booths line the left side of the wall, each featuring a massive oval-shaped glowing porthole. Each porthole looks straight into ocean just on the other side of the glass. They've actually put lights underwater for people to see.

People to see straight out into the deep, dark ocean with just a few layers of glass between us.

I'm going to throw up.

You can do this, Pip.

You have gotten over Michael.

You have braved the past few days.

You are braver than you once thought.

You are smarter than you realized.

You are worthier than you have been led to believe.

You can do *anything* you set your mind to.

YOU JUST HAVE TO HOLD ON A LITTLE LONGER.

It takes several seconds, but I manage a step forward.

And another.

And another.

My eyes begin to rove around.

I've caught the attention of the host, who comes up beside me. "Are you sure I can't help you with something? Do you see what you're looking for?"

The host prattles on, but I stop him when my eyes come upon it, and forcing myself forward ten more steps, I reach the piano.

I pick up the envelope gingerly.

Break the well-known seal.

Read the text in Hugh's infamously known scrawl.

Bravo, Pip.

I knew you would do it.

You will find me, and end the game, when you give me what I want.

Tell our story.

CHAPTER 24

"A GAME?! I CAN'T *BELIEVE* HE WOULD PULL THIS KIND of stunt on us. It's insanity, that's what it is. True *insanity!*"

I've never seen Nash this enraged before.

Actually, I've never seen him angry at all.

Nash and I are back in the room, the poor room that has been torn to shreds in my haste to try to make sense of this horrible case of murder of my boss and one of my dearest friends. A visual example of the chaos my life has been the past nine days.

For my boss and one of my *dearest friends*.

Yup. I am. I am going to kill him.

Nash has been pacing back and forth the past hour in front of the bed where I sit cross-legged in a heap of papers, tapping away at my computer. I have at least twenty-five tabs open on my laptop.

"How are you not fuming at this, Pip?"

"I am," I say calmly, continuing to type.

"But doesn't it make you want to rip down the wall?"

"Certainly," I say, flipping over to another tab on my computer. "But I've become accustomed to a certain level of chaos. It comes with the job. And then there's the fact . . . he's alive."

My rage-relief has slipped out of proportion the past few hours.

I'm more 30 percent rage and 70 percent relief now.

Still furious, but the world has at least righted itself yet again.

Hugh is alive. Neena, Jackie, Crystal, Gordon, and even eerie Ricky are innocent.

Nash is by my side.

Better yet, Nash and I are *together*.

I feel better than I have in a long time.

There's going to be one *heck* of an explanation needed for all this, and a salary increase demand of at least 50 percent or I'll sue. I'm fine. We're all fine. Life, in its most sincere and beautiful word, is *fine*.

"What does he want? It can't be money. Can it?"

My raised eyebrow is my answer.

"Is this part of the sick game then?" Nash says. "Another twisted clue?"

"The game is up," I say. "Least, the first part is over. I've solved it. Hugh isn't dead."

"And yet," Nash says broodily, "I can't believe everything he's done to us the past few days. And for what? I know he likes his little games, but this has gone too far."

"No, there's something about this one," I murmur, more to myself than Nash. I lean back from my computer and reach for my notebook. I begin flipping through my notes. "This isn't research for him. This isn't some party trick gone wrong. He's really after something. But what—?"

"I'm going down again to try to find him."

"Won't work. He's MIA. They all are."

"*Traitors*," he hisses.

I nod.

What else is there to say?

Everybody has disappeared since I discovered the envelope. I don't know who was watching me, or from what vantage point, but after combing through the lounge and finding nobody, I raced upstairs, only to find everybody gone. They weren't in the dining rooms. They weren't in the lounges or the libraries or on deck. Nobody was in their bedrooms, and believe me, I picked every single lock.

They disappeared.

The group I had thought was so broken apart is still united after all.

This time, just against us.

"I can't stand here anymore."

"I agree. You're about to pace a hole in the floor."

"I'm going to look again. I'm going to bang on every door on this ship trying."

"We made it this long without making a scene on the ship," I say. "We've only got a matter of hours left. Let's not ruin it now."

I snap my computer shut.

I can't look at any more of his old books.

The words are all starting to blur.

"I'll come with you, though. We can at least walk the halls."

This has been our rhythm the past three hours, bouncing from poring over laptops and notebooks for clues to circling the ship for people. Neither journey has been successful.

Hugh doesn't want money.

He doesn't want a bribe.

He doesn't want any *thing* that I can possibly think of.

The closest I can guess is that he really wanted to get his newest book on the front page of the *Times* magazine, but what power do I have to make that happen?

I have no control over that.

What does he expect me to do? Pull imaginary strings from my imaginary black book of influential contacts? (Okay, fine. I do have some epic contacts, I've realized.)

At any rate, what does that have to do with "our story"?

"You know what we could do that we haven't considered?" Nash says as we hunt in the halls. "We could just ignore him. Ignore them all. Let's just pretend they don't exist. We don't have to play their games."

"But we will."

"Why's that?"

"The same reason we're speed-walking now. And they know that. Hugh knows that. We're too livid not to see this through."

He growls. "I hate being Hugh's pawn."

"Welcome to the club."

We comb through the top three levels of the ship, then when our legs wear out, drop into the lounge chairs we stargazed from our first night here. The stars are out and sparkling at this ten o'clock hour, not so much as the other night, but enough to give us something to look at. Help us clear our heads.

I sigh and sit back, resting my head against the chair.

"Maybe if we just take a beat," I say. "Worst-case scenario, we *will* see them tomorrow getting off the ship. We can be the first off. Wait for the sorry group to show up."

Nash is shaking his head, looking murderous. "I don't think it's wise for me to get near him right now."

I laugh, more of a release of energy than anything.

But then I laugh again. "Can you believe I thought they had killed him? Jackie? Ricky?"

"That one's not so far-fetched."

"Neena?" I shake my head, halfway disgusted with myself. "*You?*"

"How did you know about Neena? That was a lot of points to connect."

"I just followed the trail of logic. If Neena is in love with Gordon, then she didn't really have the motive to kill Hugh, did she? And if she didn't, her influencing me to believe she could have been angry enough at Hugh for breaking her heart was a lie. And if she was lying about being in love with Hugh, what else was she lying about? And then if the so-called anxiety pills she was popping to make her calm and easygoing weren't actually the reason she was so calm and easygoing, then what was?"

I shrug.

"The only possible thing I could think of that would allow her to be emotionally restored from the death of one of her oldest and dearest friends was exactly that: that there was in fact no death of one of her oldest and dearest friends. That *in fact* she was using those pills as a cover-up for the fact she was truly going to enjoy this vacation. And if there was no death of one of her oldest and dearest friends, then somebody was making it up. And the only person I know who would possibly make up something so *stupid* is the man himself. Hugh. And where is the one place Hugh knew I wouldn't visit while on this cruise? A little karaoke lounge deep in the hole of the ship, which I would avoid after he just so happened to give me a phobia organizing a recent diving trip."

Nash pulls up to sitting from his lounge position. His

brow furrows in disbelief. "You don't think. No. He wouldn't do something *so* bad as to give you a complex—"

I raise a finger. "No? You don't think he would plan months ahead to play with my head for the point of this game?"

Nash frowns toward the dark abyss ahead. "I severely underestimated that man . . ."

I drop my head. "Okay, fine. He didn't *create* a complex in me. He probably just discovered my issues on our last research trip and decided to use it to his advantage. The reality here is he decided to use the lounge as a hangout while waiting for me to face my fears—or get *ticked* enough—to go down there."

Nash shakes his head. "And?"

"And what?"

"And how did it feel? Facing your fears?"

I take a breath. "Not *great*, per say, but . . ."—I exhale—"it was progress and that's something. Baby steps in the right direction."

"Does that mean you're going to sign up for another cruise?"

I shake my head. Laugh. *"Never."*

"What might you do? Go diving again?"

Another shake of my head. "More like I'll walk inside a basement apartment again. I'm going to look at this like *let's get my discomfort under control so I can manage average realistic situations I may end up in in normal life,* not *let's get used to confined places so I can go scuba diving for megalodon teeth in the Florida Keys.*"

"That's an admirable goal."

"Thank you."

I pause. Take a breath. "What about you, Nash? Does the

tall, strong author-cowboy have any weaknesses? Because I've been around you awhile now, and I'm pretty convinced you're not human."

"Oh, I have plenty of 'em. But I know better than to fall for that trick. I'd rather you find out my weaknesses one by one. Spread 'em out a little. Give me a fighting chance."

I laugh. "Fine. Tell me one weakness. Just one. Make me feel better."

"You really want to hear my weaknesses?"

"I really do."

Nash sits up. Leans closer. "I'm a horrible speller."

I squint. That's pathetic. "You . . . can't spell."

"My editor hates me for it. I have to look up simple words. Like *vacuum*."

"Nobody can spell *vacuum*. We're forever second-guessing ourselves on the one *c* or two."

"And *embarrassed*."

"Is it one *r* or two? We all wonder—"

"And *buoy*."

"What are you even doing using the word *buoy* in your novels? They're all in the desert, it's illogical."

"And *bellwether*."

"What's a *bellwether*?"

"And *apparently*."

"Okay, that one's on you—"

I halt. And with a sharp inhale jump to standing.

Nash looks up with a laugh. "What? *Apparently*'s too far? That's the line?"

"I figured it out," I say in shock.

My mind begins to reel.

Everything is beginning to click.

Books.

Words.

The distant words from Hugh I've heard a hundred times.

When are you going to give me what I want, Pip? I want to see that first chapter. It's all as simple as getting down that first chapter.

That's what Hugh wants.

The first chapter.

Of *our* story.

Life this week.

In a book.

CHAPTER 25

I RACE BACK TO MY ROOM AND OPEN UP THE FIRST chapter of my forever work-in-progress. It's been so long since I've opened it that I squint having to reread it again. It's painful.

Thirty-two pages of a horrible start to a horrible story that, if continued, would no doubt meet a horrible end.

Is this really what all this work was for?

This drivel?

And the worst part is, for the thirty-two-page, three-year-long project, it *still* isn't a complete chapter.

Nothing of the sort.

Just a girl wandering around aimlessly, much like me the past few days on this ship. Without a clue.

Without a goal.

At least, I guess, I had a *goal* the past few days we've been on the ship.

If the story had been about *me* these crazy past few days . . .

I suck in a breath so sharply that Nash says, "What?" from the other side of the room.

I just shake my head.

The pieces are coming together, the ideas falling into place better than this old trash heap of a working manuscript I've wasted so much time on.

I'm too scared to say anything out loud, my hope rising like a rocket from its launching pad, and so I don't say anything.

I open a new document.

Type a word.

Two.

Precisely eighty-six minutes of nonstop typing later, I sit back against the pillow and headboard of the bed. I can't believe it.

My fingers are bent with overuse and probably destined to be so for some time. They need icing. My brain needs icing. Everything needs icing.

But for the first time in my entire life, I did something I didn't know was possible.

I wrote.

I . . . as it turns out . . . can write.

I *can* write.

I had to *finally* let go of that old, dead-end story and be willing to give my mind a fresh start—as Hugh always said.

I've got a first chapter fleshed out, and better than that, even, an outline—nothing as good as Gordon's but far more polished than Hugh's—that'll guide me through the rest of the book to a complete end.

I just needed a push.

A rather big push, as it turns out.

One from a friend who . . . quite possibly . . . was willing to fake his own death to give it to me.

"Congratulations. How did it feel?"

The bed dips down as Nash sits beside me. His arm wraps around my shoulders. His gaze shifts from me to the computer.

He looked over my shoulder at some vague point, but when it was clear what I was doing, he pulled back and gave me some space. Eventually he pulled out his own computer and for some time the room was silent but for the typing on our computers.

It was quite cozy in fact.

Quite . . . special.

I'd like nothing more than a thousand more nights, ten thousand more nights, together, like this.

I'm grinning from ear to ear. "Great. Too great for words, actually. How was your writing time?"

"I just finished. Thank you for asking."

My brow rises. "You finished your book?"

He nods. "And you got your feet under yours. I'd say congratulations are in order for us both. You're one of us now, I think. You've got the bug."

"I've got the confidence. I . . . *can* do it." I'm still marveling.

"Of course you can. You always could."

"I know. But this time . . ." I pause, shaking my head. "You know, it's not as hard to write a book as I thought."

Nash laughs. A big, mirthful laugh. "I look forward to our talk when you're in edits. We'll see how you like it then." His lips brush my cheek, leaving a breezy peck before I see his smiling eyes again. "I kid, Pip. You're going to be great."

I extend a kiss, a longer one this time, and when I pull back, I say, "Hey. I don't know if you're busy tomorrow, but . . . if you're not . . . I've got another chapter to do."

"Are you asking me on a date?" His eyes twinkle. "A writing date?"

I grin.

"Oh, you've got the bug bad," Nash says with a laugh. "Even solving a murder on your first day in Europe, you're talking about work."

"I just . . . I have these ideas running through my head *now*—"

"I know the feeling, Pip. You're in welcome company. I can't imagine, though, with your drive for analyzing . . . I wonder . . ."

"What?"

"Oh, I'm just looking forward to seeing how this all plays out. What kind of writer you're going to end up being. Slow and meticulous or rabid fast."

I snap my computer shut.

Pop it open again on second thought; email my chapter to at least twelve different trusted sources. Then shut it again.

"What was that for?" Nash says.

I'm halfway to the door and stop. "I may be new to writing, but I've been around all you people enough years to know you never, *ever* trust your book to be saved in one place. I'll die if I go through one of your lost-manuscript sagas. It's in your inbox for safekeeping. And Neena's. And even creepy Ricky's. Now, c'mon."

"Where are we going?"

"To give Hugh the final piece of the puzzle."

CHAPTER 26

THE BLUE LAGOON LOUNGE IS EXACTLY AS I'D PIC-
tured it would be at ten o'clock on the final night on the
ship. The room smells of sautéed basil and steak simmer-
ing in buttery garlic—probably because a waiter just walked
past with a steaming set of steaks on a platter.

There is no shortage of dishes being passed around the
tables.

On one table, a gigantic centerpiece consists entirely of
crab.

And of course . . . there's music.

Nash and I step farther into The Blue Lagoon, and sure
enough, the person holding a microphone while singing
right at this moment is not dead Hugh, but very much a
live Hugh.

Onstage.

Dipping the microphone attached to a stand like he's
Frank Sinatra himself.

People clap when he dips again, and again when he gives

an upbeat little twirl. Nobody looks surprised to find him here. In fact, everyone looks tremendously pleased.

Almost as though . . .

"Hey, has he been here all week?" I say to a table full of ladies.

"Of course he has, honey," says a woman with a tint of blue in her silvery hair. "Ten o'clock on the dot. Hugh's Nightly Special."

Somebody elbows the woman in the ribs with a specific look my way. "That's Penelope Dupont," she hisses.

The woman in blue looks up sharply. "Although . . . I don't know . . . precisely. I just got here . . ."

Seriously?

They're in on it too?

EVERYBODY'S IN ON IT?!

"What has he been doing?" I say. "Just singing?"

"Well, and the workshops—"

She gets elbowed again and amends, "But I couldn't be sure."

I roll my neck. Face Nash. "Oh my *gosh. That's* why I didn't get a thousand angry emails. He told *everyone* to just not talk to *me.* I mean, I emailed everyone that he was ill, but still, I knew that was weird. People aren't that considerate when it comes to money. Dozens of demands should have come through for a refund. You know what? I bent over *backwards* the past week working to find replacement authors for those workshops and have them call in. I pulled a dozen big, huge strings. And here he was all this time, giving workshops *and* a show."

"It's fine to ask for favors."

"I *begged* Trudy Louis, Nash. Like on my knees begged. On FaceTime."

Nash tucks in his lower lip to keep from smiling.

I swing back to the dinner party of ladies.

"Tell me something. Did he tell you not to talk to me? What'd he say, exactly?"

The blue-haired lady opens her mouth, but the one with the crab legs smacks her and interjects. "He's right up there, sweetie. If you've got questions, you just need to ask him yourself."

"Oh, believe me, I will."

I straighten.

Hugh's blue eyes meet mine now. They positively twinkle as he carries on singing his tune.

Does he not fear me?

At all?

Out of the corner of my eye, I see the rest of the gang.

Neena calls to me, but I flash her a *deeply* intense glare, the kind of glare that says *Oh, don't worry, I'll be talking to you five in a second,* and zero back in on Hugh.

He puts a hand up.

The music stops.

"And for our workshop finale in this greatest and most highly anticipated book tour, I'd like to invite up our special guest to help us finish our time together. Ladies and gentlemen, the woman we've all been waiting for," Hugh announces. "Let's give a round of applause."

Claps go around the room, and he puts out a hand to help me onstage. I pointedly don't take it and pull myself up.

"I *should* be ripping that microphone out of your hand and hitting you on the head with it," I snap.

The room stills.

It's just me and Hugh in the circular blue spotlight onstage.

Like an act.

A few people laugh, thinking it's all a bit.

"For the record," I say, "I'm *livid*."

"But?"

"You had *no right*."

"But?"

"This was *entirely* over the line and you will be paying me back *handsomely*."

Hugh tilts his head. Waits. "But?"

"But . . ." I wait for ten long seconds, then at last I hold out my computer, open, to chapter 1. "I'll give you this."

Hugh's eyes float over the document for a brief, confirming moment. "Is this a . . . full chapter?"

"Yes."

"About this?" he says, pointing around us.

"Yes."

"And has our Pip . . . found her voice?"

And this time I can't help it. I let slip a tiny smile. "Yes."

"Aw, Pip. I knew you would."

The room swells. People begin clapping.

Neena, perfectly as expected, begins to cry.

Gordon puts a comforting arm around her.

Jackie looks stiff and uncomfortable as she puts forward a couple of tight claps.

Crystal. Where is Crystal?

I freeze, then point to two men——one older, one much younger—sitting at a round table. "Is that . . . Pogache and Carragan?"

One of them, the burly Carragan, raises a frothy glass of beer at me. "I'm Bob, actually. And you've met my son, Trent. Not too bad for a seventeen-year-old, was he?" he says, proudly grinning as he elbows his son at the table.

Hugh jumps in. "Pip, I don't think you've met Bob Moore, one of my old buddies down at the station. Good sport, wasn't he, for helping us out?"

"Thank you for the free trip," Bob says, raising his ale again.

"Fake security?" I say, dazed.

That certainly helps things make sense.

"Well, it would have been exceedingly challenging to pull it off without him, wouldn't it?" Hugh says, like *of course*. "I certainly couldn't have taken my own body away on a stretcher. I certainly couldn't have interrogated you poorly enough to make you do it yourselves."

The world truly *does* make sense again.

"I *knew* he was an awful detective," I say, pointing. "I mean, innocent until guilty, yes, but letting murderers just *roam free* in secret? And two people *dead?*"

Hugh laughs. "Without some incompetence, the competent don't rise to the occasion."

I guess that's true.

I guess . . . everybody's mind-numbing, absolutely infuriating carefree attitude about everything is precisely what drove me to solving this thing.

"Tell us," Hugh says, "what was the final clue that led to your breakthrough?"

He swings the microphone on its stand my way, like we're in a lecture hall now and not exactly where we are. Onstage. In a basement. Of a cruise ship.

I hesitate. This really is the finale of his workshops, and the finale of the cruise, and here I am, the finale guest. "I . . . I don't know where to begin," I say. "There were several clues. The knife in Nash's bag, for one. I remembered the same weapons found in different hands played out in your book *Twice Down the River.*"

Hugh wags a finger as he grins at me, then the audience. "She's a smart one, folks. *This*, my friends, is the brain behind all my research. She can tell you more about my books than *I* can. Alright, so go on. What else led you to the discovery?"

"Well, in this case, everyone had a bloody knife on their person or property that could be linked to them. Everybody was guilty; ergo, nobody really was. At first I found the knife in Crystal's room and initially was led to believe she was guilty, but then after I realized Neena had lied about her anxiety medication and it was really mints, I went hunting in Nash's room. Soon enough, it became clear everyone had the weapon."

"Good. And . . . ?"

"And then," I begin tentatively, "there was the strange way everybody reacted during the trip. At first they were devastated, but one by one they all took on surprising characteristics. Almost as though they *wanted* to be guilty. Neena hinted that she was deeply hurt, possibly to the point of committing murder, after you ditched her years ago from engagement—"

Hugh laughs at that. "I liked that one."

"And yet I realized she's in love with Gordon."

Neena makes an uncomfortable grunting sound, and I swivel my head to her to see she looks openly embarrassed by the public announcement. "Well," she says, fanning herself, "guess the cat's out of the bag."

"Jackie claimed you had discovered she has a ghostwriter—"

"I do *not*," Jackie calls out tersely for all to hear.

"And that perhaps you would have used that information against her. Except for the fact Jackie is the most rigidly academic person I know."

Jackie's chin tips up. "Thank you."

"Ricky was terrifying in general—"

"Ricky didn't have a character role," Hugh interrupts. "Ricky was just Ricky, except for his task of handing you the fake letter."

So Ricky is just in general terrifying. That tracks.

"The security was funny. Pogache had a hard time stringing together an investigation and was grossly overinterested in hoverboards while missing actual weapons entirely—"

"Again," Bob calls out in a *give him a break* way, "seventeen."

"There were just several things."

"Tremendous. The murder mystery that ends in a karaoke party. A riot of an end. Now. As for *this* book." Hugh gently takes the computer from my hands. He swivels it around. "Let's take a look, shall we? Let's see what our future great American mystery writer has in store for us."

Hugh brings the laptop over to a barstool and sits down onstage, resting the laptop on his knees.

It's the oddest of experiences. Everybody, all the fellow book lovers and readers and novice writers, wait with bated breath while we watch Hugh's expression shift from the laughable, easygoing man I've known day in and day out for five years to what I term "professor mode."

Laser focused on the manuscript.

Tiny ripples of seriousness on his forehead.

Eyes that remain in a permanent squint as he reads line by line.

Professionally speaking, Hugh's fellow authors, publicists, and editorial team love when he does this.

I always love when he does this. It's as fascinating as watching a rare, nearly extinct animal in its natural habitat.

These are the moments when Hugh's insights are crystal clear, and when they come out, they come out with incredible accuracy. These are the moments when you realize you are in the company of brilliance.

Hugh, for all his faults (of which *clearly* there are many), is rarely wrong when it comes to manuscripts.

He's guided every single one of The Magnificent Seven over the years, and that one-on-one consultation alone has been worth millions.

I don't realize I'm crossing my arms so tightly I'm about to strangle myself until my chest starts constricting.

I scan his face for clues.

Is it horrible?

Is it beyond horrible?

I jump in when I can't take it anymore. "I only just wrote it now—"

"Obviously," he murmurs, eyes laser focused on the page.

"The idea just came, so it's a bit rough."

He doesn't reply.

"And of course, this is still very new."

He puts up a finger to shush me.

I reposition myself to stare at the wall in the distance (pointedly *not* the portholes).

At some point I look down at Nash.

He's standing at the bottom of the stage, giving me space to have this moment.

I raise a questioning brow at him.

Is this going to be a good moment or a bad-talent-show wreck of one?

He tries to give me an encouraging smile, but his expression can't lie. He doesn't know either.

It could go either way.

My chest is tightening, my breaths coming shorter both from the anxiety and from the fact that being down here *still* is incredibly challenging, and Nash is just putting both hands onstage to hitch himself up when Hugh sighs.

Nash freezes.

I freeze.

We all freeze.

Hugh sits back on the stool.

Looks up.

At me.

At the audience.

At each of The Magnificent Seven at their table.

He holds out both hands toward the computer like it's a brand-new baby and says proudly, "Well. She *did it.*"

The man certainly knows how to create a climactic moment.

Applause breaks out again, even louder this time.

Some even stand.

"She did it," he repeats over the crowd as he pulls me in and begins to heartily shake my hand. "Everybody meet the future mystery writer of America!"

"That's a little generous, isn't it?" I say quietly to him as he takes my hand and raises it in triumph to the crowd.

"A plot primarily about me?"

"Primarily about *me*," I interject.

He shrugs. "We can agree to disagree. What we can agree on, however, is that this book will be a *tremendous* hit. Everyone will know it. And if they don't at the beginning—what with you being new and all that, naturally— believe me, Pip, we'll make sure it happens. You've got the lot of us by your side."

I grin.

It's the first time I've felt the force of The Magnificent Seven. Oh, how every author longs for them by their side.

Hugh tilts his head. "What are you going to title it? *The Book Cruise? The Magnificent Seven? The Greatest Murder of All Time?*"

"*Without a Clue,*" I say without hesitation. And he laughs.

It's a fitting title for a girl like me, who ends up on a book

cruise only to find her boss and mystery giant has been murdered in the middle of the Atlantic Ocean, and due to the
incompetence of the security on board realizes it's up to her
and her amateur sleuthing skills to solve the murder before
they all hit land.

"You know, if this was all just to get me writing, it was
quite the risk," I say. "Making me believe lives were at risk,
giving me a phobia by absolutely terrorizing me with that
underwater diving research—"

Hugh raises a finger. "I did not *give you* a phobia, Pip. I
just realized last month that you had quite the disinclination
to confined underwater situations and went with it. It's a
handy room to spend the week in for the most part, don't
you think?" he says, waving a hand around the blue room.
"Endless karaoke. Lots more fun than the original plan of
hiding out in a broom closet. And you'll be happy to know
I continued on with my workshops, so we have plenty of
happy cruisers."

"I noticed that," I say with a frown. "So what? *Everybody*
on this ship knew . . . except *me*?"

"Well, you *and* Nash, of course. But that wasn't by design.
I had intended to tell him alongside the others, but when it
was clear he was bent on being with you, I decided we best
not tamper with love. Ultimately, I didn't trust that he would
see the vision and keep the secret."

"He most certainly would *not* have," I say. I frown at the
others. "But the others did, huh? They were so willing to
play along?"

"When they knew the plan, of course. But some were
easier to convince than others." His eyes slide over to Jackie's.
"Unfortunately, I had to pull a card on a couple of them."

"What card?"

"Well," he says, slipping his hand behind my shoulder and guiding me offstage as the applause begins to die down. "That's the thing, Pip. People like to cling to little rumors about The Magnificent Seven. Rumors of secret handshakes and secret meetings. Most are them are terribly fun and terribly untrue, but some?" He smiles. "Some secrets are even better than you can make up. You are, as it turns out, in quite a delightful world."

I raise a brow. "Like what secrets?"

"Oh, we've got a whole booklet on it. I'll get Jackie to show you sometime. I had to use one, though. The Rule of Yes. When you join The Seven, you have the gift of one automatic yes, no hesitation, no questions asked. You only have one card like this in your lifetime, so you have to use it wisely. As for me, I used it here. You see, that first day everybody believed I really was murdered. I needed it to be so for authenticity's sake. You saw how awful they reacted when they thought they were in on the plan of me missing. They're good writers and terrible liars, which is humorous, really, as my writing helps me lie considerably. But there you have it. You saw how everyone reacted. At first, I was afraid Neena was going to lose her mind."

"She did, Hugh," I say. "That first day she was a complete wreck."

Hugh smiles and touches his heart. "It was nice to see I'm so loved, wasn't it? I found Neena and told her first. Then the others. There were, as you can imagine, several *intense* reactions. Nobody likes to be woken up in the middle of the night by a ghost over their bed. But"—he shrugs—"Jackie was the only one with whom I was reduced to using Rule #4 on."

"Which is what, exactly?"

Hugh begins walking us toward the circular table of authors.

"The Rule of Yes. One Ask with a capital *A*. Whatever the asker needs in that moment, wherever we are, and for whatever purpose, you drop everything and help out. Neena used it on Christmas Eve of 1989. Remember that, Neena? When we all had to fly out to Morocco?"

She grumbles, "I *thought* he was a prince."

"Gordon used it two years ago. Jackie, of course, will cling to her one wish until she dies."

"Did Crystal use hers up?"

"Quite literally forty-three minutes after she pledged to our group. Used it to rent out the Eiffel Tower—"

"You can't rent out the Eiffel Tower."

"They *say* you can't rent out the Eiffel Tower," he corrects.

He waves a hand at the six before him. "And I used it here to make sure everybody played the right cards in my little game. Jackie, as you saw, had the clearest, most negative reaction to this ask."

My brows shoot up. It's all clicking together. "You told her she had to play along in that room that day," I say. "The room where I ran into her and she had that knife. I knew she was livid about *something*."

"That something was me, behind the curtains, who had just given her the fright of her life."

We're standing now next to the table of authors. Everyone is here now.

"So you told her she had to act like her motivation for murdering you would be that she employed a ghostwriter and you found out?"

"She was *incensed*, as you could tell."

"It was the worst moment of my life," Jackie interrupts, fanning herself. "To even *think* I would stoop so low—"

"I liked my character," Crystal interjects cheerily.

She swings on the seat of her barstool beside the table,

legs crisscrossed. "I liked playing the angry, hidden daughter. Sorry, Pips, for getting all 'I'm going to murder you too' on you. No offense meant."

"None taken," I say. Although, in reality, she was a little *too* convincing. "And you two," I say, pointing at Neena and Gordon. "This is . . . real."

"What can I say? I love a man in a good hat." She looks fondly at Gordon.

"And you?" I say, turning back to Hugh. "You decided, in all these years of having this big, grand genie wish, to use it on me. You could've asked for anything. Why ask for something for *me*?"

And at this, he grins.

Pats me on the shoulder.

"Because if you haven't realized by now, Pip, we all love you. You have indeed been one of us for a long time. And a friend is born to love in times of adversity. We saw your adversity, and I decided it was time we gave you the push you needed. Plus, there's the small fact I have chosen you and you weren't jumping along quite as quickly as I wanted."

I raise my brow. "What?"

Hugh puts his hand out. "I've put a lot of thought into it over the past five years. And after careful consideration, given all the candidates, I could think of no better successor to my place . . . than you."

My eyes swivel to the rest of the group. "Wait. What—?"

Hugh claps me on the back. "I'm retiring, Pip. I'm ready to go on some new adventures. And I want you to take my place. My whole goal here was to help you realize you already have everything it takes to be a writer."

"And you gave me a story."

"The *first* story," Hugh clarifies. "I gave you a first. But I know it'll be no time before you have this first book written and come up with the next."

My breath is coming short now.

It's quite possible I'm going to pass out. "But . . . but what about all your friends?"

"I choose you."

"All those other authors. There are so many."

"I choose you."

"I haven't even finished a book yet, let alone *two chapters*."

Hugh's smile broadens as his hand grips my shoulder and gives it a squeeze. "Pip, I still choose you. And don't worry. I'm not, after all, dead. I will mentor you, and everyone here will mentor you, and together, my dear, you will soar."

I'm so stunned I can't speak.

"Welcome to The Magnificent Seven, Pip. It's going to be one heck of a ride."

EPILOGUE

"RULE #87," CRYSTAL SAYS, "YOU CAN'T BUY A NEW house without a hot tub for guests. And those guests being us. I made that one up."

"What?"

After three glorious days in Barcelona and two more weeks of Nash and me hopping around the European countryside, Crystal decided the fun should *absolutely* continue, given the celebratory circumstances of my induction into the group and all.

Which is how exactly two months later I've ended up somewhere in the Amazon, with some stranger yanking me up by a harness at my hip.

Some would call the view glorious.

I can only bestow such a term when my feet are firmly back on solid ground.

Today, as we've ziplined through the rainforest, we've finally begun to dig into all the secret rules.

And yes, apparently there is also a secret handshake.

It's quite laborious to learn actually.

Took me three solid weeks.

"How many rules are there exactly?"

"Ninety-six," Neena trills.

"Ninety-seven," Crystal amends. "I added one last meeting, remember? The Mandatory Fondue Christmas Eve Party."

The rules, for the record, are unreal.

They say that writing is an isolating experience.

Maybe that's the case for other people, but when you're part of The Magnificent Seven, there is never (and I mean *never*) a dull moment.

"Are we absolutely *sure* we should be doing this?" I say, trying my best to avoid looking down. "I thought I would be doing less of these moments when I wasn't getting paid to do it for Hugh."

"Now you're just doing it for free," Neena says, grinning.

"It's called friendship," Gordon says. "We do stupid things for friends because we love them."

"Bottoms up," Crystal calls, and the whole platform lurches as she hops off it and into thin air.

She free-falls for about twenty terrifying feet before her line finally catches.

"But this has ten reviews on Google," I say.

"Wheeeee," Crystal says.

"*Total!*" I say louder to everyone.

They all ignore me.

"And half of them were *two stars!*" I add.

"They lived to write those two stars, didn't they?" Neena says, as though this is an excellent point.

Neena hops off next.

Then Gordon.

Then Hugh (who isn't quite so "retired" after all).

"C'mon, Pip! It's your turn!"

Crystal's voice echoes through the trees. I can't see her. All I see is the green foliage everywhere. The thick scent of mangoes and fresh dirt and slithering snakes hidden in trees.

"Want me to nudge you?" Nash says with a whisper in my ear. I feel his hand gently on my back and turn toward him.

"Don't you *dare*," I hiss.

As it turns out, I have a natural fear of two very logical things: being underwater in confined spaces, and being one hundred feet in the air zipping through tree lines and narrowly avoiding death by tree trunk.

Gordon's nearing seventy-six and did this like a breeze.

But they all have an easier time living than me.

Just in general, I have to work harder in life to be free.

"We've got time," Nash says. He leans against the tree trunk of the tiny stand we're on as if to say, *No really, Pip, we absolutely can be here all day.* I smile a little because he means it, and for that reason, and roughly a thousand more, I love him.

"I can do this," I say, bouncing my shoulders. Hyping myself up.

"You can do this," he echoes.

"Why are we here again?"

"Because Crystal wanted to do research for her YA series while celebrating your induction, and you said last week, and I quote, 'Oh wow, that sounds like fun.' Despite the fact I told you we would end up in this situation—"

"At the time, she implied we would be staying at a *resort*—"

"Sleeping on the ground in tents."

"She said the food would be unparalleled."

"And now here we are. In a tree."

"Can someone explain to me why I continue to go on all these things?"

Nash grins. "Because you're a part of the group now, and like seven-year-olds in a treehouse club, we've decided to take our secret-yet-completely-public club entirely too seriously. And," he adds, "life's more fun with people who aren't afraid to be completely and utterly, and eccentrically, themselves."

"Of which this lot certainly is." I sigh and look down just past my toes to the bitter, bitter fall one hundred feet below.

I bite my lip and swivel round. "Nash."

"Yes?"

"I love you."

Nash's eyes crinkle as he smiles.

"And I'm going to need you to push me off."

Nash saunters slowly up to me. Reaches behind my sticky, braided ponytail and lifts my chin gently. His kiss is long and deep and the kind of kiss that makes the world swirl for just a little bit. "I love you too, Pip," he says. "More than anything else in all the world."

And then he pushes me off the ledge.

That's the thing about friends.

They may pull a little Willy Wonka on you, challenge you, and for a moment you may really think they are going to murder you.

But if they really love you, like the friends I have do, they're friends in good times and bad.

In moments of triumph and in moments of tragedy.

Friends, when done right, can be closer than family, can be the first people you think of to call in those big moments, and little. They love you despite your faults and flaws. They see you, all the little bits of you that you try to keep tucked so secretly in the corner, and they stay.

They always keep the light on for you.

They always answer the call.

Friends can even, if you are very, very lucky, fake a death.

All for you.

DISCUSSION QUESTIONS

1. Throughout most of the book, Pip has the unique position of belonging to the Magnificent Seven without really belonging. Do you have a group like that where you feel you belong? Can you name people in your life who have your back no matter what?

2. Pip has found her identity in always being the composed one in any situation. When she finally loses her composure, it's the catalyst for her to take the next big step in her life. Do you relate to feeling like you always have to "have it together"? What would it take to free you from that pressure?

3. The writers in the Magnificent Seven represent a wide variety of genres. Which genre most appeals to you, and why? Would you see yourself writing the same genre that you like reading?

4. Did you have any suspicions about the murderer's identity? If so, what led you to your suspicions?

5. Do you think Hugh was justified in his plan? How would you feel if a friend of yours did something like that?

6. Is there something in your life you need a push to do? What's holding you back, and what would be the thing to propel you forward?

7. There is a powerful moment in the book where Pip realizes she's not too much for Nash and can be her true self with him. How did you feel when you read this part and witnessed Pip's realization that she was loved and accepted just as she is?

8. Pip tells the reader, "... In the case of fight or flight, I am not the kind of person who can just let things go and slink off in the distance. I'm brave and afraid." Has there been a moment in your life where you were braver than you expected, whether that was because you had to be or wanted to be?

9. This book has a cast of eccentric and unique characters. Which one was your favorite and why?

10. If you could go on a book cruise featuring your favorite authors, who would comprise your Magnificent Seven?

ABOUT THE AUTHOR

Taylor Meo Photography

Melissa Ferguson is the bestselling children's and adult author of titles including *Meet Me in the Margins, Our Friendly Farmhouse,* and *The Perfect Rom-Com.* She lives in Tennessee with her husband and children in their growing farmhouse lifestyle and writes charming children's books and heart-warming romantic comedies that have recently been optioned for film.

Follow Melissa with over 1 million other subscribers at @ourfriendlyfarmhouse or her newsletter, melissaferguson.com.

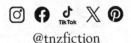

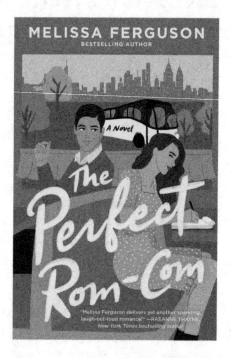